Treasured

Also From Lexi Blake

ROMANTIC SUSPENSE

Masters and Mercenaries
The Dom Who Loved Me
The Men With The Golden Cuffs
A Dom is Forever
On Her Master's Secret Service
Sanctum: A Masters and Mercenaries Novella
Love and Let Die
Unconditional: A Masters and Mercenaries Novella
Dungeon Royale
Dungeon Games: A Masters and Mercenaries Novella
A View to a Thrill
Cherished: A Masters and Mercenaries Novella
You Only Love Twice
Luscious: Masters and Mercenaries~Topped
Adored: A Masters and Mercenaries Novella
Master No
Just One Taste: Masters and Mercenaries~Topped 2
From Sanctum with Love
Devoted: A Masters and Mercenaries Novella
Dominance Never Dies
Submission is Not Enough
Master Bits and Mercenary Bites~The Secret Recipes of Topped
Perfectly Paired: Masters and Mercenaries~Topped 3
For His Eyes Only
Arranged: A Masters and Mercenaries Novella
Love Another Day
At Your Service: Masters and Mercenaries~Topped 4
Master Bits and Mercenary Bites~Girls Night
Nobody Does It Better
Close Cover
Protected: A Masters and Mercenaries Novella
Enchanted: A Masters and Mercenaries Novella
Charmed: A Masters and Mercenaries Novella
Treasured: A Masters and Mercenaries Novella

Masters and Mercenaries: The Forgotten
Lost Hearts (Memento Mori)
Lost and Found
Lost in You
Long Lost
No Love Lost
Masters and Mercenaries: Reloaded
Submission Impossible
The Dom Identity, Coming September 14, 2021

Butterfly Bayou
Butterfly Bayou
Bayou Baby
Bayou Dreaming
Bayou Beauty

Lawless
Ruthless
Satisfaction
Revenge

Courting Justice
Order of Protection
Evidence of Desire

Masters Of Ménage (by Shayla Black and Lexi Blake)
Their Virgin Captive
Their Virgin's Secret
Their Virgin Concubine
Their Virgin Princess
Their Virgin Hostage
Their Virgin Secretary
Their Virgin Mistress

The Perfect Gentlemen (by Shayla Black and Lexi Blake)
Scandal Never Sleeps
Seduction in Session
Big Easy Temptation

Smoke and Sin
At the Pleasure of the President

URBAN FANTASY

Thieves
Steal the Light
Steal the Day
Steal the Moon
Steal the Sun
Steal the Night
Ripper
Addict
Sleeper
Outcast
Stealing Summer
The Rebel Queen

LEXI BLAKE WRITING AS SOPHIE OAK

Texas Sirens
Small Town Siren
Siren in the City
Siren Enslaved
Siren Beloved
Siren in Waiting
Siren in Bloom
Siren Unleashed
Siren Reborn

Nights in Bliss, Colorado
Three to Ride
Two to Love
One to Keep
Lost in Bliss
Found in Bliss
Pure Bliss

Chasing Bliss
Once Upon a Time in Bliss
Back in Bliss
Sirens in Bliss
Happily Ever After in Bliss

A Faery Story
Bound
Beast
Beauty

Standalone
Away From Me
Snowed In

Treasured

A Masters and Mercenaries
Novella

By Lexi Blake

1001 DARK NIGHTS
PRESS

Treasured
A Masters and Mercenaries Novella
By Lexi Blake

1001 Dark Nights

Copyright 2021 DLZ Entertainment, LLC
ISBN: 978-1-951812-47-8

Foreword: Copyright 2014 M. J. Rose

Published by 1001 Dark Nights Press, an imprint of Evil Eye
Concepts, Incorporated

Sign up for the 1001 Dark Nights Newsletter
and be entered to win a Tiffany Key necklace.

There's a contest every month!

Go to www.1001DarkNights.com to subscribe.

**As a bonus, all subscribers can download
FIVE FREE exclusive books!**

Acknowledgments from the Author

I love writing these yearly "novellas" for a lot of reasons. It's fun to let some of the characters who aren't big bad operatives take the center stage for one. For another I always love working with Evil Eye and the amazing women who run it. Thanks to Liz Berry, MJ Rose, and Jillian Stein for the work they do to push the romance genre forward and for always supporting their fellow women. As always thanks to my team – Kim Guidroz, Maria Monroy, Stormy Pate, Riane Holt, and Kori Smith.

One Thousand and One Dark Nights

Once upon a time, in the future…

*I was a student fascinated with stories and learning.
I studied philosophy, poetry, history, the occult, and
the art and science of love and magic. I had a vast
library at my father's home and collected thousands
of volumes of fantastic tales.*

*I learned all about ancient races and bygone
times. About myths and legends and dreams of all
people through the millennium. And the more I read
the stronger my imagination grew until I discovered
that I was able to travel into the stories... to actually
become part of them.*

*I wish I could say that I listened to my teacher
and respected my gift, as I ought to have. If I had, I
would not be telling you this tale now.
But I was foolhardy and confused, showing off
with bravery.*

*One afternoon, curious about the myth of the
Arabian Nights, I traveled back to ancient Persia to
see for myself if it was true that every day Shahryar
(Persian: شهریار, "king") married a new virgin, and then
sent yesterday's wife to be beheaded. It was written
and I had read that by the time he met Scheherazade,
the vizier's daughter, he'd killed one thousand
women.*

Something went wrong with my efforts. I arrived in the midst of the story and somehow exchanged places with Scheherazade — a phenomena that had never occurred before and that still to this day, I cannot explain.

Now I am trapped in that ancient past. I have taken on Scheherazade's life and the only way I can protect myself and stay alive is to do what she did to protect herself and stay alive.

Every night the King calls for me and listens as I spin tales. And when the evening ends and dawn breaks, I stop at a point that leaves him breathless and yearning for more. And so the King spares my life for one more day, so that he might hear the rest of my dark tale.

As soon as I finish a story... I begin a new one... like the one that you, dear reader, have before you now.

Chapter One

Tessa Santiago stepped into the lobby of the restaurant and wondered if she could still beg off. No one had seen her yet. She could slip back out and text her host that she'd gotten caught in traffic or something.

It was weird to be invited to an anniversary party for an ex-fiancé's twin brother and his wife, wasn't it? Who did this? There were definitely times she wished her breakup had been way less chill. If she'd thrown a couple of dishes at his head, maybe left some nasty messages, she wouldn't be here. But no, she'd had to stay friends with the man because at the end there hadn't been passion between them. It hadn't been his fault or her fault.

But this awkwardness was definitely his fault.

"Tessa! Hey, I'm so glad you came." Nina Malone was a gorgeous woman with a smile a mile wide, but then what did she have to frown about? She was happily married to the CEO of a billion dollar company and had the most adorable kids. Nina wore the kind of designer gown that probably could feed a small country, and killer heels that made Tessa's feet ache looking at them.

Yeah, Nina was the kind of woman who invited exes to parties because she stayed friends with everyone. Nina was one of the reasons Tessa wished things had worked out with Michael Malone.

He was a genuinely great guy. His family had been awesome, and she'd loved them all, but the truth was there hadn't been a spark between her and Michael. That lack of true passion had been the reason they'd ended the engagement. Lately she'd been wondering if *she* was the problem, if she didn't have any passion at all.

Even as she hugged Nina, she caught sight of her ex. Michael stood across the private dining room looking stunning in his custom-made tuxedo.

Why, oh why, couldn't she have truly loved that man?

"Happy anniversary," Tessa said, stepping back. "You look

amazing, as always.”

“So do you,” Nina said in her British accent. That accent, Tessa had been told, had softened over the years Nina had lived in Texas. She’d been a McKay-Taggart employee when she’d met JT Malone and fallen in love, and now Nina ran security for Malone Oil.

Nina had been the one who had tried to help Tessa fit into the Malones’ wealthy world. They’d come from similar backgrounds, though Tessa had grown up in Dallas and Nina in London. The middle class was still the middle class, and it was a big step up into the world the Malones ran in.

Or her current bosses, the Taggarts. Tessa worked in the personal security department of McKay-Taggart. While Ian Taggart might have started out middle class, he hadn’t stayed there. None of the Taggarts had. After all, this party was being held in the cornerstone of Sean Taggart’s restaurant empire. Top was one of Dallas’s celebrated fine dining spots. It was the kind of place the wealthy frequented and the not so wealthy aspired to go.

She hoped they had tacos.

“Like I said, I’m so happy you came. It’s been an age since I saw you. How are you?” Nina asked.

She was the same as she’d been for the last year. Since she’d broken things off with Michael, she’d worked and worked and…worked some more. She took every long-term assignment she could and tried not to think about the fact that she’d walked away from a beautiful billionaire who’d been kind to her.

If she couldn’t love a man like Michael Malone, who could she love? She’d started to consider the fact that she was broken in a way that couldn’t be repaired. And the real trouble was she couldn’t even figure out why she was broken.

“I’m good. I just got back from a six-week assignment in Loa Mali.” Tessa plastered a smile on her face. “When I wasn’t following the queen around, I worked on my tan.”

She hadn’t. She’d sat in her room and read books and worked out and gone to the shooting range and took her frustrations out on paper targets.

“I seriously doubt that,” Nina said with a sigh. She waved to someone behind Tessa. “I’ve got to say hello to some board members, love. Please stay for dinner. I miss you.”

“Sure. Wouldn’t miss a free meal.” Especially if it was tacos or a nice juicy burger. She had a terrible suspicion that she would be offered neither. Oh, she could totally get those off the menu, but tonight's party would be a plated meal, and it would likely be super fancy.

She wasn't a super-fancy girl.

Nina gave her another hug and walked off, always the gracious hostess.

"Hey, how you doing?" a familiar voice said.

She turned and didn't have to smile because she and Michael didn't pretend. They'd always been good friends, and even after the breakup she still cared about this man. "It's weird, isn't it?"

"Being at my twin's anniversary party? Yes. I would have sworn JT would never get married," Michael said with a shake of his head.

He could be obtuse at times. Or rather not very self-aware. "I'm talking about me being here."

Michael frowned as though he'd never even had the thought. "I wouldn't want you to stay away. Nina and JT are your friends. At least I hope they still are."

She sighed. "Of course. It's just weird that we still work in the same office and run in the same circles. And I heard you took my mom to lunch two weeks ago."

"No, I didn't. We happened to be at Mario's at the same time, and we were both alone," Michael corrected. "The place was crowded, like it always is, and it made sense to share a table. I like your mom."

She'd heard all about how nice Michael was and how her mom wished it could have worked out. And shouldn't she try again? After all, Michael wasn't seeing anyone. "She likes you, too."

"If it helps, my mom talks about you all the time." Michael took a drag off his beer. "I'm constantly being reminded that my brother's kids are growing up without cousins, and you could have solved that problem. She firmly believes I could be happy right now if I hadn't screwed things up."

He hadn't screwed anything up. "Should I talk to her?"

He shook his head. "No. Not at all. And I promise the next time I see your mom I will be a bastard and make her thrilled we broke it off."

Maybe she needed to stop worrying about how other people might view their situation. "Don't. I'm glad you had lunch with her. My brothers are all busy, and I've been on assignment. She's lonely.

She's been missing my dad lately, and I think having someone to talk to made her feel good. And you think you catch hell from your mother about your single status? Try being the only daughter with three brothers who married young and started their own football teams. You would think my mother would be happy with eight grandchildren, but I swear until I pop one out she won't feel like she's done her job."

"I sometimes wonder how she keeps up with all the names," Michael mused.

"Years of teaching high school." That was her mom's secret. She'd had to learn roughly a hundred names every year.

"Well, I'm glad I only have to deal with JT's two." Michael frowned suddenly. "Speaking of. I should stop Jasper from climbing up that banister. They're going to kill me."

Michael ran off to save his toddler nephew from himself, and Tessa looked around the beautifully decorated room. It was filled with people from JT and Nina's lives. Tessa recognized a few people from the office. Ian and Charlotte Taggart were talking to Ava Malone. A couple of guys from Tessa's unit seemed to be working security.

She made the rounds, saying hello to the people she knew and awkwardly explaining to some of them that she was no longer engaged to Michael. It was a lot, and dinner was still thirty minutes off. She found herself making her way to the bathroom to take a break from all the small talk.

She would eat dinner, stay for the toast, and then get home as fast as she could because there was a bath and a book waiting for her. Like there was every single night.

It was a good thing, though. She'd decided to take some *me* time after the breakup. Some work-on-herself time. No dating. No hook-ups. Just time to reflect on where she was in life.

Tessa stared at herself in the bathroom mirror. She was thirty-four and took bullets for other people for a living. And even that was getting a little boring. She hadn't actually been shot at in a long time. Her last assignment had been watching over the queen of Loa Mali and her two daughters. There had been sun and sand, and an odd amount of science talk she hadn't been able to completely follow. Those girls were smart.

Was it time to try again?

From the expression she'd made in the mirror, absolutely not. A genuinely horrified look had come over her face when she'd thought about putting herself out there.

Perhaps it was time to accept the fact that there wasn't some magic person out there for her, that what her parents had was rare. They'd been soul mates, and even after her dad had died, her mom kept his memory alive, still smiled every time she said his name. She was practical enough to know that didn't happen for everyone.

She straightened her blouse, smoothed down her hair, and braced herself for a couple of hours of talking about how great she was doing and answering awkward questions and watching happy couples being happy.

She could do this. Tomorrow she would ask for the most brutal assignment her boss could find and maybe lose herself in it. If she was dodging bullets, she wouldn't be thinking about her nonexistent love life or listening to her mom casually mention how long a woman's eggs were viable.

Tessa walked out of the bathroom in time to see Charlotte Taggart exiting the private party room. Charlotte, who had set her up with Michael. Charlotte, who now wanted to make amends by setting her up with someone else.

She was such a coward, but she ducked into the bar to avoid that conversation. She was sure Charlotte had some guy in mind and he was the nicest man and they would look so cute together.

Nope. Wasn't going there again.

Tessa eased onto the barstool with the most coverage. It was in the corner, behind a pillar. Charlotte would have to actually walk into the bar to see her.

"What can I get for you?" A slender woman in a white collared shirt slid a coaster in front of Tessa.

Maybe she could hang here until dinner. The tables had place cards, and she was sitting at a table with Simon Weston and his wife Chelsea. They wouldn't be hard to deal with and totally knew what subjects would be weird for her. She just had to hide until she could slip into her seat at dinner. "I'll take an old-fashioned."

The bartender nodded.

"Hey, it's going to be okay." The man beside her was talking, his voice hushed, but then the place was kind of quiet, so she could hear him. "You know you're never going to please those girls, right? There's a reason they're called mean girls."

There was a loud sniffle and a feminine voice saying something

Tessa couldn't quite make out.

"I know it hurts, and I'm ready to talk to you anytime you want. I need you to understand that you haven't done anything wrong. I don't care what anyone else says. You're allowed to love who you want to love, date who you want to date. Shame is a weapon, and they'll use that to try to hurt you. Don't let them because there's no shame here. You stand tall and know that your family is behind you all the way. So are your real friends."

Another big sniffle and the girl slid off her barstool. Tessa got a glimpse of auburn hair and a youthful face. She hugged the man and walked away, saying good-bye.

"You're good with her. Is she your daughter?" She wasn't sure why she'd asked the question. She hadn't even gotten a good look at the man beside her. He had a stack of books and a notepad in front of him. And a beer.

Something about the way he'd spoken to the teen had made her heart twist. She remembered asshole high school girls and how they could drag someone down. Her brothers had told her to try harder to fit in. Her dad had told her maybe if she acted more feminine they would all get along.

She loved her father and brothers. It had been a different time, but she admired how this man had handled the situation.

"Only if I had her when I was…oh, god. Nineteen. I could be her dad. No. She's my sister. And thanks. I try. I'll be honest, I didn't spend much time with teenaged girls when I was a teen. I had a brother and chess club. It did not make me an expert at dealing with this kind of thing." The man beside her had golden brown hair that was slightly shaggy and warm hazel eyes.

He was cute. Not so stunning that she was put off. He was that warm guy who probably had a lot of women friends because he was nice.

"You were nineteen when she was born?" That was a big age gap. For some reason she wanted to keep the conversation going.

"Yep." His lips curled up, and he was awfully cute when he smiled. "She's my half sister, though that's a ridiculous qualification. She's my sister, and I have an even younger brother. My mom's second act was pretty spectacular. Hey, Leslie. Can I get another beer?"

The bartender slid the old-fashioned in front of Tess and nodded the man's way. "Sure thing, David. Is she okay?"

"Carys? She's dealing with mean-girl crap," the man named David said. "It sucks, but she'll get through it. She's a smart kid, and she's got a network of friends who don't go to her high school."

The bartender popped the top off a longneck and replaced the one David had finished. "I'm glad to hear it. Your burger should be ready soon."

A burger. That sounded so good. She was probably going to be eating something super fancy like pâté or Cornish game hens with caviar.

"I think you'll find Leslie makes an excellent old-fashioned," David said. "It can be a tricky one to get right."

"Don't I know it?" She took a sip, and it was excellent. "That is good. I bartended for a couple of years."

"Me, too. It's how I got through college."

"With all those books, I would say you're still in college." Those weren't fiction books. They were older tomes, reminding her of the science books her dad collected. That was when she realized who she was dealing with. Not the man, but the type. There was a reason the guy in front of her felt comfortable. "You're a professor."

He grimaced. "I'm not even wearing a tweed jacket. Do I give off ivory-tower vibes or something?"

"Nah, I just know the type. I'm the daughter of two teachers. My dad taught biology at a community college, and my mom was a high school Spanish teacher. She's retired now, but she still volunteers. And it's the books. They're older and not from a library or a college bookstore. You're taking notes. You're either a writer researching something or a professor researching something. I made an educated guess."

He tipped his beer her way. "Well, it was a good one. I'm a junior professor at UT Dallas, and I am working on a biography of a quirky South American billionaire who bought an island and created his own country."

"Oh, that's interesting. When I think 'history professor,' I think of medieval England or the Ottoman Empire." She relaxed a bit, enjoying the conversation. How long had it been since she'd talked to a guy simply because it was nice to talk to him? And not about the security industry. That was all the guys in her office talked about. Work and sports.

"I know about those, too. They emphasize European history in

American schools, but I did a semester at University of São Paulo and kind of fell in love with South American history and contemporary politics," he explained. "And I'm surprised. Your eyes haven't glazed over yet."

Oh, she liked his smile, and he wasn't wearing a ring. Hadn't she told herself she wasn't going to do this? But really, what was she doing? Talking to some random pretty man in a bar she didn't frequent often. She'd been to Top for office-related occasions and a couple of times with Michael, but she typically went to less fancy places for food. She was more of a food truck girl. Why shouldn't she spend the half an hour or so she had chatting up the attractive professor? "Well, like I said, I'm the child of two teachers, so you can hit me with all the lofty terms you like. It makes me feel at home. I come from a long line of intellectuals."

Her brothers had all gone into white-collar professions. Two lawyers and an accountant, and their precious baby girl had screwed everything up by going into the Army and then becoming a bodyguard.

"Well, that's good to know." He held out a hand. "I'm David Hawthorne."

She took it. His hand was warm and surprisingly callused for a professor. He'd done work in his time and probably still did. "Tessa Santiago. Nice to meet you."

"Same." He sat back. "You know it's funny. One of my favorite teachers was Mrs. Santiago. She taught Spanish at Bell High School."

Her jaw dropped because it was such a small world. "Seriously? That's my mom. She taught at Bell forever. Dad was at TCC."

"You're little Tess." His whole face lit up. "Sorry. Your mom talked about you. She used your name in many assignments. *La pequeña Tess no tiene zapatos.*"

"I wasn't that little, and I always had shoes. I'm roughly the same age as you." It was crazy how embarrassed she could still get. And his accent was good. He didn't sound like some Texans speaking Spanish.

"Were we in the same class?" David asked.

"I went to Trinity," she admitted. "We actually lived in Euless, so Mom taught at Bell, but all of her kids went to the enemy school." Bell and Trinity were high schools with a healthy rivalry. It was something she and her brothers had regularly teased their mom about. It was nice to talk to someone who came from her old neighborhood. "I'm sure that we passed each other at the stadium on Friday nights, though."

"Ah, you are under the mistaken impression that I attended football games. You need to meet my brother. He was the football guy. I was likely studying for Academic Decathlon." He winced. "I was kind of a nerd in high school. I'm probably still a nerd."

He was a hot nerd, and she couldn't forget how he'd handled his sister. "I only went for the soda. It wasn't allowed in my house, but I could sneak it at the games."

"Here you go." The bartender was back, and she'd brought heaven with her. She placed a burger and some of the crispiest-looking fries she'd ever seen in front of David before glancing back Tessa's way. "Can I get you some food?"

Tessa frowned. "No. I'm supposed to eat froufrou stuff. I'm here for a party."

The bartender sighed in obvious envy. "Oh, they are having the most delicious quail this evening. And the foie gras is divine. You'll love it."

The bartender turned away.

"You do not look like you love duck liver," David pointed out. "I'm going to admit something, and you can never tell a soul. I think it's gross, and I don't like escargot. I don't care how much garlic and butter you smother it in, it still tastes like snails and dirt."

She liked him quite a bit. "Why can't I tell anyone?"

"Because my mom works here, and she's proud of the food. I'm going to admit that I'm more of a Tex-Mex guy." He gestured to the basket in front of him. "But they make a fabulous burger and fries, and I can share if you like. It might fortify you for the four-course extravaganza to come."

Her stomach rumbled. She was actually hungry, and it was for more than food. She wanted to talk to this man. "All right, David. I've got a couple of minutes. So how did a kid from Bell High School end up in Brazil? Did you know your Spanish wouldn't work there?"

She sat back as he started to talk, and the night didn't seem so lonely anymore.

* * * *

David had walked into Top this evening because Carys had seemed to need someone to talk to, and he'd known she would be here since she always helped out on Friday nights. He'd spent the day on campus, grading papers in his office and researching his book in the stacks at the library. The restaurant his stepfather and mom had started was on the way back to his town house, and the thought of microwaving a burrito held no appeal.

Of course, he would have been able to eat that whole burrito. Instead he'd had to share his burger and fries with Mrs. Santiago's daughter. Little Tess had grown into a stunning woman who held every bit of his attention in a way only an article on the current Chilean political situation usually could.

He also wouldn't have ended up ordering the molten lava cake and watching her eyes close in pure pleasure. He wouldn't have sat here and talked for hours.

"Hey, guys, I hate to interrupt you, but this is last call," Leslie said. The young bartender had done her job perfectly, only disrupting the bubble they'd been in to bring them food or coffee after they'd both had a couple of drinks. The richness of the coffee had gone perfectly with the dark chocolate of the dessert.

His stepfather knew how to cook.

"I think we're good," he told her. "I'll take the bill."

"Sure you will," Leslie said with a shake of her head.

He didn't want to have to fight over this. He hadn't come in for a free meal, but his mother would likely make a big deal out of it.

"Oh, my god." Tessa had glanced at the clock behind the bar. "Is it that late?"

He checked his own watch. Almost eleven. Top closed earlier than most of the bars in the area. "Yes, it is. I guess we lost track of time."

Four hours. They'd been sitting here for four hours. They'd talked a lot about her family and his work. They'd discovered they both loved Marvel movies, and she'd been surprised that he shared her obsession with muscle cars. They'd spent a good hour talking about the 1969 Ford Mustang he was restoring. It had been a present from his mom and Sean when he'd passed his dissertation. Tessa had seemed interested in both his job and his hobby.

She was a unicorn.

She went the loveliest shade of pink. "I can't believe I did that. I missed the whole party."

He should have pointed that out to her, but he'd been too happy to sit and talk. "Sorry about that, but I had a nice time tonight. Probably the best time I've had in a while."

He dated. He tended to follow a pattern. Meet a woman, date for a couple of weeks, and then she got bored with the fact that he was far more interested in his work than anything else. He'd even dated a woman in his department, and it had floundered.

But Tessa held every bit of his focus. He'd listened to her stories about growing up with three brothers, and the rest of the world seemed to fade away.

Her long raven-dark hair fell around her shoulders, drawing him in deeper as she gave him a half smile. "Me, too. Why is that hard to admit?"

"For me? It's hard to admit because then I have to acknowledge that my dating life's been crappy lately." He knew he should play it confident and present himself like the stud he wanted to be. Except he'd never wanted to be a stud. He was pretty happy being who he was. Mostly. Though he had to admit that since his Navy officer brother had moved in, he'd noticed that he'd started to fade into the background when compared to Kyle.

But then that was what happened when one was always surrounded by heroic military men. The prof didn't quite live up to expectations. Kyle fit in with their Taggart stepfamily far better than David ever had.

"Mine's sucked," Tessa said with a breathless sigh, as though it felt good to admit that. "I was engaged for a while and since we broke it off, it's been pretty sad."

He wasn't about to let this one slip through his fingers without at least trying. "Well, what do you say we try to turn it around? Any chance you would like to have dinner with me? I promise this time I'll get you your whole own plate. I know this great Tex-Mex place a couple of blocks over."

"I would like that." She practically glowed in the low light. It kissed her golden skin and made her dark eyes flash. She was the most beautiful woman he'd ever seen, with lush hair and a generous smile. Beyond her obvious beauty, there was a warmth about her that called to him.

He pulled out his phone. This was the customary trading of digits, a sacred ritual in the modern mating game. The minute he saw her hesitate he realized he was being too aggressive. He set his phone down and decided to go the more secure route. He picked up the pen he'd meant to use to take notes on Ricardo Montez's manifesto. He hadn't picked that sucker up all night because he'd been far too interested in her. He quickly wrote his numbers down. "Here's my cell and my office number in case you want to give me a call. I would love to take you out to dinner."

She sighed and picked up his phone. "Unlock it. Sorry. I'm female, and giving out my number can be a risk, but I think I'm willing to take it with you."

That was good to know. He unlocked his phone and handed it to her. She put her number in and then her phone was buzzing, the ritual of exchanging digits complete. She handed his cell back and saved his number in hers. "I would lose the note. I'm way better at keeping up with digital things."

And they were at the awkward part of the evening, the part where it was over but they didn't want it to be over. The point where they both knew damn well it was way too soon to go any further than they'd gone. "How far away are you from home? I'm not trying to figure out where you live. I just want to make sure you get home okay."

She slid off the barstool and stood in front of him. "You are a sweet man."

He didn't like the sound of that. He'd learned that women like her tended to not appreciate sweetness. Or rather *sweet* got a man locked in the friend zone. It wasn't a bad place to be. He had lots of women friends, but he wanted something more from her. "There's more to me than meets the eye."

Her hands came up, eyes taking him in. "I bet there is, Professor. I don't know what my work schedule is going to be like, but I would definitely love to continue our conversation. And I would definitely love to see that Mustang of yours. Why don't you give me a call and we'll take it from there?"

Desire flooded his system in a way it hadn't in ages. He'd been so focused on his brain that if felt good to let his body want something. Someone. Her. "I will."

Was she going to kiss him? He held himself still, willing her to brush those luscious lips against his. He wasn't about to scare her off though. He would let her set the pace in the beginning, and then once she trusted him, he could take control and show her how not sweet he could be.

"Tessa?" A feminine voice broke through the intimacy of the

moment.

He turned, and a somewhat familiar woman was standing there. He couldn't remember her name, but he'd seen her around the restaurant.

Tessa had stepped back, and an apologetic expression crossed her face. "Nina, I'm so sorry. I...uhm..."

"You obviously found something more fun to do than my boring anniversary party." Nina had a smile on her face. The name rang a bell, too, but a distant one. His mom had mentioned someone named Nina was having a party tonight.

Malone. She was Nina Malone, and she was married to some guy who had a connection to Ian's company. Malone Oil.

Did Tessa work for Malone Oil? That might fit. She definitely seemed to know the boss's wife. If he was making the proper connections, Nina was married to the head of Malone Oil.

"I lost track of time," she admitted. "I'm sorry. I didn't mean to miss it."

Nina waved her off. "It was a bit boring, like the celebration of a long-term marriage should be. And it's closing down. Can we give you a ride home? JT's bringing the car around."

Tessa waved off the offer. "Oh, it's fine. I can grab a cab."

"Absolutely not. It's late, and we didn't even have a chance to talk. It's the least we can do for dragging you out here, and your place is on the way back to Fort Worth." An elegant brow rose over Nina's eyes. "Unless you have another ride."

Oh, he would love to give her a ride, but it was too soon, and he wasn't that guy. He was the guy who made every woman feel comfortable, who built a foundation before showing off his wild side.

He had a wild side. He just didn't indulge it often.

"I took a train, but I would be happy to escort you." He would probably look way cooler if he'd driven, but the train let off close to his town house, and there was a station right at the college he worked at.

She shook her head. "I appreciate it, but she's right. My place is on their way. Nina, I'll be right with you."

Nina nodded and moved toward the front door.

The waitstaff was winding down orders and settling up checks. Any minute now his mom would walk out of her office and start helping.

The night was over, and he was about to be left with his books and papers to grade, and normally that didn't make him as sad as it did tonight.

"It was good to meet you, Tessa." He held out a hand.

"You, too, David. Do you mind if I kiss you?"

The amount of relief he felt should have scared him. "God, I wish you would. I'm trying to be a gentleman and…"

She stopped him, pressing her lips against his and brushing them softly.

When she put her hands on his shoulders, he let his find her waist and gently dragged her closer. She'd given him permission, and he would let go the minute he sensed a second's hesitation, but he wanted this kiss.

It was his final argument as to why she should answer when he called her, why she should take that date with him.

He took over, and she seemed to easily follow his lead. He explored her with slow kisses, one wave after another, warming him and stealing his breath.

At the first tentative touch of her tongue, he knew he couldn't go any further or he would cause a scene. He gave her one last kiss and pulled back.

"I can't wait to see you again." He should play it cool, but he'd never been cool, so she should get used to that.

She stepped back, obviously as affected as he'd been. "Me, too. See you soon."

She gave him a warm smile and grabbed her bag before turning and walking away. Her backside was as pretty as the rest of her.

Tessa. Who would have guessed his dream woman would be the daughter of his favorite high school teacher? It was a strange and small world.

But for once, his own piece of it held some wonder.

Chapter Two

Tess slid into the middle row of the big black SUV. JT was behind the wheel and Nina in the seat in front of her, but there was something missing. "Did you forget the kids?"

JT started to pull the vehicle onto Main. "I can't forget them. They're too noisy."

Nina turned slightly. "They went home with their grandparents. JT and I are actually checking into the Mandarin for the rest of the weekend. It's their gift to us."

Even in the low light from the dashboard, she could see the way JT grinned at his wife. "It's the best present of all. Time alone. I love our kids, but damn I miss long mornings in bed. Most of the time I wake up to Jasper bouncing on top of me or Ryder screaming through the baby monitor. Tomorrow I'm sleeping in and we're having breakfast in bed."

That sounded lovely, and she couldn't help but wonder what the professor did with his mornings. He probably read the paper while drinking coffee, and wouldn't he look adorable with his hair all messy and his eyes still sleepy?

She had it bad. One evening with the man and she was thinking about how he would look in the morning.

How long would he take to call her? Would he play it cool and wait the prescribed three days so he didn't look too eager? That would be disappointing.

Maybe she should text him tomorrow. It would be a way to let him know she was interested and they didn't have to play games.

Not any of the yucky games. Now sexy games were a whole other story.

That kiss…that kiss had sparked something deep inside her, and it hadn't merely been about sex. It had been a long time since she'd gotten down and dirty with a man, and she had needs. But David wouldn't merely be a body in bed. They'd connected.

She'd felt a spark.

Or was she desperate and looking for something?

"How did you two know?"

The cab went awkwardly quiet, and Tessa wished she hadn't said anything.

"Know?" JT asked.

"I felt something for JT pretty much the minute I met him." Lucky for her, Nina didn't pretend to misunderstand. "Of course I might not have if I'd known he was lying to me."

"Now, I did not lie," JT argued.

Nina turned her husband's way. "Did you or did you not know I was your bodyguard?"

JT's big shoulders shrugged. "I might have had an inkling, but then I knew you wouldn't kiss me if you thought we had a professional connection. So I might have played dumb. Hey, baby, it worked out."

"Is this about the guy you were with at the bar?" Nina asked.

"She was hitting on some guy at the bar? Well, good for you, Tess. It was probably more interesting than watching Mike stumble through that toast. He is not a public speaker," JT said with a shake of his head.

"I wasn't hitting on him. I was talking to him." And then she was kissing him. She'd seen the moment he'd decided not to make a move on her, and she'd decided to make one of her own. He was obviously a cautious man, and she didn't mind that. She could be reckless. "I stopped in to grab a drink and we started talking. He was a student of my mom's."

"Really? That's fascinating," Nina said.

"Why would you go to the bar? We had an open one at the party," JT countered.

Nina put a hand on his arm. "It doesn't matter. So he was a student of your mother's."

JT deserved an explanation. She'd skipped out on their party. "I'm sorry. It was weird to answer all those questions. Some of the people there didn't know Michael and I broke up. And I was avoiding Charlotte, because she's been hinting that she wants to try her hand at matchmaking again. Apparently her latest experiment went well."

"Yes, I heard she set up Hutch with the daughter of a family friend," Nina allowed. "They're getting married, so Charlotte's on a high."

"Hutch? The young guy who hooks up with women in closets and plays video games for a living?" JT whistled. "No wonder Michael was in a bad mood. I think he's starting to feel like a wallflower. I keep telling him no one is calling him a spinster behind his back."

"No, you say it to his front," Nina accused. "He's sensitive about it, you jerk. And I did hear Charlotte mention she had recently met a few single men she thought would make lovely partners. You were probably right to run."

Charlotte tended to set up people she knew, and she mostly knew people who worked at McKay-Taggart or the investigative company run by Adam Miles and Jake Dean.

The last thing she wanted was to date anyone connected to her work. Not again. And definitely not anyone who lived in the lofty world of Dallas's elite. She'd tried, and it hadn't been a good place for her. She hadn't fit in there, and she didn't want to.

"I'm sorry about missing the party. I got caught up in talking to him. He's a professor and he knows all this interesting stuff," she admitted.

"And he's cute," Nina prompted. "Did he ask you out?"

She felt a smile slide over her face. "He might have."

Maybe she wouldn't volunteer for an out-of-town assignment right away. She'd been out of the country for weeks, and her boss liked to spread those assignments out. Wade Rycroft ran the bodyguard unit, and if she asked to work in Dallas for a couple of months, he would likely honor her request.

It would be good to be home. She could spend some time with her mom, finally get around to decorating her apartment. All the boxes were unpacked, but the place still didn't feel like home.

She could explore this thing with Professor Hottie.

He'd gotten hotter over the course of the night. He had a real Superman thing going. He seemed blandly handsome until he smiled and talked about things he was passionate about, and then he was flat-out sexy as hell.

And it was nice that his mom worked at Top. Tessa wondered if she was a server or one of the cooks. If she'd been the one to make that burger, then kudos to David's mom because it had been excellent.

It had been better because he'd shared it with her.

"I don't think I've ever seen you so glowy," Nina said with a smile. "I'm glad you came because I'm happy you met someone."

"Well, I mean it was just a couple of hours in a bar." She felt the need to tap the brakes a bit. At least with her friends. Nina had already seen one of her relationships fizzle and die.

"Did you say he's a professor?" JT asked as he sped up to get on the freeway that would take her to her one-bedroom apartment.

It was in a nice part of town, but it was bland and colorless. She would bet the professor's place was full of books. "Yes. He teaches history at UTD. David Hawthorne."

Nina snapped her fingers. "I thought he looked vaguely familiar. Isn't he a Taggart?"

"No. His last name is Hawthorne." And her brain finally made the connection it should have hours and hours before. It wasn't like Hawthorne was a common last name. She felt dumb she hadn't put it together, especially since Kyle had been working the party. "He's Kyle's brother, and Kyle is Sean Taggart's stepson. Kyle Hawthorne joined my unit a couple of months ago, but I haven't worked with him. I've been out of the country most of the time since he hired on."

"I'd heard he was back from his stint in the Navy," JT said. "I've never met his brother though. So the two of you got along?"

David's mom didn't work in the kitchen. His mom owned the kitchen and the building, and at least four other restaurants in the DFW area, not to mention the fact that his stepdad regularly showed up on national cooking shows. And he had a connection to the big boss at McKay-Taggart.

JT had asked a question, and if she didn't reply they would know something was wrong. "He seemed nice. Like I said, he knew my mom."

"So you're going to go out with him," Nina prompted.

"I don't know." He hadn't mentioned that his stepdad owned the place. That seemed odd. He definitely hadn't mentioned his brother worked for McKay-Taggart. Kyle had been in the restaurant, and David had merely mentioned him in passing. "I've got a heavy workload for the next month or so. I'll have to see if I have the time."

The car went quiet, and she wished she'd grabbed a cab instead.

"Darling, he's not really a Taggart, you know," Nina began. "He's a professor. I don't think he runs in those circles if that's what you're afraid of."

"I'm not afraid of anything." It explained the Mustang. Even a shell of that car would be expensive. The full restoration would yield a car that was worth a small house. "It was a nice night, that's all."

The fact that he hadn't mentioned his stepfather bugged her. Why was he trying to hide the connection? Had he known exactly who she was? Not that she thought he was targeting her for something. Why would he? But also, why wouldn't he have mentioned that he was in a place his family owned?

JT started talking about something the kids had done and Tess sat back, all of the sparkle of the evening washed away. She knew it shouldn't matter who the man's family was, but it did. It mattered that he hadn't mentioned them. It mattered that she worked with his brother.

It mattered that he lived in a world she didn't belong in.

She was quiet the rest of the drive.

* * * *

David turned back to the bar. He'd watched Tessa until she'd disappeared from sight.

He would text her in the morning to thank her for tonight and ask if she had any time this weekend. He wanted to get at least one date in before he had to leave for South America. It wasn't a long trip, but he also didn't want a couple of weeks to go by without seeing her. He wasn't going to be that asshole who went by some rule that it wasn't masculine to contact a woman unless he'd left her hanging for a couple of days.

"Hey, bro. I'm surprised you're still here." Kyle strode behind the bar and picked up two longnecks. He was dressed in a suit, though he'd obviously shed the tie at some point in the evening. He nodded Leslie's way. "I'm taking one of them to Chef, and this one is my tax for grabbing it for him. You got my mom's wine? She's had a day."

The only time Kyle would call their stepdad Chef was here at Top, but then Sean tended to go into "chef" mode the minute he stepped inside the doors. It was like "general" mode except with food.

Leslie passed him a big glass of Cab. "Always. Let Grace know we've got it all handled tonight. She should put her feet up and relax."

Kyle chuckled as he grabbed a tray and placed all three drinks on it. "I doubt she'll do that, but I appreciate it." He turned back to David. "You want to join us? I've been told there are plenty of leftovers. They're doing family dinner, but I think Sean's setting up a private room for us. I think they want to talk."

He was still hungry, but it wasn't for food. "I should get home. I'm going to miss the last train if I don't get a move on."

Kyle stared at him. "Come on, man. You can't run every time."

Run? He wasn't running. Except maybe he was. It wasn't that he didn't love his mom, and he liked Sean, but he had never felt like he fit the way Kyle did. Kyle and Sean got each other. Their talks were easy, and they seemed to genuinely enjoy each other's company.

Sean tried. He did. Sean asked about what was happening at the college and how his book was going, but they'd never found the easy repartee he and Kyle had. Or Kyle and Luke. Their youngest half sibling was growing up Taggart, and that meant he was good looking and popular and athletic.

At least he could talk to Carys. Carys called him for advice all the time, and that made him feel like he was a part of the new family his mother had started.

"I'm not running. I stopped by to talk to Carys. Is she still here?"

Kyle shook his head. "She went home with Ian and Charlotte. She's spending the night with Tash and the twins. Was she okay? It looked like she'd been crying."

He was glad she was spending time with her cousins. Tasha was the oldest Taggart, and she had a good head on her shoulders. She would listen to Carys and give her sound advice on how to handle the situation. And the twins would bolster her emotionally. Kenzie would cry with her and Kala would help her plan bloody vengeance. All in all, they would be a solid team. "Someone posted shit on social media about her. It's mean-girl stuff."

"That sucks," Kyle said but seemed to dismiss it. "Come on. It'll mean a lot to Mom if you have dinner with us."

He was going to have to go. "I thought you already had dinner. Didn't you go to the private party?"

"I didn't actually go. I worked the party," Kyle explained. "Apparently there's always someone after the billionaire head of an energy company. I had a taste of it though. The quail was delicious, but I would have needed four of them to fill me up. I had to sneak Ian a burger. Did you know he can eat a whole burger in two bites? That's a big freaking burger."

If he'd worked the party, maybe he knew something about Tessa. She'd been a guest, and if he knew the way McKay-Taggart worked, someone had run background checks on all the guests. Didn't a Malone actually work for MT? It had been years and years since he'd spent any time at Sean's brother's office. He'd had a couple of summer jobs when he was doing his undergrad, but he hadn't worked cases or anything. He'd filed a lot of paperwork and organized things for his mom when she'd been the office manager there.

He dropped a thirty dollar tip for Leslie since she'd taken care of them all night and she wouldn't charge him for anything. Apparently neither he nor Kyle were allowed to pay Top for anything. It was one of the reasons he rarely came. It felt weird to not pay. He wasn't some trust fund kid. He'd worked his way through school, and he made his own way in the world.

"It was for the Malones, right? The family that owns the oil company." He could tiptoe his way around this subject. The last thing he needed was his brother giving him shit about a woman.

He followed Kyle as he started for the big office their mom and stepfather shared. His mom had taken over the daily operations of the restaurant empire while Sean oversaw anything creative, including the TV deals he'd made.

Sometimes he wondered if his mom ever thought about Peter Hawthorne anymore.

"Yep," Kyle replied. "It's Nina and JT's anniversary. They usually have it out at the ranch, but she wanted something in town this year. I think they didn't want Michael to have an excuse to not come. Since he broke things off with his fiancée, he's kind of been a hermit. I mean as much as a dude with millions of dollars, a high-rise condo, and a job as one of McKay-Taggart's top investigators can be. It must be weird for them to keep working together."

Yeah, he knew all about that. He'd only gone out with Darcy Riggs a couple of times, and it was odd to see her around campus. He couldn't imagine having to work with his ex.

The question was how did he manage to ask Kyle if he knew Tessa without setting off alarm bells in his brother's head? No one in the world could annoy him the way Kyle could. In a brotherly, give-him-shit way.

Then again, he could always kick his ass out of the town house.

His brother was staying at his place, and maybe the idea of homelessness would make him more respectful.

Or he could not say a word. That was the better plan.

Kyle pressed through the door. "Hello, you two. I bring cocktails, and Leslie said we should all relax. She's got things under control. Please tell me there are short ribs left."

His mom wore a slim skirt and a tailored shirt that made her look like a captain of industry. She was sitting at a table set for four. Sean had taken off the black jacket he wore in the kitchen and was in slacks and a T-shirt.

They made a striking couple. Anywhere those two went, eyes followed them.

He couldn't help but remember how many people said his mom had been way out of his father's league. They still joked about how Pete Hawthorne had managed to land Grace Thornton.

Tessa was gorgeous. She was probably way out of his league.

"I think you'll find I saved you a couple," Sean said, gesturing for them to all sit. "Thanks for working tonight. And David, it's good to see you. It's been a couple of weeks."

"I'm getting ready for the big trip." David leaned over and kissed his mom on the cheek before settling onto his chair. "I know it's still a ways off, but there's a lot to manage, and I'm probably only getting one shot at the library."

"He wants me to watch his cat." Kyle frowned and shrugged out of his jacket. "Who let him get a cat?"

"He showed up one day and wouldn't go away." He hadn't meant to become some weird cat dad. He'd gone home one night two years before and when he'd opened the door, a thin feline had sped inside. Before he'd known what he was doing, he was opening a can of tuna, and the cat never left. He now scooped kitty litter and often worked with a tabby sitting on his desk watching him. Hamilton was a cautious cat. He eyed everyone who came into the house as a potential enemy. Sometimes he swore that cat was plotting world domination. The good news was after a long period of wariness, Kyle and Hamilton were starting to get along. "And I saw you petting him last night. You know it doesn't make you less of a man to pet a cat."

"Fine." Kyle sank into his seat. "I'll admit Hamilton's kind of cool."

His mom leaned in. "That trip is what I wanted to discuss with you. By the way, thank you for talking to Carys. She's been so upset."

"David said she's dealing with high school crap." Kyle sighed in obvious appreciation as Sean uncovered the dishes.

Okay. Maybe he was hungry. Short ribs, risotto, and sauteed green beans. He could definitely eat.

"It's a little more than that. It's a complicated situation." His mom passed him the green beans. "But social media always is. I should never have allowed her to have a page. I try to monitor it."

"You wouldn't have been able to stop this. It didn't come from her. Even if you'd kept her off the Internet entirely, it would still have hit her hard. But she wouldn't have known it was coming." He felt for his sister. He hadn't had the kind of pressure on him Carys had on her. She was pretty and popular, and that meant someone was always looking to take her down. Any deviation from the norm would be punished in that world, and Carys had one big deviation.

"Did someone finally out her for being in a threesome?" Kyle asked.

Sean nearly dropped the plate. "What?"

His brother wasn't the most subtle of men and got their mom's death stare, the one that let them know she was going to end them if they didn't straighten up and fly right.

"Kyle," she began.

"What is going on?" Sean set down the platter. "I thought this was about some girl from her school saying mean things on social media. What is this about a threesome?"

"Not like a sexual threesome." Kyle looked his way as though David could save him from the land mine he'd stepped on.

He would love to let his brother wriggle on the hook, but he didn't want Sean to suffer. "Someone is going online posting pictures of her with Aidan and Tristan and saying fairly salacious things about the three of them."

"They're slut shaming my daughter for having male friends?" Sean had gone a nice shade of red.

His mom reached out and put a hand over her husband's. "Babe, they're shaming her for having two boyfriends, and you cannot do the same. I know you've tricked yourself into believing they're nothing more than friends, but they're dating, and we don't get to have a say in it because she's smart and they're all good kids. They are not having sex."

That red shade had fled, and his stepfather had gone a pasty white. Luckily, David knew where the Scotch was. This conversation required more than beer. He stood and moved to the bookshelf behind the big desk and poured out two fingers, offering it to Sean, who took it and downed it.

"I did not think I would need to hear those words today," Sean said, his voice steady.

"She's sixteen. She's got a good head on her shoulders, and she has feelings for two young men who are also good kids." He felt a definite need to make Carys's case. It was too easy for Carys to be held to a different standard than her brothers, and that wasn't fair to her.

"How did I not…" Sean began, and then he sighed and sat back. "I knew and I didn't want to admit it. She's always been drawn to those boys."

"They're some of your friends' kids, right?" He'd met Aidan O'Donnell and Tristan Dean-Miles, but he only vaguely knew their parents. "The families are all close, and doesn't one of them have two dads?"

"Yeah. Tristan comes by the idea of sharing a girlfriend honestly. His dads have happily shared a wife for years. I just didn't think my daughter would end up in a relationship like that," Sean allowed.

"She's not," his mom said. "She's dating them. They go out together, and there's no jealousy. It's a good relationship for her."

Sean looked to his wife. "She talks to you about this?"

"A little. I think she feels more comfortable talking to her brother. She talks to David during their tutoring sessions," his mom explained.

When his sister had struggled with Spanish, he'd offered to help her out. He'd been tutoring her for two years, and he enjoyed the time he spent with her. Without those weekly sessions, he might never have gotten to know Carys. He was starting sessions with Luke soon and looked forward to a closer relationship with his youngest sibling.

"But David doesn't talk to us," Sean pointed out. There was no small amount of accusation in the words.

Maybe he wouldn't be staying for dinner. He needed to make a few things plain to his mom and stepfather. He wasn't there to narc on his sister. "I wouldn't have talked to you about it this time if I didn't feel like Carys is going to have real problems. I wouldn't betray her trust unless I thought she was in danger. This is emotional danger, and you need to know. Mom already knew some of it. But if you're looking for someone to spy on your daughter, I'm not your man."

"David, sit down," Sean said quietly. "I appreciate the fact that she can talk to her brother and feel safe. You're also the only reason she's passing Spanish. I'm sorry. It's hard to admit that my baby girl is growing up. I'm not going to shame her for something that is normal and natural. I'm going to support her. Please let me know if you think she needs more support than we can give her."

This was why he liked Sean. David might not feel like he fit in with the family, but his stepfather was a good man. When David had first heard his mom was dating an ex-Green Beret, he'd thought Sean Taggart would be some macho asshole. He'd turned out to be one of the most thoughtful, tolerant men David had ever met. "I don't think she needs a therapist, but I don't know how this is going to play out. Some people will high-five her and others will look down on her."

"That sounds like life to me," Kyle said.

"Well, everything is dialed up to a hundred when you're a sixteen-year-old girl." His mom handed him the short ribs as he sat back down. She put a hand on his forearm, and her eyes were shining with tears as she whispered *thank you.*

"She'll be okay." His sister had a big group of family and friends around her.

"I want to know who was following her around." His mom sat back with a frown on her face. "Someone took pictures of her holding hands with Aidan and Tris. Whoever did it put the pictures on her volleyball team's social media page. It wasn't someone from her school."

"Or it was someone from her school who has a fake account." He'd thought about this, too.

"I'll figure it out." Kyle had a pile of food in front of him. "I have a friend who pretty much owns the Internet, and I'm putting her on this."

He knew the woman Kyle was talking about. MaeBe Vaughn was a cute hacker who worked for McKay-Taggart, and Kyle pretty much took every chance he could to get close to her. But she was a "friend."

David did not want to be friends with Tessa Santiago.

"The Internet has been rough on our family lately." Sean sat back.

"I told you, it's a troll, and it will go away," his mom said with a sigh before looking David's way. "We've been getting some weird reviews."

"And a surprise inspection." Sean frowned. "That wasn't such a big deal. Inspections happen, and we're always ready, but the timing was shitty. I don't know. Something feels wrong. Like I'm missing some connection I should catch."

Though he was a successful chef now, it wasn't hard to remember that once Sean had investigated things like corporate espionage. After all, it was how Sean had met his mother.

"I'll look into it," Kyle promised. "Like I said, MaeBe can find anything on a computer. If someone's fucking around with the family, she'll figure it out."

"I'm sure it's all coincidence." His mom set her fork down. "You know what they say. When it rains, it pours. And that brings me to what I want to talk to you about."

That got some alarm bells ringing. "You said it was about my trip."

He had a research trip planned to coincide with spring break, and it was even to a place with a beach. Not that he would be lying out by the ocean.

"Yeah, you're going to some island, right?" Sean seemed far more comfortable talking about this subject. He'd even picked up his fork again. "This is about the book you're writing? Something about a crazy millionaire?"

"Ah, he wasn't crazy. He was eccentric," David corrected, warming up to his favorite subject. "His name was Ricardo Montez…"

"And he wanted to change the world," Kyle finished sarcastically. He straightened up when Mom's death stare made a second appearance. "Sorry. I hear this story a lot. I mean a lot. He's obsessed. The whole hidden treasure thing is cool, but David talks about the man's political beliefs to the point that I've started to fall asleep when I hear the words *social democracy*. I'm pretty sure the cat does, too."

The cat liked to nap when he wasn't being a paranoid weirdo.

God, Hamilton was the feline version of Kyle, right down to purring the neighbor's cat's way but being way too scared to actually approach her.

He wasn't going to be Kyle or the cat. "I'm going down to the island Montez bought back in the eighties to do some research. I leave in two weeks, and I'll be gone for seven days."

"I want you to take your brother with you," his mom said.

He was twelve again being told he couldn't go to the movies if he didn't take his kid brother along. "I don't think Kyle wants to go."

"I do not, but I agree with Mom." Kyle suddenly had his serious face on. "You can't go without a bodyguard. Given everything that's happening around Sean right now, I don't feel comfortable with you alone in South America. You're not traveling straight to the island. You have to land in Buenos Aires, and then you're planning on riding a bus to Mar del Plata."

"Why would you take a bus?" his mom asked.

"I'm recreating Montez's first trip out to the island." He would be taking pictures and trying to make it as authentic as possible. "From Mar del Plata, I've hired a boat to take me to the island."

"Have you looked into the business behind the boat?" Sean asked.

"They had a great rating on the web." He wasn't sure why he was getting interrogated. He hadn't thought anyone was interested in his trip.

"There are several dangerous groups in the area who fund their terrorist activities by kidnapping wealthy travelers," Kyle pointed out. "They recently held the son of a Mexican businessman hostage for two months before they negotiated his release to the tune of a million dollars. I can give you several more instances in the last year."

"It's dangerous, but Kyle knows what he's doing," Sean explained.

"It's dangerous for wealthy people." He wasn't going to have Kyle suddenly in charge of his trip. "I'm a college professor. I don't have anything."

"Do you honestly believe I wouldn't pay to get you back?" His mom had a worried look on her face, and he knew it wasn't merely about him going to South America. It was the fact that Kyle was back and obviously troubled. Carys was going through some hard times. Luke was growing up.

"I think there aren't a lot of people in South America who know I'm your son. We don't share a last name, and Hawthorne doesn't open the doors that Taggart does." He loved his mom, but this trip was supposed to be easy.

"I assure you these militia groups do their research," Sean said. "And they have people on the inside. You're a rich target. I can't force you to take a bodyguard, but both your mother and I will feel infinitely better if we know Kyle's with you. He's been doing some background checks, and he already has questions about the boat you rented."

"Two of the employees have ties to militant groups." Kyle had a smirk on his face. It was the same one he'd had since they were kids, the one that came out when he bested his brother at something. "So your trip to the island was probably going to go wrong. It's cool. I canceled it for you."

"You did what?"

Kyle shrugged. "Can't have big brother getting himself kidnapped. I don't think you would do well in captivity. Don't worry. I'll handle everything, and you can take notes. And I already asked MaeBe if she can watch Hamilton. Big Tag signed off on the time out of office. It's going to be fun."

It was not going to be fun. It was going to suck. But he sat back because there was no way he was getting out of this.

He would text Tessa tomorrow. It would give him something to look forward to.

Sean and Kyle started talking about all the ways David could be brutally murdered. It was their love language.

"Baby, it's going to be okay." His mom reached out and held his hand briefly. "I appreciate you being open to this. I've been worried. I'll worry less if Kyle's with you."

Yep, he was going on a trip with his brother. "All right."

She sighed in obvious relief and started talking about the new location they would be opening in a few weeks.

David sat there and thought about Tessa.

At least one thing had gone right.

Chapter Three

"Did you hear about Kyle?"

Tessa looked up from her phone. She'd been staring at the three messages she'd received from David Hawthorne. They'd come in over the course of three days, and she couldn't stop thinking about them even two weeks later.

Hey, it's the crazy professor from Top. I was hoping you had some time this week. I promise a full plate of your own, and I know where to get the best enchiladas. How about it?

That had been sent the morning after they'd met. Professor Hawthorne didn't play the waiting game. She'd looked down at the text and felt a smile cross her face until she'd remembered the decision she'd made the night before. She couldn't go through another relationship that involved work. Work was all she had, and the fact that David Hawthorne had the most stunning eyes didn't change that truth.

Professor Hawthorne was way too close to her bosses, and that was why she'd ignored the text.

The next message had been a voice mail around twenty-four hours after the first.

"Hey, Tessa. It's David Hawthorne. I'm not sure if you got my text, so I thought I would try calling. I had a great time the other night and would love to see you again. Maybe we could meet for lunch or even coffee. I hope to hear from you."

She'd listened to that message about a hundred times. He'd gone back to text for his last message.

Tessa, I wanted to say it was lovely meeting you. I don't know what went wrong, but I'm going to delete your number so you don't have to worry about me calling again. I wish you all the best. David.

She believed him. He wouldn't be the guy who bugged her, needing some kind of answer as to why she refused to reply to him after the connection they'd made.

He was gone, and she would have to make sure she didn't run into him again. The good news was she rarely ever worked with Kyle, and David Hawthorne didn't frequent McKay-Taggart circles.

"Earth to Tessa." Wade Rycroft was standing at her desk, and he'd said something about Kyle. "Are you okay?"

She set her phone down and tried to focus. "Yeah, boss. What's up with Hawthorne?" She'd started calling Kyle by his last name as a reminder of why she wasn't answering those texts. In the days since that night, Kyle hadn't once mentioned his brother to her, and he hadn't acted awkward, so she had to believe that either David hadn't mentioned her or Kyle didn't care. She was happy either way. "I thought he was about to go on vacation."

She'd heard him talking about a beach, but she wasn't sure where he was going. There wasn't an assignment on the board with his name on it, so she'd assumed it was a vacation. Which seemed weird since he hadn't been working for McKay-Taggart for more than six months. Vacation days didn't kick in until then, but she'd guessed that being a member of the boss's family had its perks.

Another reason to not date David Hawthorne.

Even when she wanted to. She'd sat up late the night before wondering how he was feeling. If he was hurt that she hadn't replied or if he'd already moved on.

"Not a vacation, exactly, and that's why I'm going to need you to report upstairs in thirty minutes." Wade was a big man who'd spent as much time on a ranch as he had in the Army. He started out of her office, the obvious order being that she was to follow. "Kyle was finishing up a close-cover assignment this morning. He was putting the client on her plane back home when he dropped her luggage and broke his damn foot. He's at the hospital now."

She hustled to keep up with Wade. "That must have been some

heavy-ass luggage."

"Apparently it was a freak accident thing. He was in the exact right position to have it bust three bones. It's not a big deal, but he's going to have to stay off of it for a couple of days, and then he'll be in a boot," Wade explained. He had a folder in his hand as he walked down the hallway.

"That's awful, and I'll pitch in to send him a basket or something, but I don't see what it has to do with me. He doesn't have an assignment on the board." He wouldn't if he was going on a vacation. Tessa had a job starting the next day, but it was a short-term gig. She would be providing additional security for the former president, who was coming into town to give a speech at SMU. She was working with the Secret Service to ensure that President Hayes had a quiet, totally drama free three days in Dallas. Then she would have to stare down the weekend. Again.

How could she miss someone she barely knew? The temptation to call him, to apologize, was almost overwhelming, but it didn't change the fact that it was a mistake to date someone close to her boss. And she knew she didn't belong in the world David Hawthorne ran in. He wasn't some down-on-his-luck professor. He had family money behind him, and that came with strings Tessa had already figured out could strangle a girl no matter how awesome the family was.

"This one was off the books, but it's important to Ian, so I need you to take it." Wade kept moving toward the stairs that would take them up to the main office of McKay-Taggart. She rarely went up, preferring the relative laid backness of what the rest of the company called the "Man Cave." The bodyguard unit was on the floor below the main MT office and above Miles-Dean, Weston, and Murdoch's elegantly high-tech offices. The Man Cave was comfy with a gym and a kitchenette, and sometimes Wade brought his German shepherd. She was comfortable here.

She shook her head. He was definitely not thinking about the assignment she already had. "I can't. I've got a meeting with Secret Service this afternoon."

She'd been planning this assignment for six weeks. She'd done the legwork, and now all that was left was to knock it out of the park, impress everyone, and get the promotion she deserved. The bodyguard unit was growing, and Wade was looking to break it into two teams with two leads. There was zero question Jamal would get one of those positions. She wanted the other one. Doing this job well would all but assure her of the promotion.

"I've already passed that on to Jamal. He and West will take over for you." Wade opened the door and started up the stairs.

She hurried to catch up. "Hey, you can't give my assignment away."

"I can because I'm the boss. It's literally what I do. I hand out assignments. This is your new one. I hope your passport is up to date." He handed over the folder.

He knew damn well it was. "All right. I'll bite. Where am I going?"

"Argentina. You're flying to Buenos Aires this evening. From there, you're going to a city on the coast, and then to a private island."

"So this is a close-cover assignment?" Who was she dealing with? She'd provided security for movie stars and politicians and businesspeople. South America would have its own unique problems, like any place would. Any place in the world could be dangerous under the right circumstances. "Is the client wealthy?"

"He's from a wealthy family, and he would definitely be considered a high-value target, if that's what you're asking." They'd made it to the top of the stairs, and Wade held the door open for her.

"Do we have any known threats?" It was kind of sad that she was hoping the answer would be yes. It had been a while since her adrenaline had been up. The last time she'd been shot at had been years ago. What she needed now was a good high-danger case to take her mind off the sexy professor.

She wondered what he was doing for spring break. It had to be coming up soon. Would he head out to his stepfather's lake house? Or take some luxury vacay?

Her mom used to spend her spring breaks preparing for the rest of the school year.

"Not that Kyle found." Wade started for the big guy's office.

Who was Kyle protecting? And why Kyle? There was no doubt the man was good, but he wasn't seasoned. If this was a client Taggart wanted to impress, why send Kyle?

"You've got some of Kyle's notes in that folder, but he's going to send you the rest. He worked on a lot of this at his place." A wide smile came over Wade's face. "Well, hello, pretty lady. I heard there was an angel up on this floor, but I didn't believe it."

She didn't gag the way she would have if Wade had been

genuinely trying to pick up Taggart's admin with that line. He'd already picked her up and taken her out and gotten her pregnant. Geneva Rycroft gave her husband a grin. "You still have it, babe. That would totally work on me."

When she'd started dating Michael, this was kind of what she'd been looking for. McKay-Taggart was full of happy couples who worked together and never seemed to have a single problem unless Big Tag pissed off Charlie and then got his lemon snacks taken away. That had been a rough week.

Wade leaned over and kissed his wife. "I'm glad to know I still got it. Is he in there?"

Genny nodded. "He's been on the phone all morning. And you should know that some of your guys have already been up here planning how to give Kyle as much hell as possible for letting a Louis Vuitton suitcase take him down."

"We're going to give him so much shit." Hutch leaned against the doorframe of his office. Greg Hutchins was McKay-Taggart's resident IT expert. "My fiancée knows some crazy science stuff that will elevate all of my pranks."

Yep, she had another wedding to go to. Hutch—the dude least likely to ever get married—was planning a wedding with a scientist cutie named Noelle. It would be the first wedding she had to go to since she and Michael had canceled theirs.

"Poor Kyle." MaeBe Vaughn worked IT as well. She was the classic gamer girl, with purple hair, black lipstick, and combat boots. She was adorable, and the word around the office was Kyle was sweet on her. She settled her crossbody over her shoulder. "I've got to go pick up a cat from Kyle's and pack a bag for him. He doesn't know it, but he's going to his mom's place. He seems to think he can get up and down the stairs of the town house. Is he floating up them? David's not going to be there, so he'll end up starving to death."

The mention of his name made her heart flutter.

Flutter. It was a stupid word, and an even stupider thing to do. She wanted to ask about why David wouldn't be there. Did Kyle live with him? Was David taking a trip?

All of those bricks of information fell into place and reminded her that she wasn't merely supposed to throw her body in front of bullets. She was also an investigator, and she could properly connect the dots.

David was a professor specializing in South American history and politics. Naturally his brother going on an assignment with him wouldn't be considered a "job."

David would be a high-value target given who his stepfather was. He would need security. He wasn't trained and his brother was, and now his brother couldn't go anywhere. She spoke the language and was used to international travel. She was the perfect person to slide into Kyle's spot and make sure the boss's step-nephew remained safe.

Except she couldn't.

"I can't do this." She looked down at the folder, and there was David's name. "Look, Wade, I get why you want me on this assignment, but I'm not protecting David Hawthorne. No way. I'm not going."

She couldn't be alone with the man. If she was alone with him, she wouldn't be able to hold out. She would end up kissing him again, and kissing would lead to touching, and touching would lead to a lot more. By the end of the week, she wouldn't want to leave him and wouldn't be able to protect her heart and her job the way she should.

Everyone had stopped, and all eyes were on her. Wide eyes. The kind of eyes that told a woman she'd fucked up.

"Well, I'll find someone else, then," a deep voice said. A familiar voice.

She didn't want to turn, but she did, and sure enough, there was David looking sexy in a sport coat, a briefcase in his hand like he'd come straight from a lecture.

"If it helps, I didn't know you worked here," David said. "I promise I'm not stalking you. I'll let Ian know we need someone else."

"There isn't anyone else."

Yay, the big boss was standing in his doorway, and he'd heard her completely reject his nephew. Awesome.

"I can handle the trip." David's shoulders squared, and he pointedly didn't look her way. "I was planning on going solo anyway. My mom is being overly cautious. I'll call my friend and have him send a driver out for me. I'll skip the bus trip, and once I'm on the island, I'll be perfectly safe."

MaeBe held up a hand. "Uh, I've been monitoring some chatter on the Dark Web about a celebrity's son traveling to South America."

"My dad wasn't a celebrity, and he's also no longer with us." David's tone was curt, his jaw tight. "I stay out of my stepfather's business as much as I can. So they must be talking about someone else."

"Or they don't know you've got a chip on your shoulder about your mom's husband," Hutch said with a shake of his head. "Either way, it's too dangerous unless you take a bodyguard."

"Santiago, Wade, my office now." Big Tag looked Hutch's way. "Why don't you take David to the conference room? If he slips away, I'll be shoving those Red Vines you love so much where you don't want them shoved."

"That's rude," Hutch said. "And effective. Come on, Professor. Let the big guys work this out."

She could feel the flush that had come over her. Not only had she pissed off the boss, she'd hurt David, and that hadn't been her intention. She followed Tag inside. "I'm sorry, Mr. Taggart. I can't go to Argentina right now."

"You have other plans?" Big Tag was a mass of muscle who didn't look like he was a fifty-year-old with five kids. He looked like a dude who shot people for a living, and she was likely next. "Because I thought you understood that this was the kind of job where shit comes up and you take care of it. If you wanted a nine to five, you should have applied somewhere else."

The ice coming off that man could freeze fire. "I think I should stay on the Hayes assignment. Jamal likes to travel."

"Jamal's mother is going through chemo treatments, and he's her main support system. Do you want to drive her to and from her treatments?" Tag's blue eyes stared at her like lasers.

Her gut knotted. "I didn't know. Of course not."

"Everyone but West is on assignment, and West is in training," Tag pointed out.

"I wouldn't send West," Wade said. "He's got no international experience. He's barely been off the ranch, so I'm not sending him to Argentina." Her boss sighed. "I'll go, Ian."

He was supposed to go on vacation with his wife and stepson and daughter. They were going to Disney World for spring break. "You can't cancel your trip."

They'd been planning it forever. He'd been excited, and his daughter would be devastated.

"I won't cancel. Genny and Ash can take Bella." Wade's face had gone grim. "I wouldn't be able to look Sean in the face if anything happened to David."

"Or David could understand that he shouldn't take a trip that's so dangerous," she shot back. She wasn't sure why David couldn't understand this was a potentially bad idea.

"David has one shot at getting the information he needs to document a moment in history. History is important to him. It's his whole career, and from what Grace has told me, it's always been his focus." Big Tag leaned against the edge of his desk. "Imagine being a nerdy kid who reads biographies of Napoleon while all your friends are playing video games. Except he didn't have a lot of them. Friends, I mean. He's been working on a book about this man for years. I would go with him if I could, but it's almost spring break, and half the office is taking off. Santiago, did my nephew do something he shouldn't have? Is there a personal reason you're refusing this assignment?"

The image of a studious boy reading his books and likely getting bullied and feeling alone struck her hard. David hadn't done anything but have a great conversation with her and honor her boundaries. He'd been polite and tried to put her at ease even when she'd been rude to him. "I don't think it's a good idea for me to be alone with him."

"Wade, could you give us the room? Don't change your plans. If I can't convince her to go, I'll figure out a way to do it myself. I'm not letting David miss this opportunity, and I'm not going to be the one who costs your little girl time with her dad at Disney World."

Wade nodded and then she was alone with the big boss and a shit ton of guilt. How had she not known about Jamal's mom? She'd cut herself off from everyone, built up walls around herself, and then bitched about being isolated. She thought because the people around her seemed happy that they didn't have a care in the world, but she knew Genny had a tough time before she and Wade got married and that every minute they had together was precious. West had hired on after an accident at the ranch he'd grown up on. Kyle hid his pain.

"What did my nephew do?" The question came out in an even tone.

She hated the weakness, but she had to blink back tears. "I spent some time with him a couple of weeks ago. He made me like him, and I don't want to like anyone right now."

Big Tag's shoulders came down, and a groan came from the man's mouth. "For fuck's sake. Do you have any idea how many times I've been through this?"

She sat down because this seemed like it was going to be a long lecture that ended with her going to South America.

It was time to remember that she had a team around her, and she owed them, too.

"Why can't I get clients no one wants to sleep with? I seriously think I should hire people based on their fucking sex drives," Tag continued. "I would say older people, but those suckers want some, too."

How bad could it get? Moments before, David had looked at her like she was the last person in the world he wanted to sleep with. She'd been a bitch, so maybe thinking he would be tempting was now a completely one-sided thing.

"Here's a clue, Santiago. Don't sleep with him. From what I can tell he lives like a monk anyway, so if you're not some musty old book, he probably won't notice you're there."

The boss could really go on and on.

But one thing was clear. She was going to do her job. No matter how much it hurt.

* * * *

So this was what it felt like to be in the big conference room. David had wondered sometimes since he'd heard a lot of stories about this place. His stepdad had sat here and listened to the plans for the op that sent him to Fort Worth all those years ago, to the place where Grace Hawthorne worked.

"You know you don't have to sit there. I'm not going to slip out." He wasn't going to run away, but he also wasn't about to force a woman who didn't like him to spend time with him.

Look, Wade, I get why you want me on this assignment, but I'm not protecting David Hawthorne. No way. I'm not going.

She'd been so adamant. It had been a real kick in the gut.

"Big Tag was serious about those Red Vines." Hutch had been sitting with him while Ian decided his fate.

At least when it came to a bodyguard. Ian couldn't stop him from leaving this evening. He wasn't missing this opportunity. He'd been researching this book for five years. Having access to Ricardo Montez's personal library, to the island and the treasure that was supposedly hidden there, was a biographer's dream. This book was the key not only to assured tenure, but also to getting this lost gem of a story out in the world.

"So what'd you do to Santiago? Not that it takes much these days." Hutch sat back, putting his feet up on the conference room table.

"I asked her out." That was the killer. He wasn't sure where he'd gone wrong. He'd asked her out. He'd attempted to make sure there wasn't a miscommunication, and when it was obvious she wasn't going to answer him, he deleted her number from his phone and hadn't bothered her again. They'd had such a good connection that night, but he wasn't the smartest man when it came to dating. He'd missed a cue or something.

Or he hadn't because she'd been the one to kiss him. She'd been the one to put her lips on his, her eyes glowing in the low light as she'd walked away.

What had happened between that moment and this one? It wasn't like he hadn't faced rejection before, but this one had hurt like hell.

Hutch whistled. "Damn. You stepped in it."

Obviously Hutch had been hired in on Ian's sarcasm initiative. "Yes, it was clearly a mistake."

Hutch sighed and sat back. "Tessa's touchy right now. She was engaged and it ended. It was amicable, but she still has to work with the guy. It's sad because they're both nice people. I think she's got what I like to call the thirty-year-old blues. It's when all your friends are married and happy and it hasn't happened for you."

Maybe the intimacy he'd felt had been one-sided. Maybe she'd taken a look around and realized she could do way better than a professor of history. It wouldn't be the first time. Hell, he'd had a couple of women who'd dated him so they could meet his happily married stepfather.

Maybe *he* had the thirty-year-old blues.

His cell phone trilled, and he glanced down. His research assistant. He'd only hired Luis the semester before, and the grad student was already working overtime. Luis Vasquez was a double major in history and Spanish, making him the perfect research assistant. He also had family ties in Argentina, and those had already started paying off as Luis had left for Buenos Aires the day before. David slid a finger across the screen to accept the call. "Did you make it okay?"

"Not only made it to the city, but I'm already here on the island. I managed to get a cell signal and thought I would take advantage. I hope you don't mind, but I called Eduardo and he said it was all right to come out early. I'm taking some great film for you," Luis said.

"I thought you wouldn't be out until later in the week." He'd been planning to visit with a cousin of his who lived in a seaside town.

"My cousin took off with a girl he met in his math class. They're on their way to Brazil for the week. I thought work sounded better than sitting in his place alone. I would have to clean it first," Luis said with a huff, and then a bit of static came over the line.

"I'm glad you got in okay," David said. "I've run into some problems here."

"I'm sorry. You cut out on me," Luis said. "This signal is going to drop at any moment. I wanted to let you know that Eduardo's eager to talk to you. I think he's found something his dad left, and it's in a code from what I can tell. He won't show me," Luis admitted. "He's a little manic, but he seems cool. I'm going to go out and get some footage of the estate and talk to some of the people in the town close to here. I thought I'd wait until you get here to go up to the mountain."

Montaña del Cielo. Heaven's Mountain. It was on that mountain that Montez had written his manifesto about freedom for all people, decrying the very capitalism that had granted him the money to buy the island in the first place.

Montez's story was the thing of legend. And it would also make an excellent documentary someday since Montez had at least three wives and a whole lot of exotic animals in his own personal "paradise."

"Well, enjoy yourself because when I get there tomorrow afternoon we're going to work our asses off." He had one week to get what he needed. Or to convince Eddie that his crazy dad's life was a brilliant story and he should keep the nature preserve he'd built intact for future generations. Montez had been eccentric, but he'd cared about the people on his island and the wildlife there. "My flight takes off in about eight hours, and I'll contact you when we land."

"I'm...forward to seeing...again." The call started to go in and out, proof that any cell service on the island would be unreliable.

And then the line went dead, Luis obviously losing the signal.

David frowned and set down his cell. "I didn't get a chance to tell him Kyle's not coming. The last time I talked to him I told him there would be two of us." He was going to convince Ian that all of this was unnecessary. It was one thing for Kyle to tag along, but he wasn't about to ruin someone else's vacation because his mom was paranoid.

And it wasn't like he would be alone. Luis would be with him. He was fairly certain his mom wouldn't see his twenty-two-year-old assistant as a proper guard, but there was safety in numbers.

"You're crazy if you think you're going in alone." Hutch yawned. "If MaeBe says there's talk about you on the Dark Web, there's talk about you on the Dark Web. I mean, if you want to write a book about being kidnapped and held for ransom, this would be a great way to get some research in."

"No one wants to kidnap me."

"Maybe they don't want to but they have to," Hutch countered. "They probably don't even like their jobs. Who would? It's a pain in the ass to kidnap someone. I should know. I worked for the Agency for a while, and then there's every single bachelor party we have around here. It always starts with trying to make the dude crap his pants and ends up with someone vomiting. It's why I'm not having one. Of course, if I was me, I wouldn't care that I wasn't having a bachelor party. I would still kidnap me in revenge for all the shit I've done before. I have to think about that. Do you think sincere apologies would work? My fiancée bought like fifty pounds of good card stock for our save-the-date cards. I could use those. Apparently good card stock makes things seem more serious."

Luckily the door came open and Ian strode in. Sean's brother was practically a superhero, if superheroes had potty mouths and were sarcastic. So he was Deadpool. The point was Ian Taggart was a larger-than-life hero. Many of the men and women who worked here were. Who had Tessa been engaged to? Which one of the super-muscular, knew-how-to-kill-a-man-fifty-different-ways dudes had she been in love with?

"All right. I've got everything set up. Hutch, when MaeBe gets back have her send me a full-on report on everything she's got on the threat to my not-nephew," Ian said. "Your Red Vines are safe."

Hutch hopped out of the chair and gave the boss a jaunty salute. "I wasn't worried about the vines, Tag. I was worried about where you would shove them. I'm a taken man now, and all of my bits are reserved for my gorgeous girl. Also, there's someone named Luis we're going to have to do a background check on because Kyle's workup doesn't even mention him."

"He's my assistant. Kyle's met him. He's been working with me for months." There was a reason his mom was paranoid. She'd been around security guys for way too long.

"Yeah, see, most of the time the bad guy doesn't show up at the last minute twirling his long mustache," Hutch said. "So I'll run a background check."

Was he serious? "It'll be a waste of time."

"Big Tag will tell you there is nothing I love more than to waste time," Hutch replied confidently. "It's my favorite hobby."

Ian nodded. "It's on his employee review every single time. Please, David, waste Hutch's time."

David sighed. "His name is Luis Vasquez. He's a student at UTD employed by the history department. I don't know his Social Security number or anything like that."

Hutch waved that off. "No need. I don't need numbers. Good luck not getting kidnapped, man."

Hutch was a weird dude.

Ian sat down across from him. "Hutch is going to be wishing he had that luck. I happen to know how his bachelor party's going to go."

"He said he wasn't having one."

Ian's lips quirked up in a slightly evil grin. "He's not the one planning it. It's okay. We're calling this party Karma Comes for Hutch. It's probably not illegal. Mostly."

He did not envy Hutch. But he kind of wanted to go to that party. "I'm sorry this is such a pain in the ass. I didn't mean it to be."

"No, you meant to do your thing and not have anyone notice." Ian's grin had faded. "Are you and Sean okay? You were quick to point out we're not family."

Fuck. He hadn't meant to do that. "I know we are, but it's not the same. Ian, you have to know how much I appreciate everything you've done for me and for Kyle. And definitely for my mom."

"But you get upset if someone mistakenly calls Sean your dad." Ian let a moment pass while David fumbled for what to say. "He loves you, you know."

The big guy could make him uncomfortable on every level. He was sarcastic as hell one minute and talking about his feelings the next. Often in a weird way, but the earnest Ian knocked him for a loop.

This was Ian the dad. Ian was dadding him.

It made his tongue way looser than normal. "It would be easy to slide into that because Sean has been good to me over the years. But I was an adult when they got married."

"You were in college. You weren't an adult, but I understand. It would have been different if they'd married while you were a kid."

It was more than that. "If I called Sean Dad, it feels like I erase my real dad. I'm not trying to push Sean away or keep something from him. My parents didn't divorce. My father died and for a long time it was me and my mom and Kyle, and despite the fact that my dad was gone, he was still there, you know?"

Ian nodded. "And then Sean comes in and your mom doesn't talk about your dad anymore."

"There's no blame here," David promised. "I'm glad she's happy, but I sometimes wonder if she remembers him at all."

Ian sat back with a sigh. "I'm sure she does. Look, David, you're in a hard situation."

He shook his head. "I'm not. My mom's happy. Sean's good to her, and he's great to my siblings."

"But you don't know where you fit in this big family of ours, and sometimes you wonder if you want to fit at all." Ian summed up the situation nicely. "I can understand that. We're loud and overwhelming at times, and I can be a massive ass. I know. It's shocking that I have so much self-awareness, but it's true. You've watched your mom fall in love with someone who was very different from your father, and you have to wonder about that, too."

"Wonder what would have happened if my father had lived and Mom still met Sean?" David mused. "Yeah, I sometimes wonder about that. They fit. They have a real passion for each other I don't remember Mom and Dad having."

"Well, you were a kid, and kids miss things like that if it's not right in their face," Ian pointed out. "It's precisely why I leave the door unlocked every now and then. Gives the kids a jolt they need. It also makes them nauseous for a couple of hours, so I save on food. Sorry. Sarcasm is my go-to when I find myself in a hard conversation. There's no way to know what might have happened if your dad had been alive when Grace met Sean. I have to deal with the reality in front of me, and I assure you the groups who might view you as a way to make some cash don't care about your conflicted feelings. I'm not saying that to piss you off or to be an ass. It's the truth, and I can't let you go down there without a trained guard."

His frustration was rising. "I have to go, and I'm willing to take the chance. I don't see what you can do to stop me."

"Well, there are a couple of things I can do. I can have you on a no-fly list in fifteen minutes. Hutch will be more than happy to do that. He lives to hack. He even has the T-shirt," Ian said evenly. "Or I can save you the trouble of getting kidnapped down south and do it right here. I assure you we have places to stash you. We'll set you up next to your brother."

"Okay, I get it." David felt his jaw clench. "You're bigger and stronger and smarter than me."

"Definitely not smarter on most things, but I am in this," Ian allowed. "I know how important this is to you, so take a bodyguard and listen to her. You're in charge of all things intellectual, and she's in charge of making sure you don't get hurt. Do it for your mom."

"Her? The bodyguard is a woman?" His brain went into overdrive. It would take a while to get over seeing Tessa again. He prayed Ian wasn't saying what he might be saying.

"Yes, Tessa is going to escort you." Ian confirmed his worst fear. "I know you and she have apparently had a moment, but she's all I've got unless I want to inconvenience a bunch of families who need some vacation time. And honestly, she's who I would send. She speaks Spanish, and she blends in. Blending in is important at times."

That was the last thing he needed. "Come on, Ian. You saw how she reacted. She doesn't want to have anything to do with me. I would feel uncomfortable forcing her into that situation."

Not to mention his discomfort at having to be around the woman who'd managed to break his heart and he'd barely kissed her.

"She can be professional. You can be professional." Ian wasn't backing down. "If she thinks the island is safe, she won't have to be with you every minute of the day. So basically you have a ten-hour flight that you can mostly sleep through and then a boat ride, and you're on the island. Also, she's not uncomfortable with you. She's uncomfortable with herself and the fact that you're connected to me. She had a relationship with another employee. It didn't work out, and she's still not sure why it didn't. She thinks if she starts something with you and it goes bad she might lose her job. I don't know why she thinks that since I never get to fire anyone, but that's where she is."

David could understand that. "I heard she was engaged."

"To Michael Malone. Charlie set them up, but I always thought they were too alike. Tessa needs someone who can balance her. Honestly, Kyle's been talking about setting the two of you up," Ian said.

His brother had mentioned there was a woman at his office who might fit well with him. Had his brother been trying to play matchmaker? "Why would he do that?"

Ian chuckled. "No idea, man. He's spent too much time around happy couples, I suspect, and he's not even close to being ready to go after the woman he's crazy about. So he's turned his attention to you. And he's not necessarily wrong. You hit it off, didn't you?"

In spectacular fashion. "And then she ghosted me."

"Well, now you can give her the cold shoulder and let her know how it feels," Ian pointed out. "Or you could show her that you're not Michael and you're not going to move in a world she feels uncomfortable in. I suspect she thinks you're more invested in your stepfather's wealthy world than you are. I also suspect she doesn't understand that the kind of money my brother and I have isn't the same as Malone money. We might have a private jet, but we share it between three different businesses and bicker over that sucker endlessly. We might have a lake house, but again, it's a family asset. It's amazing, but it's not a mansion. We're new money and happy to be new money. It's not the same. Although I suppose canceling your coach seats and shoving you on the aforementioned private jet isn't going to make my case."

"What?"

Ian pushed back from the table. "Yep. I canceled your tickets. According to MaeBe, there's talk of a wealthy American coming into Buenos Aires via commercial jet tomorrow, so we're going to change that up. You leave at eight this evening from Dallas Executive. I'm not doing it for your comfort. I'm doing it because of those messages MaeBe found on the Dark Web. If they don't know when you're coming in, they can't kidnap you. You'll have a car and a driver waiting for you. Or we can do the kidnapping thing. It could be fun."

He sat there for a moment, trying to figure out if his uncle was being…

He'd just thought of Ian as his uncle. Damn it. He worried about his father being erased, but somehow this crazy family his mother had married into had become his, and Ian wasn't being a dick. He was worried. Sean would be worried. God knew his mother would. "I'll do this your way. And thank you for putting up with my stubbornness."

Ian chuckled and put a hand on his shoulder. "Your stubbornness is nothing. I've had to deal with telling Boomer that a sandwich he wanted to eat had gone bad. That was stubbornness. I've given Tessa Kyle's notes, but you should know they're thin. You're going to have to fill her in on some aspects of the op. She'll meet you at the airport."

Where he would have to survive an all-night flight with the most beautiful woman he'd ever met. A woman who wanted nothing to do with him.

Because he was some wealthy dude with connections that could cost her a job she loved.

Except he wasn't.

He was being pessimistic. The way she'd ghosted him had thrown him for a loop.

"You honestly think she rejected me for my family connections?"

A brow rose over Ian's blue eyes. "She told me so. She also told me she said what she said today because she's afraid if she's alone with you, she'll rip your clothes off and ride you like the intellectual stallion you are."

That got him sitting up straighter. "She did?"

Ian shrugged. "Not in so many words, but you get the gist. Tessa's fierce when it comes to some things. She's a genuine badass, but she took some losses she hasn't dealt with yet. I don't even think she realizes how they're holding her back. If you want her, I would bet you could have her. It wouldn't take much, but be careful with her. She's oddly delicate. You might need some of that stubbornness. And I can answer the real question that's going through your head. You need to answer it and be sure before you go after anyone."

That made David wary. "What question is that?"

"Was your father the prologue to a great love story?" Ian asked in a quiet tone. "Was he the warm-up act? Is that all you can expect to be?"

Damn, but the man was perceptive. "I guess I do ask myself that question. I look at a woman like Tessa and wonder why she would settle for me. That's what everyone joked about when my dad was alive. My mom was too beautiful for him, too vibrant. He was a fairly boring guy."

"Not according to your mom," a familiar voice said.

David winced because his stepfather was standing in the doorway.

"Excellent timing, brother." Ian stood. "I've got David all set up, and now you can do the stepdad thing. Also, the bodyguard I hired for him wants his hot bod bad, but she's real gun-shy, and he's going to turtle on her. If Grace wants grandkids anytime soon, you better talk to him."

"I'm not turtling." David wasn't so out of touch he hadn't heard the term. He didn't go into his shell when things got slightly emotionally tough. Did he?

Sean's brows came up in that way they did when someone said something dumb. "Sure you aren't." He slid into the seat Ian had vacated. "And you're wrong about your dad. He wasn't boring. He was incredibly smart, and he was tenacious. You do know he put himself through college, right? He worked two jobs and had a family. Your mom said he was Superman because he would get up and work four hours at UPS, then manage to make it home to have breakfast with her before he took his classes. He'd come home and eat dinner with her before he worked another shift at a video store. When he slept she had no idea, but he did it because he loved her and they had you by then. He could have taken a job somewhere and y'all would have gotten by, but he wanted more for all of you. He wanted to ensure that he could take care of you the way he thought you should be taken care of."

The way Sean was talking about his dad…well, he hadn't expected it. "How do you know all of this?"

"Because I asked your mom. After we got married, I asked her to tell me everything about Peter. I love your mom, and I wanted to know everything about her and her life, but beyond that, I wanted to know who your dad was because we had a connection, he and I. We both love your mother, and we both love you and your brother. I wanted to know what kind of a dad he was because I didn't know how to be one, and he seemed to be good at it."

Damn, the Taggart brothers seemed determined to get him emotional today. He was a man who liked to live inside his head. When things got real, he tended to draw in on himself and get lost in his work.

Fuck. He really was turtling. Had he been doing that for the last twenty or so years? Had he been doing it since his dad died?

"I didn't realize you were talking to her about him. I guess I thought once my mom met you she kind of forgot about him. I wouldn't blame her."

Sean leaned in. "Of course you would. David, you are not going to hurt my feelings because you loved your dad and you felt something when your mom got remarried."

David needed to make something plain to his stepfather. "I'm glad she's happy. I didn't want her to be alone."

"But you think I'm different from your dad," Sean said. "So different that you have to wonder what she saw in him. And that's where you're wrong. Your father and I are similar in a lot of ways. You know his dad wasn't exactly kind to him. He survived a lot."

Now David had to wonder if Sean didn't know things about his dad that he himself did not. "I know he used to talk about how important it was to keep my temper in check."

Sean nodded. "Because his father couldn't. Because his father was abusive. You never knew your grandfather because your dad wouldn't let him near you. Your father was intensely protective. He might not have gone into the military, but he was a guardian. He was fierce about his family."

So many memories flowed over David. "He was a good dad."

"Yes, he was, and he is not forgotten," Sean promised. "You aren't some side note for your mother. Or me. You might not share our last name, but you do belong. You might find yourself in this weird family where almost everyone is ex-military, but who do they call when they need to know something other than a football score? You are the reason most of the kids in our family are passing their classes because you help with homework. And you're handy with cars. It's a gift."

He felt a smile spread across his face. "I'm afraid I get my muscle car addiction from my dad. After he made sure we were all comfortable, he bought this 1955 Ford Thunderbird. He spent five years rebuilding that car and then he sold it after driving it for three months. Said the fun was in rebuilding it. I think he also liked how much he could sell the sucker for. He bought Mom a new car from that."

Sean sat back. "I know what would have happened if he'd lived, David. He would be with your mother today. He would have made sure she was never put in a position where I got to meet her. Even if I had, she would have been happily married, and I would have respected that. I'm not happy you lost your dad, but you have to know that I am happy I got to be in your life."

David groaned because he had to let this go. "You're good at this, Sean."

"I'm glad. So I can tell your mom she doesn't have to worry about you?"

His mom had her hands full between Kyle's damage and Carys's scandalous young love. "I'll go with Tessa."

Sean stood. "Good. I appreciate it, and I look forward to reading that book of yours when you finish it."

David followed his lead because if he was going to make that flight, he probably should get a move on. Sean wasn't lying. He would read the book when it came out. Sean always read his articles, even the ones his mom could barely get through because she wasn't interested in voter trends in newly emerging democracies.

His dad would have liked Sean.

When Sean held a hand out, David made his decision. That hand was out because David had held him off. Sean was a hugger when it came to his family.

David gave his stepdad a hug and practically felt the relief go through him.

Maybe he hadn't been the only one who worried if he fit in.

"Do you need a ride out to the airport?" Sean asked as he started for the door. "I don't think you've been on the jet before. The airport is this tiny thing."

He could take a cab. Or… "Do they have a place to park?"

"Of course, and it's secure," Sean explained. "I want you to call me if you need anything at all. And please leave your cell on. I know it's weird, but your mom feels safer when she can see a little blip on her phone."

His mom still tracked him, and he didn't mind. It wasn't like he went anywhere interesting. But he was wondering if he shouldn't drive himself. And maybe make a point. "I'll leave it on, though you should know cell service is sketchy on the island. And I think I'll drive myself. Thanks, Sean. I'll see you when I get back, and tell Mom that Kyle is a whiny man baby when he's sick and she should prepare for that now."

Sean sighed. "I'll let her know. I think he's going to be stubborn."

David chuckled. "You have no idea."

Sean strode off toward Ian's office, and David felt something settle deep inside. Why hadn't they had that talk before now?

Sean wasn't trying to take his dad's place. He was simply trying to find his own. Like everyone was.

He noticed Tessa was standing outside the conference room, a worried look on her face. "Hey, I thought maybe we should talk. I should explain what happened."

He was absolutely certain she would give him the "it's me, not you" talk, and in this case apparently it really was her and not him. The trouble was that made him think he might have a shot with her if he played his cards right. It might be time to take a chance. But he had to do this right or he would lose her again. Luckily, he knew a lot about politics, and sometimes a smart man had to know when to bluff.

He gave her a bright smile. "Hey, don't worry. It's all good."

She stared at him like she wasn't sure she could trust him. "David, I should have called or at least replied."

"It's not a big deal." It was huge, but he wasn't going to tell her that. "I appreciate your willingness to go with me. I was going to take the Mustang to the airport. I don't want to leave it in the garage when no one's going to be home for a week. Do you want a ride?"

Her eyes went wide, and he could see plainly she did. "Uhm, I don't..."

"We're going to be stuck in a small metal tube for nearly ten hours," he pointed out. "If you can't handle a twenty-minute drive with me, maybe we should rethink." Another thought hit him, one that made him sad. "Unless you don't want me to know where you live."

Warm brown eyes rolled. "What would you do with my address? Send me flowers?"

"Not now since you ghosted me."

Her lips curled up. "Fair. All right, give me your phone and I'll put it in."

He handed her his cell. "You'll have to put yourself in. I really did erase your number."

She frowned. "That seems extreme. I thought you were just saying that."

It was good to know he could surprise her.

He intended to surprise her a lot over the next week. Maybe a book wouldn't be all he came out of this with.

Chapter Four

What the hell was she doing?

Tessa glanced down at her watch. She was standing in front of her building ten minutes early, and there was a big part of her that wanted him to be late. Really late. Annoyingly late.

There had to be something about the man that wasn't perfect beyond his connection to her employer.

She'd come down when she realized if she stayed inside one minute more she was going to decide to change again. Because she'd been halfway to convincing herself that she could do a fine job as a bodyguard in that curve-hugging dress that gave her so much confidence. Lots of bodyguards wore four-inch heels and a push-up bra. Yeah, sure they did.

Coming down here had saved her so much discomfort because in her line of business, slacks, a sensible shirt and shoes, and a blazer were the only way to go. The blazer hid her shoulder holster in a way that off-the-shoulder sex dress never would. And she didn't care that Hollywood assassins could stuff any number of weapons between their thighs. Hers did not work that way.

It's not a big deal.

The words David had said haunted her. What did that mean? It's not a big deal. It had felt like a big deal. Not texting that smart hottie back had been a big fucking deal to her. She'd agonized over it, and he'd just kind of let it wash over him. He'd taken his shot and moved on. She had thought of nothing but him for weeks.

Or he was saving face by playing it cool and she was being ridiculous. The man was making this easy on her and she was inwardly complaining that he wasn't making it harder. It was perverse, but then she had deeply conflicted feelings about David.

Feelings she could maybe work out over the course of this week. She could get to know him and then she would see he wasn't as perfect as he seemed to be. Most men showed their true colors when a woman spent too much time with them. He wouldn't be as patient as he seemed. His charm would wear off when she took charge and he got annoyed.

Yes, this could be exactly what she needed.

Especially if he was late.

A deep purr caught her ear, and she turned to see a gorgeous muscle car rolling down the road. It started to slow as though it was going to turn into the parking lot but then righted its path as the driver seemed to recognize her.

That car was a dream. Navy blue, with a wide black stripe running over the hood. David had done a spectacular job. He'd likely spent months restoring her and making her glow.

And that suddenly seemed sexual. The man was obviously good with his hands.

He pulled the car to a stop in front of her, put it in park, and hopped out.

Would being around him make him less attractive? Because a couple of weeks apart had definitely not done that trick. He was dressed more casually than he'd been earlier in the day, and the T-shirt he wore showed off muscular forearms. His hair was a bit messy, like he'd taken a shower and simply ran a towel over it and let it dry naturally into waves. Even the glasses he wore were sexy.

He was the college professor equivalent of a dreamy boy-band singer. Except he was a man, and that scruff on his well-defined jawline did something for her.

"Hey, I'm sorry. Am I late? I was going to come up and help you with your luggage."

Of course he was going to do that because he was a gentleman and he helped people even when they were horrifically rude and ignored his polite texts.

She was definitely the asshole in this situation.

She hefted her small bag. "You're early, and I travel pretty light. You were right about that car. She's a beauty."

Small talk. She could make small talk with him, and then they wouldn't have to feel weird and awkward.

The biggest grin came over his face, and it took everything she had not to sigh. "Thanks. She's the outcome of many, many hours of work. Although it doesn't feel like work. It's a way to shut off my brain. Like muscle memory. I used to help my dad work on cars. It was his hobby, and I think I feel close to him when I'm restoring a car. Sorry. I was reminded of that today. I think I told you this was a present from my mom and stepdad when I finished my doctorate. I thought it was my mom's idea, but now I wonder if it wasn't Sean's. And I am talking entirely too much. Let's store your bag and we can head to the airport."

He moved around to the trunk and had it open in a second. She placed her bag beside his and tried not to think about how sweet it was that he'd restored this whole car so he could feel close to a father who'd been taken too soon.

But she couldn't because she knew that feeling so well. "My dad had this vintage record collection. Like all the oldies. Elvis and Frank Sinatra and Sam Cooke. When he died all I wanted were those albums. When I listen to them I feel close to him. He used to put on a record and he would stop my mom from whatever she was doing and they would dance in the living room."

That was how she always saw her dad—dancing in the middle of the day, his eyes closed because he didn't need to see. They fit together perfectly. She and her brothers used to gag and make fun of them, and now she would do anything to see them together one last time.

Why had she told him that? She was supposed to stay professional toward the gorgeous man who could easily get her fired.

Though that wasn't what she was really afraid of.

He grimaced as he moved to open her door. "Okay, so this is one of those coincidental things. I need you to understand that I had no prior knowledge of that story."

"Of course you didn't. I haven't told it to anyone." Not even Michael. She'd been engaged to the man, lived with him for six whole months, and she'd never taken those records out of their box. They hadn't fit in that magnificent, state-of-the-art mansion in the sky of his.

She'd never opened herself up to him even though he was a good man. He simply hadn't been the right man.

David slid in behind the wheel and turned the key. "Remember that. I play it because it goes with the car."

Sam Cooke's brilliantly smooth voice filled the car. "Lovable." It was one of his early songs and one that a person who was only passingly familiar probably would overlook.

"You do not." She stared ahead as he pulled out onto the road. "You're a fan."

"I like music, and I love that man's voice. I had a professor who taught Contemporary Black History who introduced me to him. Opened my eyes about a lot of things, he did," David said. "So I thought we could talk on the way to the airport. It's probably best if we try to sleep on the plane. I need to hit the ground running, so to speak. It will be roughly ten a.m. when we land in Mar del Plata."

"I'm sorry about that." She'd made the decision to skip Buenos Aires entirely. Since they had a private plane, they could fly straight to the coast. She would have taken them directly to the island, but there wasn't a landing strip. The island was mostly jungle, and the owner wasn't interested in developing it past the two small towns on the coast and the tiny village in the center of the island. "I know you wanted to take the route the guy did."

"Montez," he supplied. "Yeah, I did want to take the same route, try to get the feeling of wonder he must have sensed when he first saw the island after that long bus ride. But the bus will still be around later. I'm afraid the island might not."

"Is it going to explode or something?"

"Ricardo's son is now the owner of the island. He'll change things. It's inevitable. I want to see the house and the grounds before Eddie renovates." David pulled the Mustang onto the freeway and eased up to speed. "I think he'll hold off on the renovations for a while. At least until he finds the treasure."

That engine was purring perfectly, and she wondered how fast it could go. "The treasure?"

"You haven't heard the story of Montez's treasure?"

"No." Though she had to admit she was becoming more and more intrigued by this hero of David's.

"Wow. It's kind of a big deal," David murmured, obviously unimpressed with her knowledge. "Though I guess it's a big deal in academia and treasure-hunting circles."

"There are treasure-hunting circles?"

David flashed her a grin that threatened to make her melt. "Oh, yeah. There are treasure hunters across the globe. Mostly they look for shipwrecks or historical objects that were lost. Montez's treasure is a contemporary thing, so it's unique. Montez became an urban legend when it was hinted that he hid a treasure on his island. Then shortly after he died, a poem that he'd written was released, and it seems to hint that the treasure is real and it gives clues to its location."

"What kind of treasure?" Tessa asked.

"No one knows exactly. It's been speculated that it's a small box that includes gold coins and some artifacts he collected. Some people think it's a larger treasure. Montez liked to collect historical objects. Some think it's cash. But more importantly, some believe he hid his final manifesto on the secret to life. As a biographer you can understand why I would want to read that."

She could understand why it would be important to him. "So you want to look for this treasure?"

He nodded. "It's one of the things I intend to do while we're there. I've got an assistant who's already on the island. He put together camping equipment for us. Well, for him and me. I certainly don't expect you to traipse through the jungle looking for treasure."

What did he think she was going to do? "Uhm, that's exactly what I'm supposed to do."

For the first time since she'd gotten into the car, he seemed a bit awkward. "I thought once we were on the island, you were off the hook. Ian told me if the island seemed safe, you would likely treat the rest of the trip as a vacation."

Was that why he was so comfortable with her? He thought he could ditch her when they got to the island? She wasn't about to lose the big guy's nephew. "I'm not a big vacation girl, to tell you the truth. I would rather stay close to you and do my job."

His eyes were back on the road. "This is jungle territory."

"Then it's good I brought my hiking boots." She'd looked up the island they were going to this afternoon. It was rugged, and she was likely in for a week without her cell. The island had power and water, but cell service was notoriously bad, and there weren't tons of cars there either. It looked like an interesting place—a place trapped in time.

"We're going to be eating MREs and sleeping in tents," David pointed out.

"I've done both before, Professor. And if you mention the mosquitos, I'll let you know I've survived those, too. I did my time in the Army. They didn't take into account my delicate femininity, and neither should you."

His hands tightened on the steering wheel. "I wasn't saying you can't handle it. I'm sure you'll handle it better than I will."

Something about the way he said the words made her wary. He lived in the city and had a very intellectual profession. And they were sitting in his hobby, which also didn't lead to lots of time spent in the great outdoors. "You have hiked before, right?"

One big shoulder shrugged. "A little. I've camped before, too."

They might have two different versions of camping. "How old were you the last time you camped?" She remembered that Big Tag had bought a lake house with David's stepdad. "Lake houses do not count. When was the last time you slept outside in a tent you had to put together yourself?"

He sighed. "All right. I was probably twelve. Right before my brother went into the Navy we went out to Big Bend National Park and did some hiking and some rock climbing, but we stayed in a cabin so it probably doesn't count."

She tried to envision the sexy professor climbing his way up a rock face. It was hard. Kyle, though, now that she could see. But a national park in Texas was way different than what they were getting into. "How many jungles have you been in, Hawthorne?"

He seemed to think about that for a moment. "There are some parts around Seattle that are considered a rain forest."

She snorted. "Oh, it is so not the same, and now I know I have to go with you. I thought I would be protecting you from criminals. Now I get to protect you from yourself."

For the first time she saw some genuine irritation in his eyes. "I can take care of myself, and I'm not going in alone. Luis is coming with me. He camps a lot."

She felt a brow rise. "Luis, your graduate assistant? In history?"

"Just because he's an academic doesn't mean he can't camp."

"Given that he's here doing his graduate work, and from my very cursory look into his background, he's not on a scholarship. That means he's likely from a wealthy family. He glamped. You can't glamp in the jungle." Glamorous camping—otherwise known as glamping— was what she suspected David had done as well. Somehow she couldn't see Grace Taggart roughing it out in the wilderness. His mom was an elegant woman who was always flawlessly put together. "Not that I don't think a good glamp isn't fun. I would far rather enjoy nature from the comfort of a pimped-out tent. However, I suspect that isn't what we'll be doing."

"I didn't think *we* would be doing it at all," David pointed out.

"Well, plans change." Hers sure had. She'd thought she would go home and get ready for an evening of standing outside an ex-president's hotel room. She hadn't expected she would be going to South America with a history professor. A hot as hell, "Oh, Dr. Hawthorne, I didn't turn in my project, you might need to spank me" history professor.

How many of his students screwed up an assignment so they could get some private attention from him?

"We only have two tents. Kyle wasn't planning on camping with us. He thought we would be safe enough on the island. So we have two tents and now apparently we have three people."

It was her turn to shrug. "Then I guess you and Luis are going to be sharing one."

"They're small, Tessa."

"You can cuddle."

Although the more she thought about it, she should be the one sharing a tent with him. They called it close cover for a reason.

His hands tightened around the wheel. "I thought I would have more freedom if I agreed to go straight to the island."

He was starting to get the reality of the situation. "We can turn this beauty around if you like."

He sped up. "How hard are you going to make this on me, Tess? Is turning around what you want me to do?"

She wasn't sure. Turning around would be the smart thing to do, but she was starting to think she wanted to be dumb when it came to him. "I'm not trying to make this hard on you at all. I'm trying to do my job, which is to ensure you make it back safely. Look, the jungle is dangerous. I've spent some time in a couple. We trained on all kinds of terrain. I'm going to stay in the background most of the time. You'll barely know I'm there."

"So first you nix my bus ride and now you want control of my search for the treasure. I understand you don't want to be here, but I need to know if you're going to…I don't know…sabotage me in some way. It would be easier to call it all off if that's your intention."

Ah, there was the irritation she'd expected. It was good because they couldn't talk about the problem if he didn't acknowledge it existed. "My only intention is to do my job, David. I'm sorry if I didn't make that clear. Can we talk about it now?"

"We don't have to." At least he wasn't playing dumb.

It would be easier to ignore the problem, but the truth was she didn't want him to dislike her. And she was starting to think they needed to work this out or she would never be able to stop thinking about him. "I think we do because you think I'm out to get you or something."

"You made it clear you didn't want to see me again and now you're being forced to spend a week with me," David pointed out. "If I were in your position, I might try to find a creative way out of it, too."

She hadn't tried very hard when she thought about it. She could have gotten out of this job. "I know this sounds like a cop-out, but it wasn't you. It's me."

"Sure." His eyes stayed on the road, but she didn't miss the way his jaw tensed.

"I mean it. I told you that night that my last relationship ended. What I didn't tell you was my fiancé was Michael Malone, the son of a ridiculously wealthy oil baron."

He shook his head. "You don't have to explain. You don't owe me any explanations."

"Stop being the good guy." She huffed in frustration. "I know I don't owe you anything, but I want to explain. We're going to be stuck together for a week, and it's best if we both know where we stand."

"Okay," he agreed.

"I didn't fit into his world. I didn't even want to. It's not that they weren't lovely people, but I felt uncomfortable there. He was raised in an entirely different way than I was. I know that sounds weird, but we would fight about things like paying too much for groceries. He didn't understand why I was upset he didn't use the coupons I found. He thought it was silly for me to try to keep costs down when he has all the money in the world."

"But it wasn't your money and it never would have been," David said. "Even if you married him, you would have still felt that way."

It was one of the things she'd worried about. They'd come from two different worlds, and she simply didn't fit into his. And she hadn't loved him enough to truly try. "Yeah. Like it's hardwired in me to be frugal. I didn't like the parties we went to. I always felt like they were watching me, waiting for me to screw up. Again, it wasn't his family, though I was always worried about embarrassing them. Reporters actually followed us around when we went to visit Nina after she had her last kid."

"Yeah, I understand that," David replied. "It's weird. I don't know how or why anyone would want to live that way."

"Sean's been on TV." She hoped he could start putting two and two together. "He's on TV a lot."

"Sean's got actual groupies. I don't know why people watch shows where other people cook. It's not like you can eat the food."

She could understand. She'd actually watched Sean's shows. "I don't know. There's something soothing about it."

"So you decided not to take me up on my offer because you think I run in those circles?" David asked.

Good. At least he understood. "I think you're Sean Taggart's stepson. You're related to Ian Taggart. He might not be TV celebrity, but he's a rock star in my world. He knows presidents and prime ministers."

"He also once threatened to punch a reporter if he didn't walk away." David chuckled, though it was obvious he wasn't amused. "Sean's a little better but only because his agent forced him to take media training. You know they nicknamed him Sean the Viking Chef, right? Once this group who call themselves Sean's Shield Maidens showed up at Top. These are not nice women. They like to troll my mom and tell her she's too old for him or too fat for him."

"What?" His mom and stepdad were one of the most gorgeous couples she'd ever seen.

"Yeah, the celebrity thing sucks. Anyway, they show up and they're waiting in the parking lot, and Ian happens to be there that night. No one wants to tell my mom that five crazy fans are waiting for Sean to walk out into the parking lot and they'll likely heckle her. So Ian goes out to talk to them."

"Oh, shit." She hoped the big boss had buried the bodies well.

"He talked to them by turning the hose on and spraying the hell out of them," David explained. "He said they were obviously overheated and needed a cooldown. They did not come back, and my mom never even knew it happened."

"That sounds like Ian."

"Yes, it does. Do you know who it doesn't sound like?" David asked. "The Malones. They're always in the public eye, and they've learned to navigate it. My stepdad still kicks people in the balls when they deserve it. The Taggarts aren't the Malones. Ian might know how to put on a tux, but I assure you the minute he can take it off it's gone. But none of this matters. You don't owe me a date. All you owe me right now is the promise that you'll let me do what I need to do."

It was completely perverse that she didn't like the sound of that. Wasn't he offering her exactly what she wanted? He was offering up a completely professional relationship with no hope of slipping up and whoops, we didn't mean to end up in bed together. The one tent thing was sounding better and better. He was right about Ian not being anything like the Malones. The guys she worked with talked about how he used to get in the ring with them when he was frustrated and let everyone punch him. Of course, he punched back. "As long as it's safe, I promise."

"Okay." He kept his eyes on the road. "And there's this app I use. It shops around for the cheapest price on the groceries you want, and it even applies coupons it finds online."

Naturally they even liked the same apps. "Grocery Pro. I love that one."

"Yeah, I do, too." He went quiet and took the exit that would lead them to the private airport.

And Tess wondered if she'd made a big mistake. The good news was she had some time to think about it.

* * * *

David yawned as he looked out over the ocean and had to admit that he hadn't been all that great at tempting Tessa so far. He'd brought out the big guns when he'd picked her up. He'd hoped showing up in the Mustang would buy him points, and then there had been that completely coincidental choice of music.

He wasn't a man who believed in fate, but damn the universe seemed to be pointing him directly at Tessa Santiago. They liked the same things. He'd never known a person he could talk to as easily as he did Tessa.

Unfortunately, he seemed to be the only one who felt that cosmic pull.

He was never telling his brother he'd thought those words. Nope.

Kyle would give him the emotional equivalent of a noogie and never let him forget what a romantic douche he could be.

Except he wasn't. At least he'd never been before. He was a focused academic. He was the guy someone had to pull away from a book. His mom used to have to remind him to eat at times.

It wasn't that he didn't have needs. He absolutely did, and he certainly indulged them, but he was a guy who sometimes scheduled his sexual encounters. Everything in his life was organized. There was study time. There was teaching time. There was perverted fun time. Until now he hadn't had sit-and-think-about-Tessa time.

He'd had ten hours on a flight, and he'd barely cracked open his notes. When he wasn't napping, he'd been wondering what Tessa was thinking about and if it was anything but him.

"Is that the island we're going to?" Tessa had been inside the cabin of the boat trying to get a cell signal for most of the thirty minutes they'd been sailing. "It's pretty."

It was a lovely place to be. He would like to show her all the sights. There was a pool in the middle of the island where the water glowed from the phosphorescent algae found there. "Montez bought it in the late eighties. He'd sold his first company for almost a billion dollars, a number unheard of then."

Her pretty face had a quizzical expression on it. "Why haven't I heard of this guy?"

There was a simple explanation for that. Americans focused almost exclusively on their own world. Even at the university he taught at almost all the classes were focused on Western history. "Because his business was based outside the US. Tell me how many billionaires do you know who aren't Americans or Richard Branson? Yet, they exist now and they existed then. Montez wanted to get away from the stress of dealing with his company, so he bought this island as a place to unwind and get back to nature. I don't think when he started out that he meant to write entire manifestos that would change politics in the Southern hemisphere. He was an engineer, after all. But he was changed by the island we're about to go to. By the end of his life, he'd given away almost a billion dollars, and world leaders would flock here to get his guidance."

"Okay, maybe I'm going to have to read this book of yours."

He wasn't expecting it to be some crazy best seller. It would be an academic tome. What it might get him was tenure, and that was better than gold in his world. "He's an interesting man. His son became a friend of mine when we were in São Paulo together. Eddie was a late in life kid for his dad. He was Montez's only child, so he inherited the island, but you should know Eddie's not a billionaire. Remember the part where Montez gave it all away? The only thing Eddie inherited was the island and the trust his dad set up to keep the island running. By the time he died, there were over two thousand inhabitants and a pretty decent scientific presence. So he set up a kind of government, and it's been run that way ever since."

"Wow, that must be interesting for the political historian."

It was completely fascinating. "Obviously."

"So your friend lives here?"

"No. He lives in Buenos Aires. He often visited his father on the island before he passed two years ago. The money left over kept up the big house Montez had built out here. It's pretty much a mansion in the middle of the jungle. At one point in time, Ricardo Montez had these crazy week-long parties where famous people would come out and have these long dinners and discuss politics and metaphysics. And they did a lot of drugs, of course."

"As one does." Tessa's lips curved up, and the wind blew her hair to the side, showing off the long line of her neck. She looked back out to sea. "How much longer do you think we have?"

"At least fifteen minutes. Maybe twenty. Then we'll have a drive out to the estate."

"I thought I read there weren't many cars here."

It was good to know she'd done some research. He happened to know what Kyle had left her was on the thin side, but then his brother hadn't taken this all that seriously. He'd thought their mom was overreacting, too. "There aren't, but there are a few buses and some all-terrain vehicles. There are several scientific teams studying the wildlife on the island, and they're allowed to use Jeeps. We'll hop on one of the buses and then we'll have to walk about half a mile from the stop to the villa."

It was a nice time of year to be out here. He'd intended to make that walk by himself, to take in everything Montez must have seen and heard on that first trip to the place that would eventually be his home.

Now he was pretty sure all he would be able to think about was Tessa. "Of course, I can also radio him from the boat and ask him to send a car out."

She probably didn't want to sit on a minibus and then walk through the jungle.

A single brow arched, and she stood up suddenly. Her shoulders squared as though she was about to perform a task she'd had to build herself up to. "I think I can handle it, Professor, but we should talk about something else. Something that might help us both, but you have to promise me if you choose to tell me no, you'll still remember that I'm in charge when it comes to the business stuff."

His gut tightened because she looked so serious. He thought they'd handled all of this. "What is it?"

"I've given this some thought and I've come to one conclusion," she said evenly. "I think we should throw down."

"Throw what down?" She couldn't be talking about what he thought she was talking about. She wasn't standing there looking totally professional and suggesting that they have sex.

"Throw down, as in get nasty, do the deed." She nodded as though confirming to herself that this was the way to go. "I think we should fuck and probably soon because I need my mind on the job, and you need to concentrate on your work. I thought at first that you didn't care about the whole I-never-called-you-back thing."

"You weren't the first woman to not call me back." She wouldn't be the last either. Probably.

Or he could be optimistic for once. He wasn't some shrinking violet when it came to sex. It was often his stealth weapon. Women saw him as an intellectual, and he was. But there was another side to him, the side that had spent months studying in one of Dallas's most exclusive BDSM clubs. Not the one his mom went to. Yep. Even thinking the words made the world a less sexy place.

"But I am the one who's been on your mind all day." Tessa brought sexy back real fast as she moved closer to him, and he wasn't thinking about the fact that he'd trained at The Club instead of Sanctum. He would bet Tessa went to Sanctum. "I'm the one who's got you closing those books you should have been studying. Tell me I'm wrong."

He couldn't. "I've been thinking about you for weeks."

She let out a breath, and her shoulders relaxed. "And you're the one I can't get out of my head. I think we go all in sexually tonight and get it out of our systems. Then you'll be able to write your book, and I'll be able to take out the bad guys. If there are any bad guys."

He did not hate this plan. When he looked at it intellectually it was a good plan. It was logical and practical since they were only spending a couple of nights at the mansion where there would be nice beds and they wouldn't have to fuck in a tent. The only thing he hated about it was her utter conviction that one night would be enough.

So show her it's not. Study her like you studied for your freaking GRE and give her something to be distracted by—your talented dick.

Sometimes his inner voice reminded him he'd been around Taggarts for a long time. "Let me see if I have this straight. You think we spend one night in bed and then we'll be able to forget the chemistry between us?"

"I think we'll be getting rid of the tension between us," she corrected. "I think we made a weird connection that night we met. I don't know what it was about. I think maybe I was vulnerable."

"Vulnerable?" She hadn't seemed vulnerable. She'd seemed almost luminous to him. She'd seemed happy and vibrant and bright.

"I was at an anniversary party with the family I could have had, and it reminded me that by this time in her life my mom had been married ten years and had three kids." Every word that came out of her mouth sounded sensible. It made him wonder how long she'd been thinking about this. Had she sat there on the plane and justified a reason to have him that she could handle?

He did not miss the fact that she'd talked about the family she could have had and not the man. He knew for a fact Michael Malone had been there that night, and yet she didn't mention him.

"So you think you met me and I felt safe," he posited.

She seemed to consider that for a moment. "I don't know that *safe* is the word I would use. You were easy to talk to, and it felt like somehow we fit together in a way I hadn't with anyone in a long time."

"I've never felt that instant connection before." He wasn't going to play mind games with her.

Her lips firmed, and he realized she didn't want this part of the conversation. She wanted him to jump on her and probably prove that the sex wouldn't be as good as she thought it would be and then she could go on her merry way and put him in the box with all the other men who hadn't quite fit. The sneaky brat was trying to get her taste and get out.

Maybe they would play a few games together.

"Look, that night was special, but we have to live in the real world," Tessa began. "That's why I didn't reply to you. The two of us—it's not something that's going to work out, but we're stuck together for a week. So we should go ahead and do it, and then we'll see that it's just sex and we'll be cool with each other."

Ah, so he'd called that properly. He'd been blown over by the attraction he'd felt for her. He'd thought this was it and how awesome that he hadn't had to jump through hoops. But there were always hoops. There was always work to be done, and he had the distinct feeling that she would be worth it. Maybe it was time to stop wondering what had gone wrong and try to make things go right. "And if it's not?"

"Not?"

He moved in, getting closer to her than he'd been all day. She wanted to fuck him out of her system? He leaned over and brought his lips to her ear, letting their bodies brush together. It was time to show her getting him out of her system might not be possible. She'd seen the soft side of him, the brainy side that was cautious about relationships and ensuring that the woman he was with felt safe at all times. He would still make sure she was safe, but he'd let her lead this for far too long. "What if it's not just sex, baby? What if it's something more?"

She stepped back but not before he'd heard the breathy gasp she'd emitted the moment he'd touched her. Her face had flushed, and while the air around them was warm, her nipples were perfectly visible against the material of her shirt. The gentleman in him probably shouldn't have noticed that, but the gentleman in him had also been the one she'd rejected the first time.

Maybe she needed a hint of bad boy in her good man.

"David, I'm not going to start a relationship with you."

He couldn't help but grin because she couldn't even say the words in a firm tone of voice. They'd come out shaky. Like he'd offered her something she wanted but knew she couldn't have. "I understand. You've made yourself clear. You can't have a relationship with me because of my jet-set lifestyle. I wish you could have seen my town house with its stunning views of the parking lot. When the wind is right, you can smell the fried chicken from the fast-food restaurant down the block. And you should meet my purebred cat. When I say Hamilton's a purebred I mean he is one hundred percent grump. I didn't even pay for my cat. He walked in one day and now he won't leave. Like my brother."

Her expression softened. "It's not about money. I work with your brother. I work with a bunch of your family members, and that could make things awkward. I don't need more awkward in my life."

"And after this, you won't have to see me again." It was precisely why she was willing to sleep with him.

She frowned, and her arms crossed over her chest. "I didn't say that. I'm sure I will, but we'll both go in knowing that it isn't forever, so we'll be okay with each other. You don't seem like a man who would get angry with a woman because things didn't work out."

"Is that what your fiancé did?"

"Not at all," she said with a sad smile. "Our breakup was one of the easiest things I've ever been through. We were logical and practical and we're still friends."

"And that's why you're not married to him." She was one of those people who thought logic could dictate the selection of a partner. Maybe in the work world it did. She was likely paired up with someone who was perfect on paper, and she thought that was how she should do it in her romantic life, too. "There's not a lot that's logical about love and passion."

She took a step back. "Maybe this was a mistake. I was only trying to make things easy on both of us."

He knew he could lose her if he pushed too hard, but he had to make a few things plain. "It's definitely a mistake if all you want is a quick lay to prove I'm not really the man for you because I am, and I think you know it."

She pointed his way. "I knew it. I knew there was an arrogant jerk behind all that nice-guy charm."

There was always a jerk down deep. The key to being a good man was knowing how to resist the temptation to let the jerk roam free. "If I'm arrogant because I know I'll be good for you, then so be it. You want to play it this way, then let's go. Eddie doesn't know I'm bringing a woman with me. I couldn't get in touch with him before we left. Communication on the island can be hard. So that leaves us with some options. I'm telling him you're my new girlfriend and we'll stay together in one room. Every single night you'll come to bed and we'll play."

Her jaw dropped, and she stood there for a moment. "Play?"

Oh, she hadn't thought he was kinky. That was a surprise. Since he'd started training at The Club, he'd learned pretty much everyone had a kink of some kind. She'd thought she could ride the vanilla boy a few times and walk away with the full knowledge he couldn't give her what she needed. "Yes, play, baby. As in I'll tie you up and have you any way I want you, and you'll beg me to do it again the next night."

"You're a Dom?" The question came out with what felt like equal parts horror and intrigue. "You don't go to Sanctum."

"Sanctum isn't the only club in town." And thank god for that.

She blinked a couple of times as though allowing herself to absorb the shock of what he'd said. "I wasn't…I wasn't thinking that we would have that kind of relationship. I was thinking we would just have sex."

"So you don't like D/s sex?" David asked.

She seemed to think about that for a moment. "Uhm, I do. I've been going to Sanctum for a couple of years. Ever since I started working at MT. I wasn't expecting to have it with you."

"Because I'm not the guy for you?" It was a theme with her.

"I guess I didn't think you would be into it," she explained. "You seem so…"

He could help her out. "Staid? Buttoned up? Intellectual?"

Her eyes flared as though she'd finally figured out how to deal with him. "What makes you think I'm a sub? Maybe I'm a top, too."

He didn't hesitate for a second. While he enjoyed topping, what he really liked was exploring with his partner. He liked the openness of D/s. He didn't need to be in control all the time. Unlike his brother, who seemed to need it on a pathological level, but that was a problem for another day. "Cool. I can bottom. I've done it before. It can be fun."

"You've bottomed?" She was right back on her ass. Not literally, of course, but she definitely hadn't been thinking that he was as perverted as he was.

"Of course. I've tried almost everything. It's part of the program. Big Tag doesn't make his Doms in training bottom?"

She nodded, and her eyes were wide enough to make him think she was still surprised to be having this particular conversation. "Yes, he does. You're really a member of The Club?"

This would likely reenforce the idea that he was some kind of rich boy, but it was more about his family connections. "Ian and the owner of The Club have ties that go back decades. As their kids get older, the ones who want to experiment don't want to do it at their dad's club. I say kids, but right now it's me and Kyle. I think it will probably be even weirder in the future."

"I wondered why I never saw Kyle at Sanctum," she replied. "All the other guys go. Now that I think about it, I totally understand. It would be weird to run into my mom in a dungeon. Not that she would."

"How would you know?" He would bet she hadn't talked to her mom about sex. He knew way too much about his own totally sex-positive mom's sex life. She and Sean were all about teaching acceptance and the rejection of shame.

Her nose wrinkled. "Because she's my mom."

"Yeah, and if I'd said that about mine I would have walked into Sanctum and had a complex it would take fourteen shrinks to fix." He'd dealt with this a long time ago. "But you know what? I'm glad she has Sanctum. I'm happy she's got a Dom who adores her and fulfills her. Our parents are humans, too. There's nothing wrong with them having sex lives. But some things should go into different compartments. So Kyle and I are at The Club. We pay our membership dues through service. We both take dungeon monitoring duties, and I tutor a whole bunch of kids in history and Spanish. Now I would be surprised if you're a switch, but like I said, I'm happy to experiment."

She was back to blushing. "I'm having a hard time seeing you as a top. You're a history professor."

She was thinking inside the box. It was time to give her a good sharp shock to the system. "Do you think only badass security guys can be sexual dominants? Or any kind of kinky? Because you've obviously never been to a Revolutionary War reenactment."

"Excuse me?"

"Oh, those are full of freaks," he said with a fond chuckle. "I call them sexual mullets because upfront they're all business. I mean these people take costumes and details seriously. But the minute the battle's called, it's one big orgy. I dated Betsey Ross for about a year—obviously not her real name—and the things she wanted me to do with her sewing needles would shock you. I say that because I was open about my experiences with Julian Lodge, and it even freaked him out a little. So should we have a contract?"

She was quiet for a moment. "I don't know. I probably should think about this. This conversation didn't go the way I thought it would. And I don't know that we should share a room."

"But then how will you protect me?" She didn't get it both ways.

"They don't know you're bringing a bodyguard? Shouldn't you have prepared them for me?"

"As far as I know, they still think I'm bringing Kyle." He waved that off. Eddie had always said the more the merrier, and he wasn't always the host when he offered it up. He'd once shown up in Dallas where he was supposed to sit for an interview with David with three women he'd picked up in an airport. Needless to say, he hadn't gotten much of an interview out of the man. "It wouldn't matter if I'd brought three or four extra people. It's a big house. There's plenty of room. Of course that also makes it easy to slip into a bedroom and kidnap me. After all, I'm a professor. I won't be able to defend myself with historical facts. Though I might be able to put the kidnappers to sleep. Ask my Contemporary Latin American Politics class."

"I thought there was nothing to worry about once we got to the island," she replied, obviously not willing to let him have it both ways either.

Good. He liked a challenge. It looked like he would only have a week to convince her to give him a real shot, so he was going for broke. "All right. Let's pick a path and stick to it. You're right. We're stuck together for the next week, and then if you choose to, you never have to see me again. So let's call this one week out of time. No expectations on what happens after because we know nothing happens after. When this trip is done, we go our separate ways. Until then we see where this connection we have takes us. If you decide not to sleep with me, I'll take the couch because I happen to know I'm staying in one of the bigger guest rooms in the house. I won't lay a hand on you unless you want me to. Can you trust me that much?"

Her eyes rolled. "I don't think you're going to attack me."

"Neither did Betsey Ross."

She shook her head. "You're joking about that."

Oh, he was not. She'd enjoyed some role-play. "She had very particular fantasies, so I am joking about her not knowing. But she didn't know when, and that was all kinds of fun. Did I mention I do a killer British accent? And I have an actual red coat."

She stared at him for a moment. "I don't know that I like this side of you."

"I think you like it a lot."

She huffed, a flustered sound. "What are you doing?"

"Opening up and showing you more of who I am," he admitted. "I've been on my best behavior around you, and I think it's given you the wrong impression. You say I get one week? I'll take it. If you reject me at the end of this it'll be because you truly don't like me. The real me."

"I'm serious about the relationship—about not having one," Tessa insisted.

He wished she didn't sound so sure. "Okay, then what's the problem?"

Her eyes went soft. "I don't want to hurt you. You seem like a guy with a lot of feelings."

"How about I worry about my feelings and you trust me to know what I can and can't handle? Like I said, think about it. I can always tell Eddie that you're the walking, talking symbol of my mom's paranoia, and then you take the bodyguard role and hang in the background. No muss. No fuss."

"Ah, and no sex if I don't stay in the room with you and play your girlfriend."

He held his hands up to ward off the accusation in her tone. "Hey, no machinations here. If you don't want to sleep in the same bed with me, that's cool. You want sex, you can sneak in and slip out, and no one knows I'm fucking my bodyguard. Also, I would like to remind you that you're the one who brought this up."

She huffed, a frustrated sound. "Yeah, well, I didn't think we'd make such a big deal out of it. I thought we'd be one and done."

"And I think it's going to be more fun my way. Is this a take it your way or leave it deal?"

She shook her head. "No. We can negotiate, but I thought I wouldn't have to."

Yeah, he'd gotten that vibe. "Because you thought the vanilla boy would just be happy for the sex?"

She shrugged one elegant shoulder. "Something like that."

If he played his cards right, he would slip that shirt off her shoulder later tonight and run his lips across her golden brown skin. "Like I said, if I've only got a week, I'm going to make the most of it. So how about we do this? I'll explain who you are to Eddie and you'll take a room close to mine, and if you decide to go through with it, you knock on my door and then we'll negotiate." He wasn't willing to push her too much because he might lose her. "If vanilla sex is all you want, then we'll talk about that."

She took him in with those warm brown eyes. "But you would rather be in charge."

"I think you would enjoy it, too. I'm right, aren't I? I'm right about you being sexually submissive." He would bet a lot on her answer.

She sighed. "Yes. I find it relaxing. I can be kind of intense."

He could see that easily. She would need a place to relax and let someone else be in charge. It was likely why she'd fallen into the relationship with her fiancé. He'd been a dominant male, and they'd seemed to have a lot in common on the surface. But the historian in him knew it was always in the details. Something that looks like it should work could fall apart because it often didn't matter that a couple liked the same things. It was in how they lived, what they valued underneath the basics. Two very good people could simply not make it work because their core needs didn't mesh. He could meet all her sexual needs, but if he couldn't fulfill her core emotional ones, then it wouldn't work.

But he rather thought he could if she let him try.

"Well, I stand ready to help you if you need some stress relief."

An exasperated huff came from her lips. "I thought you would be weirder about this."

"You thought you could either shock me and then I would prove I'm the uptight academic you think I am, or I would jump on you without another thought and then the sex would be bad. Either way, you could safely forget about me. How about we go into this with open minds? You tell me how you want to play it going onto the island and we'll take it from there. If you want to keep your options open, I'll still promise to sleep on the couch if you want to stay in my room. If you want your own, then I'll make sure to leave my door unlocked."

Her eyes narrowed in pure challenge. "Don't bother. If I want to get in, I'll get in."

He liked the sound of that, but he had to hope she wouldn't shrink away again. "I'll make it easy on you."

"I don't think any of this is going to be easy on me," she replied.

"It's only as hard as you want it to be. You get to make the choices. You're in control."

"Until I give it to you." There was anticipation in the words.

"Even then." He needed to make it plain to her that he knew the rules of D/s and he followed them. "It's an illusion that you're giving up control. What you're giving yourself is really permission. Permission to enjoy your body, to let go for a while because you trust your partner."

"Can I trust my partner?"

"Yes. You can trust me to take care of you in bed."

"And you can trust me to take care of you out of it." She turned and looked out over the sea. "All right, Professor. I'll think about it. I don't know about this whole go-with-the-flow thing, but I still think we'll both be more focused if we get this out of the way."

She was making excuses, rationalizing something that wasn't rational. But she needed that wall between them.

For now. "I'll wait for you tonight. I'll wait for you all the nights we're here. But I'll make it clear to Eddie that you're working."

"I should have called you," she said quietly.

He wanted to touch her, but she wasn't ready. "I wish you had."

She looked back at him, her lips quirking up. "We could have already thrown down, and this wouldn't be a problem anymore."

He sighed and leaned on the railing, the smell of the sea surrounding them. "You're a brat."

She leaned against him. "Yeah, probably."

When he put an arm around her, she didn't protest, and he was perfectly satisfied to stay that way the rest of the trip.

Chapter Five

Tessa didn't mind the heat of the day as she walked alongside David. It was way easier to deal with a little sweat than the heat that had flashed through her the minute she'd realized David Hawthorne was kind of a freak.

What if it's not just sex, baby? What if it's something more?

Her whole body had gone gooey when he'd leaned in and whispered those words in her ear.

She was not the girl who went gooey, damn it. She wasn't a girl at all. She was a grown-ass woman who didn't melt at the thought of having a man's hands on her.

She wasn't the woman who sighed and rested against him and let the waves rock them as they approached the ridiculously romantic island she hadn't expected to visit today. Nor had she thought she would be walking down a dirt road toward a magnificent house in the middle of the jungle. She stopped as she got her first glance at the big house they would be staying at. "Wow."

David stopped beside her, and she could practically feel his satisfaction at her awe. "Yeah, it's pretty amazing. Montez designed it himself. He wanted it to seem like the whole place had risen from the jungle. Like a wave coming off it."

It was a glorious structure made of wood and glass intertwined with vines and trees, as though the jungle was trying to reclaim its space. Or the two had found a way to live in harmony. "It's beautiful."

"He spent years making this place shine." David started walking again, his big body moving with grace. "The last ten years of his life he never left here. Eddie had to bring out doctors when they realized Ricardo had cancer. Some people think Ricardo could have lived longer if he'd been willing to get treatment on the mainland, but he had no interest in leaving. He said this was the place where he'd truly learned to live, and this would be the place where he died."

There was something lovely about that, about being able to make that choice. She moved back to his side. The bus ride had been perfectly pleasant. She'd imagined some broken-down vehicle no one with a brain would consider safe, but it had been a lovely, comfortable if older bus. The few people on it had been chatty and more than willing to talk to the professor when he introduced himself. He'd proven he could switch from Latin American Spanish to Castilian without breaking a sweat. The Spanish they spoke in Argentina was a bit more formal than what they spoke across Latin America, but David eased into it with a flair that her mother would approve of.

He was ridiculously charming. He'd sat with an older woman for a long time listening to her stories about working in this building for years. She'd gone on and on about cleaning products and how hard it was to keep the place sparkling when the owner refused to shut the windows. She'd listened in and it had been boring, but David had made that old woman feel comfortable, and he'd thanked her profusely for speaking with him.

He hadn't flinched when a massive, kind of stinky dog had bounded onto the bus and walked right up to him as though that dog knew who the sucker was. He'd simply found some beef jerky in his backpack and petted the old thing while its owner had settled his luggage.

Then he'd talked to that guy for what felt like forever.

They'd loved him. When the bus had reached the town they were stopping at, everyone who was going on down the line shook David's hand and wished him well. Some promised to talk to him further if he needed more information. They were all excited about his project.

He wasn't the quiet guy who stood in the background. Not when it came to this. He was the shiny center of the universe, the benevolent scholar who made everyone feel important.

When had she learned to cling to the shadows? To hang in the background and try to go unnoticed?

Maybe there wasn't one thing or moment that had taught her. Maybe it was simply part of who she was, and there wasn't anything wrong with that, but being around David was a nice contrast to her normal day.

His fascination with the world around him was infectious.

How would that translate to sex?

"The whole place is powered by solar and hydro." David had gone into teaching mode. "He was one of the first adopters of green energy."

It should be obnoxious, but she found it oddly soothing. "Didn't he make his money off something to do with solar?"

A brilliant smile lit his face. "Yeah. He invented some of the components that they still use on solar panels today."

Yep, there was that gooey feeling again. She forced herself to look back at the house or she might stare into his dreamy eyes and turn into a drooling idiot. "How did he do it? I mean, if this place wasn't inhabited before, how did he build all this stuff?"

"It wasn't completely uninhabited. The town on the east coast was here. It was a fishing village at the time. It's bigger and more modern now. Montez brought workers out here. He paid them, and when they were done, he offered them all the materials they would need for homes of their own and leased land to them at very little cost, locking the rent in for a hundred years. He did the same with businesses."

"So this whole place runs on his money?" She wasn't sure she understood how it worked.

"There's a fund that's managed by Eddie's company. The interest alone on the money Montez left for the island is incredible. But they do have some tourism on the island, and the scientific projects bring in cash. The people who live here aren't ever going to be wildly wealthy, but they also don't have debt, and they get to live here," David explained. "On this small island they've got waterfalls and great surfing and fishing. They've got this glorious wilderness around them, and they're taught from a young age to value it. It's a slice of paradise."

"I'm afraid I would miss high-speed internet." She was more of a city girl these days.

"Oh, I would, too. I mean, look, I'm fascinated by this place, but I'm not longing to move here," he admitted. "I would definitely miss being able to get anything I wanted delivered in a couple of hours. But it's cool to get a glimpse of another world. That must be the butler."

She glanced up ahead, and the big doors that looked like they belonged in some fantasy movie set had come open and a large man stepped out. He was dressed in khakis and a lightweight shirt that didn't quite hide the gun on his belt. "Butler?"

"I guess he's more of a manager. Eddie isn't here year-round, so Mateo runs the place. It's a big house, and the grounds need tending as well," David explained. "I know the manager who was here when Ricardo was alive recently retired. Ricardo called him a butler, so I still do, too."

"He's got a gun."

David stopped and shrugged. "It's the jungle. There's a population of predators out here. I suspect there are many guns."

Yeah, but she would think a rifle would work far better than a handgun, though she would allow it wasn't practical to carry around a rifle.

Another man stepped out, this one shorter than the big "butler." He was in shorts and a T-shirt, sneakers on his feet. He wore a Yankees hat and waved. "Hey, Professor!"

David raised his hand in greeting. "Luis, hello!"

She had a decision to make, and though she'd had a long bus ride to make it, she'd spent all her time watching David. Actually, she'd made the decision. She'd decided to play it safe and be open and honest about why she was there. It was the best way to protect herself.

He'd surprised her when she'd laid out her plan. She'd expected him to jump on her and maybe do her on the boat before they even made it to the island. Then she would be able to think and he would be just one more guy she'd had decent sex with.

Instead he'd challenged her. Like they were playing a game and he wanted to win.

And maybe she was the prize he thought he would get at the end. He was willing to be patient, to compromise, but only so far.

He was dangerous, and putting walls between them at night would be a good idea.

"The butler guy wasn't on Kyle's list," she pointed out.

David stopped at the beginning of the circular drive that led up to the house. "We're on the island. We're safe here. I didn't think I had to give him a staff list. I think Eddie might be offended if I try to vet his employees."

She thought about telling him they were leaving, like turning right around and marching back to the bus stop. "I wanted to vet everyone you come in contact with, Professor."

"That would be hard to do." He was frowning at her. "Tessa, Eddie's a smart man. He lives in this world. He's fine."

Luis was a friendly-looking man in his mid-twenties. He was smiling widely as he jogged down the steps. "Hey, it's so good to see you, but wow, man, where did you pick up the lady?"

David started walking toward his grad student, a hand held out. "She's…"

It was instinct, she told herself. Something felt off. Something about the big guy still standing by the door was wrong. He didn't look like the kind of guy who was into land management. There was something about the way his jaw was tight, as though he was waiting for trouble.

Why would he expect trouble from a college professor?

"I'm his girlfriend." She slipped her arm around David's waist and cuddled up to him. "Sorry about the surprise. I'm afraid I got a last-minute chance to sneak away, and I took it."

They were alone on an island, and she had no idea who was working here and where they came from because David had convinced Kyle this was paradise.

Had the man not read the Bible because even in paradise there were snakes waiting to pounce.

She felt David go still, but then his arm wound around her shoulders and she couldn't help but notice how perfectly they fit together. "We're a new couple, so we're really into each other. My brother thinks it's gross. We are very affectionate."

She gave him an inch, and it was obvious he'd decided to take a mile. And steal kisses.

Luis's brows had risen in obvious shock. "I didn't know you were dating anyone. The last time we talked, you were hung up on that woman you met at your stepdad's restaurant."

Score one for her. David's skin had flushed. At least she wasn't the only one feeling the heat. "That would be me. Tessa Santiago. I finally got some time and called him back. I think he was worried I would run again, but here I am. Don't worry. I know he needs to work. You'll barely know I'm around."

The big guy on the verandah had visibly relaxed. He'd been caught off guard by her appearance, but now that she was nothing more than some chick David had brought along, he chilled out.

She didn't like that either.

"Well, that's a surprise." Luis shook his head. "I thought you had ghosted him."

She had, and it made her feel guilty since he was a genuinely nice guy. Still, she had a part to play and a cover to put together really freaking fast. David hadn't known who she was until the night before. He'd had a name and what she'd told him. Which was very little about her work. It had been a breath of fresh air that night to not talk obsessively about open cases and what was happening in the security world. Now it gave her some cover because he couldn't tell Luis what he didn't know. "I was working. I work at Malone Oil, and I was on a business trip. Some of our sites are pretty remote, so I didn't have a signal for a couple of weeks. I felt bad when I got back and realized he'd actually called me. Lucky for me, I now have some time off, and I get to spend it with him."

"I thought we were working." Luis looked to David. "We only have a week here. And I only brought two tents. They're not big."

"We'll make do." She had no idea how she was going to convince David to share one with Luis now that she'd introduced herself as his girlfriend.

She wasn't. She was going to let herself fall into this trap. Now that she thought about it, she worried that maybe that was precisely why she'd done it.

David was looking down at her, his lips curled up in the sexiest smile. "I suspect we will."

Oh, she was in trouble, but she also suspected he might be in trouble too, and it was her job to make sure nothing happened to Sean Taggart's stepson. Ian's nephew. She needed to remember that at all times. Especially when she was in the same room with this man tonight and there was only one bed.

Had she really told him they should throw down? She'd been awfully bold in that moment. Or maybe she'd simply underestimated him.

What had he done with Betsey Ross's sewing needles? She'd been thinking about that a whole lot, thinking about what the buttoned-up professor did when class was over.

David looked back to his research assistant. "She's good at entertaining herself. Don't worry about Tessa. We'll get everything we need. Where's Eddie?"

Luis seemed to force himself to focus. "He's taking a nap. He hasn't been feeling well the last couple of days. Nothing serious. He's had some kind of bug, but he's been better today. He promised to join us for dinner. I can show you around and get you settled in. Mateo prepared two rooms since we were expecting you to bring your brother, Dr. Hawthorne."

"I dumped Kyle when Tessa said yes. We only need one. Like I said, we're very affectionate." David had the sexiest, evilest grin on his face as he dipped his head down and kissed her.

She hated that it did something for her. She could maybe resist the nice-guy professor, but meeting the pervy hottie under the tweed was like finding out not only was Clark Kent Superman, he could also find a G-spot faster than a speeding bullet.

"Well, let's go and look around the house." Luis seemed to find his footing. "Although I suspect Dr. Hawthorne could give this tour himself."

David's head was back, his eyes taking in the front of the house. "Not at all. I've only studied the place in pictures. It's different being here. Everything is so vivid."

She liked watching him, enjoyed how curious he was about the world around him and how open he was to learning. Too often lately she'd spent her days moving through like a zombie, doing the things she needed to do to get to the next one only to find herself on a loop.

Meeting David Hawthorne had tossed her off that loop and forced her to think about something beyond getting to the weekend where she could visit with her family and wonder why she didn't feel like she belonged with those happy people.

David had walked to the edge of what seemed to be a parking circle, stepping over to the place where the jungle began.

"Be careful," Luis cautioned. "There are snakes out here."

She reached for David's hand to bring him back to the house. She rather thought he might need someone to ground him at times. "I'll be on the lookout for snakes."

She glanced back at the man who hadn't left his post and worried more about the predators she might find inside the mansion.

* * * *

David was astounded by the beauty of the home Ricardo Montez had built. From the big mural at the front of the house depicting the jungle and the river, to the skylights that let in sun, every detail had been thought through. Every hall he walked down, room he took in, reminded him that he was walking in the steps of giants. So many of the people he studied about had walked these halls, sat in these chairs. History had been made here.

Too often people only thought of history being made in the big spaces—the White House, Parliament, the world's battlefields. But so much happened in the private places. In the living rooms and over dining tables, the fate of the world had been decided again and again.

He couldn't help but wonder if his own personal history would be decided here, too.

"That mural was beautiful," Tessa said. She'd been great during the tour, asking lots of questions and getting a lay of the land. "I'm glad I got pictures."

He was fairly certain she'd gotten pictures of everything so she could study the layout and prepare for whatever threat might come their way. But she'd seemed like a happy tourist.

"And this is the room you've definitely been waiting for. I saved the best for last." Luis had walked the halls like a long-time tour guide. "The library."

David stepped inside and stared for a moment. Books lined every wall, going all the way up to the ceiling, and he was comforted by the smell. Bibliosmia. It was the technical term for that woodsy, earthy smell old books had. The smell actually came from the compounds in paper breaking down over time, but he'd long ago dismissed the obvious metaphor. Some things didn't need to have a deeper meaning.

He'd always loved libraries. They were his happy place. From the time he was a child, he'd felt safe in these spaces where books and knowledge were supreme.

"Are you going to break into song?" Tessa whispered.

She seemed determined to drag him back to reality. He looked down at her. "Why would I do that?"

Her lips quirked up and she tucked a long strand of raven hair behind her ear. "It's what Belle did in *Beauty and the Beast*. Her eyes got as wide as yours just did and she burst into song."

Such a brat. She also seemed determined to make him smile. "I guess that makes you the beast."

Instead of getting offended, her grin amped up. "Don't you forget it."

She stepped away, strolling around the circular library, her graceful hands skimming along the spines of the books. He'd been surprised at how she'd handled the tour. She'd held his hand through most of it, and instead of asking Luis questions, she'd looked to David. When that woman focused on him, he felt like the world was a softer, warmer place.

And a place where his dick suddenly wanted to take over for his brain.

"I have to admit I was surprised you showed up with a girl." Luis moved close to him, keeping his voice down.

"She's a woman, and I didn't expect it either. It happened pretty fast."

Luis glanced his way, his jaw tight. "What do you know about her? I mean, I know you met her one night and then she seemed to disappear."

They'd gone over this. Tessa had been quick with the perfectly reasonable explanation. It made him wonder exactly how long she'd been thinking about it. She'd seemed torn over how to handle their situation on the boat, and then on the bus, she'd been quiet. She'd sat in the back watching him as he'd talked to the other travelers. The walk had been perfectly pleasant but pointed to the fact that she was right. His brain was more on her than the work he was supposed to do. He'd wanted to make sure she was comfortable, content.

But he was pretty sure she was wrong. He was almost certain sleeping with her would do nothing but amplify his preoccupation. He imagined seeing her naked now. Even as she walked around the library and the sunlight hit her skin, he was wondering how it would caress her body in the early morning, how she was practically glowing like the goddess she was.

Knowing exactly how gorgeous she was wouldn't make him stop fantasizing about her.

"Professor?"

How long had he been thinking about her? The woman was playing hell with his concentration. He shook it off and looked back to Luis. "I'm sorry. I got distracted. What were you saying?"

Luis looked at him like he'd grown an extra head. "I was asking how much you knew about her."

"A lot. Why?" He knew the important things. He knew he was crazy about her and she was crazy skittish about him. That was a problem he was working on.

"She said she worked for an oil company?"

She'd said that. It had been a good call. If she needed to, she could likely get her former fiancé's family to back up her cover. And it gave her an excuse to have not called him that didn't include her being a scaredy cat. "Malone Oil."

"And you know that for a fact?" Luis asked.

He wasn't sure what was going on in his grad student's head. "What's this about?"

Luis looked over as though to ensure Tessa couldn't be listening to them. "You're close to starting your plan. Have you thought about that? You're going to write the *History Journal* article when we get back, right?"

He had a publishing plan. It was a strategy he'd put together with the help of some of his colleagues. He would write a couple of shorter articles for professional journals, try to get some magazines interested, and then he would write the actual biography. It was a good way to keep his name out there and build some word of mouth for the book. "Yes. I've already got most of the first two articles ready. Coming here and writing about the trip will give the articles some personal experience."

He'd written the historical aspects. It wouldn't take him long to layer in his personal thoughts and how coming here had impacted him. He was targeting a journal that specialized in "lost" late-twentieth-century history.

There was a journal for everything.

"What if she's...you know..." Luis had an expectant expression on his face.

"No, I do not know." He was interested in whatever Luis said next because he was lost as to what this conversation was truly about. Luis was always so practical, so easy going, but he seemed nervous about one woman.

"What if she's from another college?"

He laughed out loud at that. Luis's anxiety became crystal clear, and David found nothing but humor in it.

Tessa's head turned. "You okay, Haw...David?"

Getting her to start calling him by his first name was a definite plus. "Luis thinks you're an academic spy and you're going to steal my ideas and claim them for your own in a ruthless attempt to get tenure at your own university."

She frowned. "And you think that's funny why?" The frown

disappeared like she couldn't quite keep it up, and a sunny grin hit her face. "Okay, it's pretty funny. I fall asleep writing a grocery list much less some academic paper. Your work is safe with me."

Luis had flushed slightly. "Sorry. She shows up out of nowhere, and I have to worry. You can be naïve about the more ruthless parts of our business."

David felt bad about putting Luis in this position without any warning. "Tessa's not here to steal anything."

Anything but sex, and he was going to make sure she didn't get away with it. A little thief could get caught in a trap.

"Ruthless parts?" Tessa sank down to the brown chesterfield sofa in the middle of the room. "Is this that publish or perish stuff?"

"Both your parents were teachers," he chided. "You should know this."

She shook her head. "A high school teacher and a community college freshman bio teacher. The only thing they published were quizzes. Though my dad was often featured in the letters to the editor section of the *Morning News*. He believed in the power of a sternly worded letter."

Oh, he liked it when she relaxed. When she decided to lower those walls of hers they clicked, and he could feel the energy between them. "See, Luis, she has no designs on my work."

Her expression softened. "Though I do admit I find all of this interesting. This man you're writing about lived a fascinating life."

"Don't I know it?" a familiar voice said. "David, it is so good to see you again. You look so much older, and I have no idea how you managed to convince this beautiful creature to even stand in the same room with you. *Mi ángel, me dejás sin aliento.*"

A brow rose over Tessa's eyes. She got to her feet and strode over, though when he thought she would hold a hand out to Eduardo Montez, she moved to David, slipping her hand in his. "I take it this is our celebrated host?"

Eddie looked more and more like his father the older he got, which was a good thing since Ricardo Montez had been considered an attractive man. He'd always had a way with the ladies, and his affairs were legendary. Eddie was busy following in his father's footsteps by playing as much of the field as he possibly could.

He wouldn't be playing with Tessa, though, since she'd made her choice when she'd taken his hand in hers. "Yes, baby, this is Eduardo

Montez, and he's what they like to call in these parts *un chamuyero.*"

She looked up at him, obviously confused. "A what?"

Tessa might speak exquisite Spanish, but she hadn't spent a lot of time in Buenos Aires where they had their own language of the streets. *Lunfardo.* Not that he and Eddie had spent time on the streets either, but he found it fascinating. "It means he's a smooth talker."

"I am, pretty lady." Eddie gave her a high-wattage smile. His eyes were on Tessa, but he leaned toward David. "When Mateo told me you showed up with a woman, I assumed you'd brought another grad student with you. I thought she would look like the female version of Luis."

"I only have one grad student. I was lucky to get him." His concentration wasn't the most popular. The professors who taught American and European history typically had several.

Eddie smiled Tessa's way. "You are so much better."

"I'm not that bad," Luis complained. "I get some action. Sometimes."

Eddie sighed and looked her over again. *"Entonces ella no es mi regalo de cumpleaños?"*

Like he would hand over Tessa as a birthday present. *"Vos faltás seis meses para que cumplís años. Ella es mía."*

"Hey, you promised to speak English around me, babe." Tessa had a frown on her face.

Another surprise. She didn't want them to know she spoke Spanish? "Sorry. We can speak English."

"Of course we can, though she should know everyone here will be surprised that such a beauty can't speak the language of her ancestors. Where are you from, pretty girl?" Eddie asked.

"Dallas," came Tessa's even reply. She was excellent at playing a part. "Though my parents immigrated from Mexico, if that's what you're asking. I was born in the States, and my parents wanted me to fit in. I used to speak a little, but not anymore."

He had no idea what she was doing. Half their conversation the night they'd met had been in Spanish. He enjoyed going back and forth, but if she was lying about her skills then she probably had a reason. He was going to let her lead, and they would talk about it when they were alone.

"Well, then we shall have to speak in English from now on around you," Eddie offered. "First, let me apologize for not being awake to greet you. I had a long night and overslept. I've been excited about seeing my friend again after all these years. Now I see that he's changed since he's somehow managed to convince a woman to put up with him. You'll have to tell me how you did it. I am sadly alone."

"He's rarely alone for long," David retorted. "He likes the ladies. Sometimes two or three at a time."

Tessa looked between the two of them. "And you were close friends in college?"

"Opposites attract," David reminded her. "And maybe I was different in college. Maybe I was a player."

She tilted her head up, and her words came out soft. "No, you weren't."

There was approval in that denial, an affection for him he hadn't expected. She didn't mind his good-guy side.

He hoped she liked his big bad Dom. She would find that while he could get nasty, he still wasn't a player in the common definition of the word. She would be the only one he played with if she let him.

"Oh, I can tell you so many stories." Eddie moved to the bar. Naturally there was a bar. He pulled a bottle of champagne from the small wine fridge and opened it with an expert hand. "You should have seen the poor kid from Texas trying to find his way around São Paulo. He spoke perfect Spanish and bad Portuguese. I felt sorry for him. And then he was amusing."

"I'm glad I could keep you entertained," David said, leading Tessa back to the sofa.

"Well, my friend, I can pay back the favor." Eddie poured the champagne with a flourish, handing them each an elegant glass. "I told you I'd found some of my father's notes."

Yes, it had been one of the reasons he'd been so excited about coming. "You said the cleaning staff had found a bunch of notebooks up in the attic."

Tessa clinked glasses with Eddie. "Sounds like something my David would get excited about."

He liked the sound of *my David*. "I've always thought Ricardo had more work than what we've seen. He made notes on everything he ever wrote, but we've only seen a small percentage of them."

"Why would you want to see his notes?" Tessa asked, taking a sip. "Isn't it better to read the actual work itself?"

"Ah, but the notes often tell us what the writer was thinking."

Luis had refused the champagne, but that wasn't surprising. He'd never seen his grad student drink. "Sometimes what gets left out tells us about the thought process and what the writer values. It can also tell us what he did or didn't want the audience to know."

"And sometimes my father liked to invent puzzles." Eddie downed his entire glass and poured himself another. "My childhood was all about being tested. He would give me these stupid treasure hunts."

"I always thought they sounded like fun," David said.

Eddie finally sat down across from them. "I suppose they were. He liked to hide presents for me around the house, and I would have to decode the clues he would leave. I wasn't good at it. I still wonder how many gifts are hiding in this place because my old man wouldn't give in. I had to find the treasure or it couldn't be mine. And that is another reason why I'm happy you're here, my friend."

He couldn't wait to get his hands on those notes. "I'd love to study anything new you have."

The door to the library came open, and a woman strode in with a big tray in her hands.

Eddie looked up and nodded. "Marta, thank you. Please bring it here." He looked back to his guest. "I thought we would have an afternoon snack. We keep Argentine hours here, so dinner will be late. This is Marta, and she runs the kitchen."

Marta set the big charcuterie board down on the table in the sitting area of the library. It was loaded with meats and cheeses, nuts and local fruits. He glanced over to see if any of it seemed tempting to Tessa, but she wasn't looking at the food. She was watching Marta.

"Professor Hawthorne, welcome to Montez House," Marta said with a nod. She was a stern-looking woman. She wore all black, with seemingly no allowances for the heat of the jungle. He would guess her age around fifty from the beginnings of lines around her eyes to the steel gray that streaked her dark hair. "Dinner will be served at precisely nine."

"Like in PM?" Tessa asked, and suddenly she seemed more interested in the food on the table.

"That's actually pretty early in this part of the world," David replied. He hadn't thought about this when it had been Kyle who was coming with him. Kyle started to whine around five thirty, and if there wasn't a plate of food in front of him by seven he started looking like

Hamilton on the hunt.

Tessa grabbed one of the small plates. "Well, then I thank you for the afternoon snack. This is all lovely, Marta."

Marta nodded. "Mr. Montez, don't forget that we have a staff meeting in an hour."

Eddie blinked and then nodded. "Of course. Thank you for reminding me."

Marta gave him a tight smile and nodded. "Let me know if you require anything else."

"Staff meeting? With your actual staff? How many are there?" He was curious on several levels. He wanted to know how the house ran. He was also interested in how Eddie handled things since he'd thought Eddie wouldn't handle anything at all. He was a hands-off kind of guy. But then it had been a few years since they'd gotten together in person, so perhaps he took things more seriously now.

Eddie watched Marta leave, a frown on his face that disappeared a moment later as he went back into charming-host mode. "We've had a few recent additions, and they need guidance. It's important to keep this place up, you know. The jungle is always trying to take it back. But that's nothing for you to worry about. I would like for you to take a look at this." Eddie pulled a slip of paper out of his pocket. "I'd lost the actual card he'd given me. This was a puzzle he made for my fifteenth birthday."

"You didn't get birthday presents unless you could solve the puzzle?" Tessa sounded the tiniest bit outraged. She'd made a plate of cheese and crackers and fruit.

Eddie shook his head. "No. These weren't for major items. He would have these big parties for me and he would give me gifts, but this was something private between us. The gifts were more personal. My father would never have told me there was a bike hidden in the house and then not give it to me. No, these were things like books he thought I would like, or trinkets he would bring home from his travels. My father was a complex man, but he was kind. I wish we'd had more time together."

There was the Eddie he knew, the one that was buried under all his charm and bravado. "Did you find his notes on the puzzles he created?"

"Several notebooks' worth, but I wanted you to look at this one." He handed the paper over to David.

Oh, this was a treat he hadn't expected. He tried to play it cool. Tessa was watching him, and he probably shouldn't geek out over some code written by a guy who'd died years before.

"Go on," Tessa said with a shake of her head. She stood up and glanced around the library again. "He's going to be useless to me for hours now. I suppose all of these are in Spanish and none of them have murders in them."

Luis huffed. "There are books in English, in many languages. Ricardo Montez spoke five, but he certainly didn't read anything so inconsequential as murder mysteries."

That got Eddie laughing. "Oh, he did, but they aren't in this library. He loved thrillers, but he didn't talk about them outside of a few close friends. He had a reputation to protect."

Tessa's eyes rolled. "Well, I don't. And lucky for me I have an e-reader. I'm going to take this to our room and enjoy my champagne and snacks with a nice side of murder that will be solved by a badass chick who also gets the guy. I'll be quiet about it because my guy here gets distracted by me."

"I do not." He totally did.

She winked his way. "Do too. I'll see you later this afternoon. If you need me, I'll be in our room reading or maybe taking a nap."

He didn't think she would do either of those things. Something was going on with his bodyguard, but he couldn't ask her about it now. He had to trust that she knew what she was doing and that whatever she was doing was for the right reasons.

Oddly, that wasn't a hard thing for him to do.

He caught her hand as she started to move past him. "You know I'm going to get caught up in all of this and I'll likely forget to eat."

"I'll remind you," she promised. "You do what you need to and I'll see you at dinner, okay?"

She was giving him permission to get lost in his work, to not tend to her needs the way he probably should. Or maybe she was simply playing a role, and he was reading way too much into it. "Okay. I'll be here if you need anything."

She dipped her head down and brushed her lips against his in a kiss that seemed to linger a bit longer than it had to.

It was an innocent kiss, the kind two people in a relationship had every day. Casual and loving, and it knocked him on his ass because he wanted so much more from her.

He watched as she walked out of the room.

"Damn, my friend. You have it bad," Eddie said and then immediately switched to Spanish and started explaining the notes and how this particular one had him flummoxed. He was sure this was the first draft of a puzzle he'd been given on his fifteenth birthday and lost when he'd given up on it.

It was a series of numbers, but something about them was familiar.

He started on the problem but didn't miss the way Luis had also watched Tessa leave.

His assistant still didn't trust her, and he hoped that wouldn't cause trouble.

Then the puzzle took over, and he wasn't thinking about anything but how to solve it.

Chapter Six

David closed the door behind him and felt his body hum with awareness.

"I don't understand how people here can eat so late." Tessa strode over to the closet where her suitcase had been placed and toed out of her shoes. "But I will admit the conversation was interesting. I can't believe you figured out all those numbers."

It was late, the moon illuminating the balcony, and he wondered if he could coax her into going outside with him.

The day had gone by in a flash. One minute he'd been putting together the puzzle that had led to a book in the very library he'd spent hours and hours in today, and the next he found himself here with her. He knew he should be tired, but there was a restless energy running through his veins because he finally got to be alone with her. "Once I figured out how the numbers and letters related, it was fairly easy. It was making the connection that was hard."

He'd figured out he was looking at Dewey decimal classifications, and from there he had to find the right books in the library to lead him to Montez's ultimate hiding place. The present for Eddie had been a baseball card. Sammy Sosa.

Eddie had studied that card with wonder, as though he could still see his father putting it there, waiting for him to find it. He'd explained that he'd loved American baseball as a kid, and one of his fondest memories of his father had been going to New York with him and seeing a Yankees game.

"Well, it was easy to see that they were all impressed with your deductive powers. They were talking about it in the kitchen earlier," Tessa remarked.

He'd been surprised that she hadn't been in the room when he'd come to take a shower and change for dinner. She'd shown up in time to walk with him to the dining room, but they hadn't had a chance to talk. "Is that why you're pretending to not speak Spanish? You wanted to be able to listen in?"

She wore a pretty gold sundress that showed off her toned arms and shoulders, her hair in a neat bun at the back of her head. "If they don't think I understand, they'll speak more freely around me. I want them to think I'm nothing more than a pretty piece of fluff the professor gets to bang."

He frowned at the thought. "You're far more than that."

"I don't need you to build me up. It's a convenient cover. I know you don't think that. You're practically perfect," she said, her nose wrinkling. "You even caught all my cues. It was a seamless performance."

"Oh, like the not speaking Spanish?" He'd simply allowed her to lead.

"Yes, some men would have corrected me," Tessa explained. "I've met the type. They don't like to be wrong, and they're always putting in their two cents."

"I can be wrong. I'm wrong a lot. So what did you actually do when you said you would be reading and taking a nap?"

"After I made sure there are no listening devices in our bedroom, I walked around the place, into some of the rooms Luis didn't show us."

"I'm sorry, listening devices?" he asked because that statement had surprised him.

"Yeah, I wanted to make sure we can speak freely in here. I didn't find anything. We're good. What I did find was a stairwell that leads into the staff quarters. I was shown out of there quickly," she said. "I don't like the butler."

"How can you know if you like him?" He wasn't going to argue that Eddie had no reason to listen in on them. It was her job, and he was going to let her do it. He hated that they were chatting about inconsequential things when all he wanted to do was ask her if she'd changed her mind about playing with him. "He barely said two words to me."

The big guy had been around though. He'd been waiting outside the library when they'd taken a break. David had been surprised since there had been a staff meeting Eddie had been called away to, but he'd figured Mateo was there in case he or Luis or Tessa needed something.

"I wasn't talking about a personal level, though I doubt we would have much in common," Tessa said. "He wasn't in Kyle's notes, and he's a recent hire. I heard two of the gardening staff talking about how he took someone else's place, and they don't understand why Eddie would replace the old butler since he was nice and Mateo apparently is not. They also said he's lazy and should go back to the city if he doesn't want to work."

"You know the rural urban divide is pretty much the same everywhere. The people from the country think the people from the city are lazy and don't know how to work hard." He wasn't sure why she'd focused in on Mateo, but she was smarter at this than he was.

"I suppose, but I don't like the timing of his hire. He came down with Eddie a few days ago after the old butler decided to retire suddenly. I find him suspect until such time he proves he isn't. Does he look like a butler to you?"

"What's a butler supposed to look like?" He bet most people would think of some elderly English dude, but the wealthy had butlers all over the world.

"Well, they don't usually look like they can lift two twenty and eat nails for breakfast," Tessa said with a frown.

"Eddie mentioned he's ex-military and he trained with an academy when he got out."

"All of that should have been listed in a report," Tessa pointed out. "Kyle should have checked to make sure Mateo's credentials are real. I don't even know the dude's last name."

"Kyle focused more on the people we would come in contact with before we got to the island." He pulled his tie off and slung it over the nearest chair. They'd been given a large suite of rooms with a living area, bedroom, and massive bathroom with a shower big enough for the both of them. They would fit in the tub, too.

He couldn't help but think about the fact that the bed was big enough for a whole lot of play if she decided to say yes. That bed was big and soft, and after they were done with play they could cuddle together all night.

It had been a long time since he'd slept with a woman. Sex had become something perfunctory for him, an itch he and his partner needed to scratch and then move on with life. He didn't want that with her. He wanted to indulge with her.

He wanted to study her. To read her like a book, savoring every line, closing the book only to open it again because he'd probably missed some subtext. He was fairly sure it would take a long time to become an expert on Tessa Santiago.

"Kyle was being lazy. He should have checked out every single person who works here or we might come into contact with," Tessa complained.

"He's not lazy. He's going through some stuff right now. He's still adjusting to being out of the military, and I think something bad happened to him. He has some terrible dreams he won't talk about." David felt the need to defend his brother. "And he came on the job very late. He was basically doing a favor for me. I told him everyone on the island was okay, and he believed me."

She seemed tense. He'd noticed all the way through dinner her smile hadn't once reached her eyes, and she seemed to be watching every move the staff made. "It's not a favor. It's a job, and he should have taken it more seriously. I spent the afternoon and early evening getting a lay of the land. I spent some time in the kitchens while they were making me some tea. They're surprised that you brought a woman with you instead of your brother, but I heard Mateo say that would make it easier. I have to wonder what he meant by that. I only caught the end of the conversation."

There was a simple explanation. "Kyle would have required another room. I think they're happy they didn't have to clean another one every day. This way they're responsible for three rooms instead of four. And if they knew anything about my brother they would be happy because he's pretty much a slob."

She frowned his way. "David, this isn't something to joke about."

"What has you worried?" He didn't get it. He'd had a nice day. The staff seemed competent if not entirely friendly. The food had been tasty, and the conversation at dinner had been entertaining.

She seemed to think about what to say next. He rather thought she was trying to decide how to deal with him. "I don't like how they look at you."

He hadn't been expecting that. Tessa seemed like such a logical woman. "How do they look at me?"

"Like they know something you don't," Tessa replied.

"What would they know that I don't?"

"I get the feeling Eddie wants to use you for something," she admitted. "How many of those puzzles did he give you?"

Eddie had given him two notebooks filled with Montez's notes on codes and puzzles. Eddie's father had deeply enjoyed games. He'd been known to throw elaborate treasure hunts during his parties that could go on for days. "They want me to take a crack at finding Montez's treasure, the one he hid somewhere on the island."

She pointed his way as though he'd made her argument. "The one that's rumored to be worth millions of dollars."

She was forgetting that looking for the treasure was already on their agenda. "I was planning on taking a crack at it. It's why we've got the camping gear. They don't have to use me for it."

"And if you find it?" she asked.

"I would give it to Eddie. It was his father's."

She stared at him as though trying to figure out if he was being honest. "Millions, David. The person who finds it is supposed to keep it. That's the whole point of the challenge."

The actual treasure was the least interesting part to him. "I don't need the money. The reward for me is the history I'll find. I'll honor Montez by returning the treasure to his family."

She sighed and strode across the living area. "I don't get you, Hawthorne."

Ah, they were back to Hawthorne. She was trying to put distance between them, and he didn't want that. He caught her arm, gently stopping her. "I think you do. I think that's what bothers you. Tell me if you've changed your mind."

Her eyes were wide as she looked up at him. "I should. This situation is more complex than you're making it."

"And it won't get less complex if we sleep together."

"That's where you're wrong," she said softly.

She obviously hadn't thought this problem through the way he had. All through dinner he'd thought about how to argue his position. "I'm not. If you choose not to play with me tonight, I'll still have feelings for you in the morning, and we'll still be right where we are now. We've got a couple of days and then you're determined to never see me again."

"I'm not that dramatic."

"Then you'll date me when we get back?"

She shook her head. "I won't avoid you, but I still think a relationship is a bad idea."

"Then nothing changes by playing with me tonight," he said, his voice going low. "You're not going to protect me less because we slept together. You're still going to give the job everything you have. You're not going to let yourself catch feelings for me. So you're safe to indulge. Tell me you don't want to indulge, Tessa."

Her chin tilted up, and there was a light of challenge in her eyes. "I'll feel safer if you promise to keep your eyes open around here."

"Are we negotiating?" He should have known she would try to get something out of it. Of course the fact that the thing she was trying to get was him to be more serious about his own safety was a mark of what kind of a woman she was. Smart. Capable. Protective. A little sneaky.

Her hands went to her hips, and he could see her steel herself. "Yes. I think we are. You're right. Spending a restless night isn't going to fix things. And having sex isn't going to change things."

He hoped she was wrong about that, but he was going in with his eyes open. "I promise I will be more careful. I'm not going to give you hell about protecting me."

"There's a reason Big Tag almost never puts a female bodyguard in charge of a male client."

He could imagine. "Because some of us are assholes who think we can do any job better than a woman. I'm not that man, Tessa. You're the expert here. If you think it's too dangerous, then we go, and I won't fight you on it."

"Seriously? If I told you my gut thinks something's wrong here, you would pack up and go with me?"

The whole idea of leaving gave him a headache because he might never get this chance again, but there was one correct answer here. "I trust you. You say the word and we leave."

"You are too good to be true."

He thought that was part of the problem. She didn't want to trust this thing between them because it felt too good and therefore had to be false. He needed to show her how wrong she was. "Then I will inevitably disappoint you, but it won't be by questioning your authority when it comes to our safety. So let's play. I trust you to keep us safe. Trust me to bring you pleasure."

A soft sigh came from her mouth, those full lips of hers parting slightly. "I worry I'll think more about you than I will the job if I sleep with you."

"I know I won't be able to think about anything but you if we don't."

"You seemed to do okay today."

He'd wondered if it bugged her that he'd gotten lost. He released her arm. "I'm sorry about that. I didn't realize where the time had gone."

She shook her head and moved back. "That didn't bother me. I know what you're here to do, and I'm glad you had fun with it. It's my job to make sure you can do yours. And it was cool how you put all of that together. But I have to admit I'm nervous about moving forward. I do want you."

He could compromise. "How about you go and take a shower and get ready for bed. I'm going to go out to the living area and make a couple of notes on the things I learned today. I'll close the door between us. If you come through the door again, we'll start a scene and play. If you choose to go to bed then I'll see how you feel in the morning. This is not an all or nothing offer. If you change your mind, I'll be here. But you have to promise me something. When you're in the shower, think about me. Think about what we could do if I was in there with you. If you decide you don't want to go through with this, leave the door closed. You take the bed and I'll sleep out here on the couch."

"That doesn't seem fair to you."

"Fair doesn't matter. What matters to me is that you feel secure and comfortable and you make the decision you need to make because if you do want to explore this chemistry between us, I'll be in charge." He moved to the door that separated the bedroom and that decadent bath from the living area where his laptop was already set up.

She stood there, watching him with wary eyes. "All right then. I'll think about it."

He closed the door between them and prayed she found the courage to open it again.

* * * *

Tessa stood in front of the door and realized she was being a coward. She'd taken way too long in that shower, and the whole time she couldn't stop thinking about how if she'd been a little braver, he might have been in there with her, his hands moving over her body.

He was too fucking good to be true, and she'd had that before. She'd been in this exact place with a man who should have been forever and just wasn't, and what if that was her fault?

It had seemed like such a perfect idea on the plane. She'd had hours to think it over, to come to the conclusion that they could find mutual pleasure and walk away satisfied. One night to get David out of her system had sounded like a logical, practical thing to do. Then he'd turned the tables on her on the boat. The minute she'd realized her buttoned-up professor was kind of a freak, she'd known she was in serious trouble. In some ways it still didn't compute for her. The tops she knew were men who were dominant and dangerous even outside of Sanctum. She was sure her friends would tell her she needed to hang out with people who didn't take bullets for a living, but that was her experience. She equated tops with alpha males.

Or was she equating alpha males with military men. There were other types of alpha men. She would bet David could take charge of a classroom easily. Why did a guy have to carry a gun to be an alpha?

She was stalling again. She wasn't this woman, damn it. She wasn't a woman who worried over every decision. She wanted David, and she was going to have him. They'd made their deal, and everyone knew the score, so this was easy-peasy.

She opened the door and stepped into the living area. And stopped because he was sitting at the desk, his face illuminated by the laptop screen and the soft light coming from the lamp. He had his glasses on, and he was staring at the screen intently with that look she'd quickly come to associate with him being lost in thought.

He was beautiful, and she wasn't sure how she could fit in his world. Was his world as far from her as Michael's had been?

His head came up, and suddenly it wasn't the screen he was studying. "Hello, Tessa. Come here."

The smile might have been friendly, but his tone was lower, the hint of a command in the words. She resisted the urge to lick her lips and stepped into the room. The door made a heavy, final thunking sound as it closed behind her. As tense as she'd been before, now she found her shoulders relaxing, the calm she normally felt in the changing room at Sanctum starting to slide over her.

She was suddenly so much more aware of her body, of the way the silk of her pajamas felt against her skin, the cool breeze from the fan overhead caressing her. Her feet sank into the thick carpet of the rug, and she could smell the soap she'd used.

She shook herself out of those thoughts and back to the problem at hand. They had things to work out. "We need to talk. I meant what I said about throwing down, but also—"

"No." David tucked his hands into his pockets and smiled. He was wearing the same khakis with a brown belt and a white dress shirt he'd worn to dinner, though he'd lost the tie and jacket. The top two buttons of the dress shirt were open and the sleeves rolled up. He was barefoot. It was a far cry from the leathers and boots she was used to. So why did she find it so fucking sexy? Even his glasses were hot. Hot professor.

Wait. He'd said no.

"No?" She crossed her arms. "No you don't want to have sex tonight, or no—"

"No, *we* don't need to talk." He picked up the straight-backed wooden chair he'd been sitting in and moved past her. He opened the door to the bedroom again, walking through.

She watched as he settled the chair near the foot of the massive four-poster bed. All the furniture in the villa was well-made, if simple in design. It looked like most of it had probably been made here on the island and assembled in the rooms given the size of the pieces. If he tied her down to that bed, arms and legs spread, there'd be no way of getting away. She could pull on the ropes all she wanted. That bed wasn't going anywhere.

She would be at his mercy. No arguing. No fighting her own wants. All she would be able to do was take the pleasure this man could give her.

If tonight was about throwing down, maybe she should do exactly that. Tackle him and use a soft takedown move to get him on his back on the floor. Then she could straddle him and—

"Tessa, I asked you to sit down."

With a start she glanced at him, then backed up a few steps and sat. She'd missed that first command. The second hadn't been given in Dom voice, that had been *teacher* voice. A reprimand mixed with an order and all coated in a slightly disappointed tone.

"Damn," she said in admiration. "You're a college professor. I didn't think you'd have that pissed-off teacher thing happening."

He grinned, his lips quirking up in a smirk she shouldn't find so sexy. He stepped in front of her, just close enough that she had to tilt her head back to see his face. Just enough to let her know who was in charge.

"I'm going to talk and you're going to listen." He stared her down. "We're going to address the issue of your preconceived notions about what qualifies a man to be a Dom. I sensed that you were surprised when I told you, and I think I know why."

She was getting a lecture? She hadn't expected that, but then she was starting to get the idea that David was way more of a mystery than she'd imagined. "I don't think that you can't be a Dom. I was just—"

"Please do not interrupt."

Tessa closed her lips, eyeing him from under her lashes.

He fiddled with his glasses, adjusting them slightly on his nose. He started to circle around the chair, looking down at her. It was like a predator circling his…

No. It was like a curator looking at a newly acquired piece of art. An archaeologist examining an artifact. He was looking at her as if she were unique and special. Treasured.

He stopped in front of her then dropped to a crouch. "I might not have an ex-soldier's instincts to take command, to give orders, but I have something better."

"And what's that?" Tessa asked, happy that she managed the question in an even tone and not filled with the breathless anticipation she felt. This wasn't going how she'd thought it would, how her other scenes had gone.

It didn't feel like a scene at all.

"Curiosity. I like to learn. To study." Dropping to one knee, he wrapped his hand around her ankle, sliding his fingers under the fabric of the loose pajama pants she was wearing. "And then I take that knowledge and I apply it. I develop theories." His hand pushed her pant leg up to her knee, exposing her lower leg. "I test those theories. I seek out evidence to support them." He ran his fingertips up her calf, then gently teased the skin at the back of her knee.

All he'd done was touch her leg and her whole body was on fire with need. She could feel her pussy getting wet and soft and wanting. She usually needed time to get ready. It was one of the reasons D/s had been good for her. D/s had taught her that whatever she needed to make sex good was all right. That she could go at her pace and expect her partner to be okay with it. D/s had taught her to take sex seriously, to be thoughtful.

She didn't want to think with this man. She was pretty sure she wouldn't have to.

"You have a theory about me?" She tried to make the words flippant, but they didn't come out that way.

David kneaded her calf muscle for a moment, then stood. When he held out his hand, she took it, responding to the unspoken command and letting him pull her to her feet.

"I do."

Was that all she was getting? "What's your theory?"

"If I tell you it will skew my study," he said almost absently since he was staring down at her like he was trying to memorize her face.

"You're going to study me?" She wasn't sure she would be able to handle all that intensity focused her way. When David was fascinated with a subject, it held all of his attention. What would it be like to have this gorgeous, smart man give her every bit of his focus?

"Yes. I am." He reached out and put two fingers under her chin, tilting her head up and forcing her to look into his eyes. "You want that, don't you?"

"Yes." The word was almost a plea. She was so turned on that each breath felt heavy and wet with need.

"Do you think that's an appropriate way to address me?" The question was asked on a soft tone, but there was steel beneath it.

"You want me to call you 'Sir'?"

"While that would be appropriate, what we have is special, so I think we'll use a different, special, term."

She winced, briefly pulled out of the moment because the word *special* was too close to home. She was afraid what was happening between them was special, and that scared her. "David, I told you. This is just sex. Maybe we shouldn't be so…"

"Professor," he said, ignoring her outburst. "You will call me Professor when you're submitting."

"Professor." She'd been sort of hoping he'd make her call him "Master Hawthorne." She was more than willing. But then she'd called a lot of tops Master this or that. She'd never called one *Professor* and never would in the future. Even if she never touched him again, David would always be her professor.

"You called me professor as a joke before. Tonight the word is going to have a different meaning." David once more touched her chin, but this time he slid his curled fingers back, grazing the sensitive skin below her ear. Then his hand slid under her hair, around the back of her neck, sending a shiver of anticipation down her spine.

"But before we go any further, there's something we need to do," David said.

They should talk about limits, safe words. If they weren't simply going to go at it hard, they should—

"Something I've needed to do since the first night I met you," he murmured.

David closed the distance between them and sealed his lips over hers. Tessa's eyes widened before fluttering closed. His kiss was sure and strong but not forceful. When his tongue touched the seam of her lips, it was a request not a command, and she yielded to him, opening her mouth to let his tongue sweep inside. She tasted him as he tasted her, and the arousal he'd kindled to life in her both flared hotter and burned deeper, touching parts of her soul that a simple kiss shouldn't be able to reach.

The first time they'd kissed, she'd made the move. It had been good, but this was something more. This felt like a beginning.

David broke the kiss, leaning his forehead against hers for a moment. His breath washed over her face as he sighed.

"That…that was just for us," he said as he straightened.

She met his eyes and realized this was going to be everything she'd feared. She wasn't going to get what she wanted—a quick and easy getaway from feelings she didn't want. She was going to fall for this man, and her heart would break when she forced herself to leave him.

But she couldn't stop. She would take the pleasure and she would take the heartache.

His hand on the back of her neck had turned soft, his fingers sliding into her hair in a massaging caress while he kissed her. But now they clamped down once again, a firm, controlling hold that brought her right back to the kink moment that amazing kiss had interrupted.

"You're to call me *Professor*. And from now on, any time you hear *anyone* call me professor, you're going to remember everything I'm about to do to you." His fingers tightened, and he jerked her forward.

She fell into him, his chest hard against her breasts, their faces so close that he could have easily kissed her again. He didn't. Instead, she felt the puff of air from his next word.

His next order.

"Strip."

Tessa looked up into David's eyes. What she saw there made her want to submit. What she saw there made her want to forget her gloomy-fucking-Gus philosophy of life and try with this man. Made her want to hope that maybe this time it would be right. This time it would be forever.

She dropped her gaze to his chin and reached for the waistband of her PJ pants. He kept ahold of her, that unequivocally dominant grip on the back of her neck as she wiggled out of her pants.

She hadn't bothered with underwear. She'd hadn't seen the point since some part of her had known exactly how this would end—with her naked and in his arms.

Still holding her close, David dropped his free hand to her hip, fingers tracing a slow, circular pattern up her waist until they slipped under her fitted cotton T-shirt.

"I'm going to release you and then you're going to finish taking off your clothes. Once you're naked, go stand by the post at the corner of the bed. Do you have any issues with being tied up? Any restrictions you want me to honor?"

"No, Professor."

"Very good."

David released her and took a step back. Tessa quickly stripped off her shirt but hesitated when she reached around behind her back for the fastening of her bra.

"Hesitating in hopes of earning a punishment?" he asked with that same disappointed and commanding teacher voice.

Why did she find that so hot? Oh, because she was kinky as fuck and David was her Professor Hottie.

Professor. Damn it. That word did things to her and they'd barely even started.

"If you need to be bent over my desk and have a ruler taken to your ass to improve your performance, I'm more than happy to facilitate your learning in that manner." David crossed his arms. "But I won't be manipulated into doing it. Finish taking off your clothes and go stand at the post." He pointed to the bedpost closest to her.

Tessa unhooked her bra and stripped it off, tossing it aside. She straightened her shoulders, prepared for him to look her over. She was in good shape—she had to be—but that didn't mean that she didn't have her self-conscious moments, especially being naked in front of someone for the first time. Especially when that someone was too gorgeous for words.

But David wasn't looking at her. He'd turned away and was shuffling through the bag he'd carried with him the whole trip, which was on the dresser against the far wall. He pulled out a piece of paper and started reading it. Was he seriously getting distracted while she was standing here naked?

Outrage, and a little bit of hurt, flooded her. And yet at the same time it was almost…endearing—in a very irritating way—that her professor could get distracted in the middle of a BDSM scene. She stood for a moment, her emotions cycling. In the end outrage won.

She eyed the chair, considered throwing it at him. No, breaking the client was bad business. Maybe she should punch him. Big Tag would understand.

She took a step toward him, and David whirled, as if he'd been waiting for her to move.

He raised a brow, glancing from her to the bedpost. The step she'd taken had been away from the bed, not toward it.

Shit.

"Tessa, your inability to follow simple instructions doesn't bode well."

"A trap?" She gestured to the dresser. "Trick me into disobeying so you can spank me?" She rolled her eyes. "I'm down for a spanking, clearly. You don't need to trick me into it."

His jaw tightened, eyes going hard. "Rest assured that if I want to spank you, or if you need to be spanked, I will—"

The brat that lived inside her welled up. She'd been taking this way too seriously. "Said that before. Promises, promises, Professor."

"—put you over my knee, the chair, the dresser, the bed…"

Her breath caught as he stalked forward. He held the piece of paper in one hand and a necktie in the other.

"But that was not a trick." He gestured toward the pack. "I went to get my list."

For each step he took she retreated, until she backed into the bedpost, the hard wood colliding with her backside. "List?"

"Yes. While you were out listening in on the kitchen staff, I was making a list."

Tessa eyed him. Had he been prepping and planning for their scene? Had he sat in this room and carefully plotted out all the things he wanted to do to her? Damn it, that was hot. She could still save this.

She bit her bottom lip and gave him her widest-eyed look. "What's on your list, Professor?"

"It's a quick outline of my study."

"Your study?" Her brain was addled by the sight of the tie in his hand.

"Yes, Tessa. Like I explained before, I'm going to study you. If you let me, I'll study you all week long." He held up the piece of paper, and she got only a glimpse of a few words before he tossed it so it fluttered down onto the bed behind her.

Nipple play preferences? Pinch, twist, pull, suck, flick, abrade.

How many fingers can she comfortably take in her ass?

The idea of having David working his fingers into her ass was so hot she was light-headed with need. Tessa licked her lips. "David, no more playing around. Fuck me."

She reached for him, prepared to use that takedown move she'd been considering earlier to get him on the bed.

But he was fast—faster than she thought he had any right to be. He grabbed her wrists, forcing them above her head, backs of her hands against the bedpost. He wrapped the tie around both wrists and the bedpost, securing them. It wasn't enough to actually restrain her...at least it wasn't until he added his belt.

When he whipped his belt from his pants, she froze. He smirked and ran the cool metal buckle over her nipples. Tessa hissed out a breath and arched her back.

"I don't have proper cuffs, so using the tie in conjunction with the belt, to be sure I don't put pressure on your nerves, will have to be enough." He climbed on the bed behind her, kneeling and wrapping the belt over her wrists and the post, buckling it in place. The bondage was still loose enough that she could get out if she wanted to, and the fact that he knew better than to try and use the belt by itself due to the physical risks it could pose told her everything she needed to know about the quality of training at The Club.

She expected him to get off the bed and come around to face her once she was bound, but his hands slid around her from behind. Broad, warm palms cupped her waist, then moved north along her sides. His fingertips brushed the outer curves of her breasts, and all she could think about was what she'd seen written on that piece of paper. The things he was planning to do to her. In particular her nipples.

"I think I'll start my study here. At these lovely breasts." He cupped them, lifting with a gentle reverence that reminded her of the way he'd looked at her earlier. As if she was some precious piece of art or an artifact to be treasured. Some fascinating work he wanted to study, to understand.

His thumbs flicked her nipples, and she was so ready, so needy, that she cried out.

"Pleasure or pain?" He whispered the question against her ear.

"Pleasure." She could barely breathe. "I'm so fucking turned on." She arched her back. "Professor, please…"

David gently grasped each nipple, applying enough pressure to hold them. "Please hurt you? Play with you? Fuck you?"

"Everything. Give me everything." She was past the point of arguing with herself. She was going down this particular rabbit hole, and she wasn't going to be able to turn back. When they got home, when the job was over, she would be able to go on with her life, but for now she wanted to belong to him in these dark hours. They had six nights together. Why shouldn't she spend them with him? Study him the way he was studying her?

His fingers clamped down on her nipples, a vicious pinch as tight as any clamp. Tessa moaned and arched up into his hands, needing, wanting, more. He released her and she cried out in protest, but he didn't leave. Instead, he jumped off the bed and when he faced her, there were spots of color high on his cheeks, his eyes glittering with a need that matched her own. It was good to see that desire stamped on his handsome face, to know she wasn't alone in this.

He reached out, caressing her breasts, squeezing them gently, and then contrasted that sweet touch with a vicious flick to her nipples, hard enough to have her up on her toes. Hard enough to send a straight line of desire to her pussy. She was wetter than she could ever remember being, could smell the musk of her own arousal.

When she arched her back as he rolled one nipple, David let out a tortured groan. His head dropped to her breast, and he took her other nipple in his mouth. The warm heat was wonderful, yet not enough. She needed so much more from him.

Needed everything.

"David, Professor," she moaned.

"I wanted to go slow," he panted against her breast. "But you tempt me." He bit her nipple, a small punishment.

In response, Tessa wrapped one leg against his hip and tried to jerk him forward. That earned her a bite on the other nipple that had her groaning her frustration. But as he soothed that hurt with his tongue, his hand slid down her body and finally, finally between her legs.

She knew she was wet. Every time she shifted her weight from foot to foot she could feel how wet the insides of her thighs were getting. Her clit was pulsing in time with her heartbeat, and when his fingers found the nub and started to circle it, the spike of pleasure was so sharp she thought for a moment she'd orgasm from his mere touch.

No man had ever made her feel this needy this fast. If he could do this to her with no more than his words, a piece of paper, and some men's accessories, what would it be like to submit to him in a club? Where he had access to toys and tools.

She'd probably explode.

She was going to explode now.

"I'm close," she panted.

"Damn it, me too. I want...I want to do more to you. I want to take my time but I..." With a groan David jerked back. Before she could protest, he was yanking a condom from his pocket. She got only the barest glimpse of his dick as he pulled it out of his pants and rolled the condom on. Then his big body was pressing her back against the bedpost. Trapping her, but she didn't want to escape.

"Tessa..." Her name was a benediction on his lips.

"Please." It was the only word she could manage, but it was enough.

David grabbed her hips, lifting her, and she wrapped her legs around his waist. The head of his cock bumped her clit then slid down the valley of her pussy.

"I'm not going to be gentle," he warned her.

"Fuck me, Professor." She didn't want gentle. She wanted him raw and hard and male. She wanted this side of the man every bit as much as she was coming to need the intellectual, thoughtful side.

David surged into her, his big, thick cock filling her with one hard thrust. The sudden penetration. The fullness. It was nearly enough to take her over the edge.

She twisted her wrists, wiggling them out from under the strap so that instead of holding her wrists in place she was using it as a handle, her arm muscles tense as she held on tight.

David hitched her further up the smooth post and adjusted the angle of their bodies enough for him to slip a hand between them. His thumb touched her clit, and that was all she needed.

Tessa's back arched as she screamed between gritted teeth. The orgasm was sharp and hot. As sudden and fierce as a summer storm, and every bit as powerful. Her pussy clenched down on his cock, and she heard him groan, felt him speed up his thrusts. She wrapped her legs tighter around him as her orgasm went on and on, intensified and bolstered by his own.

She could have stayed in that moment, locked in his arms, knowing, feeling that he was just as affected by her as she was by him, but nothing lasted forever. Not even the best orgasm of her life.

David let out a long, groaning breath, leaning his temple against hers.

"Holy shit," he muttered.

"Mmm," she agreed.

"Give me a second and I'll untie…"

She released the makeshift strap and wrapped her arms around him.

"…or you can get yourself out," he finished with a chuckle.

To her surprise, David grabbed her ass and, with the head of his cock still inside her, took two steps to the side and flopped back onto the mattress, her on top.

"That…didn't go exactly as planned. But it was really, really hot." He peered up at her, clearly waiting for a response.

She could still feel him inside her. "You didn't even get out of your clothes."

"Well," David said at last. "I think it's clear we'll have to do that again, since what just happened didn't satisfy either of our objectives."

"What are you talking about?"

He grinned, shifting easily from the hard-voiced top to the adorable, sexy, cuddly man she'd known he would be. "You said throw down…but we had sex standing up. Doesn't count."

"Semantics? Really?"

"And I…well, I barely even got to start my study." He slid a finger down her bare side, and it lit up every nerve ending in her body. "I'm not ready to give up on my study of Tessa."

She started to move, letting his cock slide in and out again.

She wasn't ready to give up on him yet.

She might never be.

Chapter Seven

David felt Tessa move in his arms, the soft morning light from the windows giving the whole bedroom a dewy glow.

Her hair had gone everywhere. He was caught in it, the long tresses laid out over his chest and arms.

She was way cuddlier than he would have imagined. She sighed and rubbed her cheek against his chest, her legs moving against his.

He'd had her three times the night before, and his dick should still be sleeping, but nope. His dick—which so often took a backseat to his brain—was standing at attention and demanding to take the lead this morning.

His dick had taken over, and he hadn't even worked through half his list. He'd meant to make a long, slow study of her nipples, to test how sensitive they were and what kind of play they responded to.

His dick just wanted to fuck her again.

"Did we sleep in?" Her eyes came open, and she yawned against the back of her hand.

"It's not too late." He didn't want her to think he was eager to be anywhere but here. In between bouts of sex, they'd talked. The conversation had been an easy flow of their own personal histories. He was sure she would have told him she was only talking, but he'd been soaking her in, learning about her life. Becoming closer and closer to her.

She blinked and looked up at him, and he saw the moment Doubting Tessa showed up. He'd decided there were two Tessas—the one who teased him and kept getting closer and closer, and the one who remembered what it felt like to cancel a wedding for four hundred of North Texas's elite.

The key was to get Doubting Tessa to stop thinking. When she went on instinct they were good.

He kissed her, meshing their mouths together in a luxurious embrace. She immediately went soft in his arms, and their legs tangled together.

When he started to move down her body, she rolled over and let him.

"You're going to kiss me every time I start to get weird about this, aren't you?"

She was a smart girl. He kissed his way down her neck. "What's weird about it? This feels perfectly natural to me."

She sighed. "I work with your brother."

"And it would be weird if he was here with us, but he's not. And he won't make fun of you or act like an idiot if he finds out we've slept together. He'll just try to get you to feed him if he finds you at my place. Don't give in. He's an adult, and he knows how to make ramen. If he whines too much, put in earbuds. He'll get the message." He kissed his way over her skin, pausing above her nipple. "But that won't be a problem because we're not going to have a relationship after next Sunday. So relax and enjoy the time we do have."

"You don't believe me." She said the words on a sigh. "You don't think I'll walk away."

He had a few days to make her change her mind. After all, she'd said they would "throw down" once and then be done, and she was still in his bed. "I can't make you stay with me. All I can do is enjoy the time I have with you. Sometimes in my line of business you only get so long with a subject. Like the time I got to study a seventeenth century priest's account of his mission. They would only let me study it in a clean room, and only for two hours at a time."

Her body started to move restlessly, as though she knew exactly where he was going. "You're killing me, Professor."

That was not his intention. He kissed across her belly and started down toward her pussy. His cock had spent a whole lot of time inside this gorgeous part of her, but he hadn't had a chance to taste her yet. "Tell me why you think my brother can't handle working with someone I'm involved with."

This was one subject she hadn't mentioned the night before. He needed to ease her into talking about her broken engagement. He believed her when she said she wasn't hung up on the man himself, but it was obvious to him that the relationship and its breakup still affected her.

"It's not that I think Kyle would give me hell," she replied in a breathy voice. "I mean at least not more than he gives anyone. Your brother can be sarcastic."

He kissed his way from one hip to the other, skimming over her pelvis, well aware he was building anticipation. "I know he's obnoxious, but I'm happy he's joking again. When he first got home, he was so unlike the brother who'd left. He's starting to show signs of the old Kyle. Does anyone treat you differently?"

"No. Not really. I mean I'm sure we were talked about, but it was a mutual decision." She was looking down her body, her teeth worrying that decadent bottom lip of hers. "Is it stupid that I felt like I let Charlotte Taggart down? She set us up. It should have worked."

Now they were getting somewhere. "Spread your legs wide for me."

She immediately moved her legs, giving him all the access he could possibly want. There was no shyness in her. It was obvious she trusted him physically. The emotional part was their problem.

She felt like she'd failed.

"I've spent some time around Charlotte. I happen to know she likes to set people up, and it doesn't always work out. Oh, she'll say she's the best matchmaker in the world, but she's the one who set up Boomer with that woman who ran the coffee shop she liked. The one that turned out to be a front for smuggling illegal foods. Boomer nearly got killed with a giant wheel of unpasteurized cheese. She never talks about that one." He gripped her thighs to give her the illusion of being held down. She seemed to respond beautifully to being controlled during sex.

Sure enough, there was a sigh that came from her lips, and she relaxed against the bed. "I hadn't heard that story. It's good to know I'm not the only one."

He breathed her in, glorying in the smell of her arousal. Her pearl of a clit was poking out of its hood, desperate for affection. "So you feel like you failed when all you did was be brave enough to acknowledge when something wasn't working."

"I know what you're doing, David."

"I wasn't being subtle about it." He pressed a soft kiss on her clitoris and felt a shudder go through her. "When I said I was going to make a study of you, I didn't mean only your body. Though I have to say, your body is the most beautiful thing I've ever studied."

He kissed her clit again, dragging his tongue over it and reveling in the way she groaned.

"It won't work," she said with a whimper.

He thought it was working fine, but then they were probably thinking of two very different things. "Then there's no harm in answering my questions."

"If I tell you what the real problem is, will you get to the point because I'm dying here."

He sucked one side of her labia and then the other. "Yes. Tell me what truly bothers you about the thought of dating me because it isn't that my uncle is going to fire you if you break my heart. He'll say some sarcastic shit to me about not being able to hold on to a woman and then ask me to help Seth with his math homework. So tell me the truth and I'll eat this pussy all morning if you want me to."

Eating her pussy had definitely been on his list. And he would have to do it several times before he could truly judge what she responded to. A soft tongue or a nip? Maybe both. He was willing to experiment to her heart's content.

"I don't want to be that chick who's dated everyone at the office and is still single. I'd rather admit that I'm supposed to be single and move on."

Her last relationship hadn't worked out, and it was still a sore spot for her. It might be for a while, but she would come out of it, and he intended to be there when she did. He intended to spend the next few days blanketing her in pleasure so when they did get back, she wouldn't be able to deny him. Even if all she wanted was a D/s relationship, he would take it because he knew they were meant to be.

He speared her with his tongue, taking in her taste. She shuddered and moaned as he explored every inch of her pussy. He fucked her with his tongue and let his thumb press down on her clit as she shook and came.

Then it was his turn. He got to his knees and started to reach for the condoms.

A loud banging cut through the lust cloud he was in.

"David! David, get your butt out of bed. It's time to go to work, my friend. It's almost noon, and my cook is going to be angry her whole breakfast buffet went to waste."

"It's noon?" Tessa gasped and rolled out from under him. "I can't believe we slept so late."

He fell to the bed, his cock still throbbing. It was going to be a rough day.

* * * *

This morning had been a near thing. Tessa was still thinking about how close she'd come to telling David that she was being silly and of course they would see each other when they got back to Texas. How could they not when they fit so perfectly together? She'd woken up all happy and warm, and she'd had to force herself to remember that this wasn't some fantasy where they lived happily ever after.

Your parents did. Why shouldn't you? Stop beating yourself up. You made a mistake and now you're never going to try again?

This. This was why she shouldn't have even thought about getting in bed with David. Or rather she'd thought she could avoid this by doing precisely that. She'd thought she could quell all these questions if she did the man and got it out of her system.

Turned out he was pretty hard to get rid of.

She glanced down at her cell. No bars. Someone had to have a phone because she needed to call back home and get started on finding out who Mateo was.

David was in the library again, his nose in a book, of course. They'd had breakfast with Eddie and Luis and then the men had hidden themselves away in the library, and she'd been left to wander around the house. She'd gone into the gardens and strolled around, took a couple of pictures so anyone looking would see nothing more than some full of herself American tourist taking selfies for her social media.

The last thing she wanted them to realize was that she was hella suspicious and thinking seriously about pulling David out of here.

But there was also a piece of her that wondered if she wasn't the one she was trying to rescue because she wasn't sure her walls would hold up against the professor.

It was exactly why she shouldn't have come on this job. She wasn't sure she trusted her instincts when it came to him. She might be more invested in protecting herself than him. At least on an emotional level.

If she was a phone, where would she be?

She'd walked around this floor yesterday, and it was all guest bedrooms. Luis had the room across the hall, and two others in this wing were unoccupied. She stopped in front of a big display case. There were pictures of Ricardo Montez with different world leaders. Those were displayed in ornate frames, but there were other pictures, too. Ones of Ricardo with Eddie. A few of them were of Eddie as a child, holding a fishing pole and showing off a gap-toothed grin.

She stopped on the picture of Eddie standing with a younger David Hawthorne. They were both wearing the caps and gowns from their graduation ceremony. Eddie was giving the camera a thumbs-up, but David's expression was tight, like he was smiling for the camera but something was missing.

His dad, probably.

"We were twenty-four when that was taken," a deep voice said. "Though I will admit David has always seemed older to me."

Eddie stood behind her. He was dressed for the heat in cargo shorts and a loose button-down. He was an attractive man, almost a mirror of his father, though all the pictures of Ricardo showed gray at his temples and Eddie's hair was still pure black.

"He doesn't look happy in this picture," she commented. Of all the people she wanted to underestimate her, this man was number one. She wanted him to see her as nothing more than David Hawthorne's girlfriend, someone who held his hand and enjoyed the ride.

Someone who could handle his quirks. Who didn't mind that he got lost in work because she was cool with reading a book while he studied or wrote.

She kind of wanted to meet his cat.

"This was shortly after his brother was in a car accident." Eddie picked up the frame, looking down at it. "I think someone died and his brother felt…like it was his fault. Kyle was being self-destructive at the time, and David felt that strongly."

"Because he'd lost his dad years before and couldn't stand the thought of losing his brother, too." She'd heard rumors that Kyle had gone into the Navy because he'd had some focus problems. She also knew he didn't have a car. Kyle was notorious for hitching rides with anyone who was going close to where he lived, and she'd heard him talk David into picking him up more than once. He kept saying it was because he hadn't gotten around to buying a car, but now she wondered about her fellow employee. Kyle seemed so serious. He held himself apart, but he'd also recently hired on, so she understood that. What if it was something more?

David had a lot going on in his life and yet he was so focused on her. Was she being selfish? She didn't ask him to talk about himself because she knew damn well he would only drag her in deeper. Knowing about his family and his life…just made him feel closer to what she wanted for her own.

She wasn't ready for this and yet she couldn't pull away.

"Yes, I suspect that was true," Eddie agreed. "He felt the loss of his father quite deeply. When my own died, I called David. He helped me through that rough first year. He's a good man. There is no one I would rather have write my father's biography."

"He's kind of obsessed with your dad. That didn't make you uncomfortable?" She was curious about their relationship. They seemed like such opposites.

Eddie shook his head. "David never took advantage of our friendship. Not once. My father didn't give interviews. He was a reclusive man when it came to the press. He didn't like to leave the island in his later years. David never asked to come out here. He only met my father once. He was polite, and when my father didn't want to talk about his personal history, they discussed baseball. It's only been recently that David started talking about writing the book, and he promised I could read it before it was published. I know he'll have to talk about some of my father's darker moments. My father wasn't a perfect man. He had some problems with drugs and alcohol. He didn't pay much attention to me until I was twelve. He was here on the island, and my mother preferred to live in the city. They never married, so it wasn't until I called him and told him my stepfather was abusing me that he stepped up."

"I am so sorry to hear that."

"It's a pain from long ago, and honestly, my father coming to protect me…that helped me heal. He stayed in the city for several years because he wanted me to get a good education, but we would come out here for breaks and on the weekends." He picked up a picture of a dark-haired woman holding an infant. "It's funny how we always seem to repeat the mistakes of our parents."

"Is that you as a child?" The woman in the picture had her hair pulled back, holding a tiny infant wrapped in a blue blanket. It had obviously been taken at a hospital as she was sitting up in a hospital bed, a tray to the side that held a small bouquet of flowers and some other objects.

He put the picture back on the shelf. "I was a handsome boy." His bravado was back, along with his devil-may-care smile. "I was going up to my room to grab a book for David. He thinks he's found something with one of the maps my father left behind for this treasure hunt of his. I noticed you wandering. Is there anything I can do for you? There's a pool if you want to swim. I can also schedule some activities for you, if you like."

Ah, so they wanted to make sure they knew where she was. Or he could simply be a good host, but she wasn't sure about that. Unlike David, Eddie seemed like a man who didn't hyper focus and worry about the details. "I'm fine. I might go swimming later. I was just walking around looking. I find this place fascinating."

"I was surprised David brought a woman with him. He's usually very focused," Eddie remarked. "He's had a handful of girlfriends over the years, but I've never actually met one of them. You're a first."

She was surprised by that because David was so sweet that she couldn't imagine he didn't have a woman in his life most of the time. He was sweet right up until he decided to be dirty, and then he was even sweeter. "He didn't date while the two of you were in college?"

One shoulder shrugged. "Casually. He didn't go out with anyone more than a few times, though he did have a woman he slept with. They were more friends than anything else. Well, he was friends with her. I think she was using him. He ended up writing most of her dissertation. He's not good at telling when a woman is seeing him for the wrong reasons. He can be naïve about relationships. I worry it's gotten worse since his stepfather became such a famous man. You know who he is, right?"

Here it was. Yes, she remembered this feeling quite well. Maybe she'd lied a little to her professor. In the moment it had felt like the truth to tell him she didn't want to fail at a relationship again, but the way Eddie was looking at her brought up an entirely familiar feeling. One she hated. "Of course. I met David at his restaurant."

All the times someone told her how lucky she was to be marrying into a wealthy family came rushing back in. The subtext was always that she didn't deserve it, that she'd done something wrong to be in the place she was in. That she was a little bit of a whore. Some people didn't even make it subtext. Eddie wasn't being subtle.

But then she wasn't David's girlfriend. She was his fuck buddy until the end of this trip, and she shouldn't be so offended.

"David doesn't take money from them, you know," Eddie said. "He has wealthy, powerful friends, but he doesn't have money himself and likely won't."

"Then it's a good thing I have an excellent job and can take care of myself financially." She was done with this conversation. "Speaking of my job, I need to find a way to call back to the States. Cell service doesn't work. I was hoping I could use your phone. Your landline."

Eddie frowned. "Oh, there's no phone. We had a satellite phone, but it no longer works. I think something went wrong with the company that serviced it. We're trying to find a solution, but for now if we wish to contact someone off the island, we have to go into the small village a few miles down the road. It's where some of the biologists stay. Sometimes you can get a signal there. But only sometimes. It's very small. You don't want to go there, I assure you. I don't think it would be safe. We have radios if we need to speak with the mainland."

That was odd since David had assured her how safe the island was, that there was no real crime. She wasn't going to argue with Eddie though. She would simply find her own way. "Of course. I'll talk to David about it. We'll figure something out. I promised my boss I would check in once I got settled."

"Well, David should have mentioned how hard communication is out here. I'm sorry to disappoint you," he murmured.

She wanted to tell him that she would be okay, that she would find a way, but she didn't want to tip the enemy off, and in that moment he felt like the enemy. "Well, then I'll have to check out the pool."

"I hope you have a lovely afternoon." He turned and walked away, but not before picking up the picture of himself as a baby in his mother's arms. He took that with him.

She wanted to look into him more, too.

A young woman opened the door to the room Luis was staying in, a bucket of cleaning supplies in her hand. She gave Tessa a bright smile. "*Hola*," she began and then winced. "I mean, hello, ma'am. I am going to start your room soon, but I need to go into town to buy...supplies."

Oh, she wanted to tell the young woman she didn't have to cater to the American, that she could speak her own language, but she had to play dumb. Still, she wasn't about to let this opportunity go by. "How long do you think it will take?"

The young woman's eyes widened. "Oh, not long. I'll be back in twenty minutes or so. It is close."

"Excellent. Then you can show me the way." She could make it into town and back before anyone knew she was gone. "I need to make a phone call, and the big boss here tells me there's no landline."

"*Si.* Yes, we haven't had a phone since the storm took it out a few weeks ago. It's hard to get people to work out here." She started for the stairs, her ponytail bouncing.

Tessa followed, determined to get the information she needed.

Ten minutes later she stood in front of a small building that claimed to be a bar and a hostel and a general store all in one. And apparently they also made great empanadas. The building itself was charming, with open windows overlooking the small bay and allowing a breeze to run through the space. She'd found a group of young men sitting around a table with their laptops open, arguing over something to do with sea turtles and someone miscounting.

No danger there. Her escort, who she'd discovered was named Lara, had waved her in like she wasn't worried at all. She'd promised to come back for her after she'd picked up her supplies.

Tessa stared down at her cell. Not even the hint of a bar.

"Lady, it doesn't work in here. You have to go to the roof." One of the scientists hopped out of his chair and gestured to the stairs. He was a lanky young man with dark hair and a scruffy beard that was barely short of being scraggly. But he had a wide smile and curious eyes. Even if she hadn't seen him with the science group, she would have pegged him as some kind of an intellectual. She seemed to be surrounded with them these days. "You staying at the big house? I heard they were having guests this week. That's pretty cool since the guy who owns the place is almost never in residence anymore."

She nodded, taking in that information. "Yes, I'm staying with my boyfriend who's doing some research of his own, but I need to call back to the States."

She glanced down at the clock on her phone. It was almost two thirty, so it was pretty much lunchtime back home. It wouldn't matter. Someone would answer their line if she could get a call out.

"Well, since they took out all comms a couple of weeks back, this is pretty much it," the young man said. "I'm Joe, by the way. I'm with the biology department at Stanford."

"You're definitely studying biology and not freaking math," one of his colleagues snarked.

Joe rolled his eyes. "I know how to count. You don't know how to add. Sorry, we're doing a study on the sea turtle populations on the island. The man who used to own it put protections in place on the beaches here thirty years ago, and we're trying to prove that it's actually changed some of the migratory habits of the animals. But we can't because someone doesn't know how to use a calculator."

It was good to know that boys were the same no matter their professions. She followed the scientist up the short flight of stairs and onto the rooftop lounge. There was a bar and some tables. There was also a barbecue with the most delicious smells coming off it. "This is nice. I was told this place was sketchy."

"Not at all," Joe said. "I love this island. I mean, it's small, but you can get pretty much everything you need. The island is safe. Even with the occasional treasure hunters, there's almost no crime here. Obviously there are animals out there who will eat you if you give them a chance. There are some big snakes crawling around the interior of this island, but other than that, it's kind of a paradise. Good food, nice place to stay, friendly people. All in all, I couldn't have pulled a better job. I have a friend who's in Antarctica studying penguins. She would kill to be here. The one complaint is how hard it is to get a cell signal."

She was confused about this. Eddie had told her something had gone wrong with the satellite phone, but Lara had talked about a storm taking out the landline they'd used. "But they have phones out here, right? Or they did?"

Joe nodded. "Sure, but something happened a couple of weeks back."

"The storm?"

"I mean that's what they said, but it wasn't that bad a storm," Joe replied. "I've seen way worse and not had service drop. And it didn't affect the electricity at all. We're more used to that happening. I mean we didn't have a single outage."

That was odd but not completely incomprehensible. Still, things were starting to not add up, and when it came to something like this, she *was* good at math. "Where is my best chance at a signal?"

"It's the far edge. Be careful. There's no railing." He pointed to the corner the farthest from the bar. "Most of the time you can get a signal there, but it can drop on you at any moment."

"Thanks." She moved over to the corner as music started to float up from down below. It was a soft ballad she didn't recognize, but the sweet sound made her think of David and how much she'd loved being in his arms.

Who the hell was she? She was not the soft, mushy girl who forgot about her job the minute she got some good dick. The problem was it had been more than good dick. It had been great dick, superlative dick, with a side of mind-drugging intimacy.

She had to stop. Call. She had a call to make, and it wasn't to a girlfriend to giggle about how nice her night had been. She had most of her team's numbers in her cell. Wade was likely at Disney World with his family by now, and Kyle was laid up at his mom's house. She wasn't about to get Big Tag on the line, so she dialed the number of the person who would probably be the most helpful while also being the least sarcastic.

"Hey, girl. How is Argentina?" MaeBe Vaughn's sunny voice crackled over the line. "And can I come with you? Because here is not so great. I swear to god if you don't take that pill I will force it down your throat."

"Is everything okay?" Tessa could hear a masculine voice complaining in the background.

"I'm here at Sean and Grace's place bringing the grumpiest man in the world some lunch. He's supposed to take his meds, but he's…than the doctor. I do not know how…hasn't smothered him yet. I got the better…the deal because the cat…better behaved."

She was dropping in and out. Tessa tried to lean out a bit, and the signal seemed stronger. "Hey, I don't have much time. Did you get the background check done on the grad student?"

"What? I'm sorry, you're cutting out."

She twisted a little, and the static went away. It seemed best if she leaned into the signal. "Grad student?"

"Oh, yeah, he was clean. No police records of any kind. He's in the US on a student visa, and it's perfectly in order. The only thing he's got is an eviction notice on his apartment, but he's been applying for campus housing. Do you want me to go deeper? I didn't check into his family. The household staff checked out, too. All good."

"Who's listed as household staff? Is there a Mateo? He's a recent hire," Tessa explained.

"I don't remember. Hutch did…" More static. "I don't have it in front of me, but I can send you the files when I get back to the office."

Ah, MaeBe could send them, but Tessa wouldn't be able to receive them until she had a strong signal. Or she could sneak back here and try to get a connection long enough to download the files. She would have to try. She didn't exactly have another choice. Or she could catch a boat back to the mainland and download the files there.

But she didn't want to be that far away from David. If she left the island there was a chance something could go wrong and she wouldn't be able to get back.

"It's right beside you, Kyle. You don't need mine," MaeBe was saying. "Your cell phone is on the table beside you. Right by the meds you are absolutely going to take. Okay…wants to talk to you."

How long did she have before she needed to get back? They'd been locked away in the library, but someone would miss her if she didn't return soon.

"Hey, Tess. You have to watch David like a hawk. He gets distracted by shiny objects." Kyle came over the line loud and clear.

"He's not that bad. He's intense when he's studying a subject he enjoys," she replied. A subject like her. She could still feel his hands on her body.

"Shit. Now I owe MaeBe ten bucks."

"For what?" Tessa asked.

"You slept with him."

It was a good thing she wasn't standing in front of Kyle because she could feel herself blush. "You don't know that."

"Yes, I do, because you're defending him," Kyle explained, and she wondered why it was now that she seemed to have found the perfect spot because every word was clear. "I wasn't being an ass. I didn't get a chance to talk to you before you left. David sees the best in everyone. He's naïve and he'll miss cues. You have to watch out for him. Eduardo Montez isn't his father. The business he runs has some unsavory connections, but I don't think they have anything to do with David or I would have called off the trip. That said, I still want you to watch him. I don't like the timing. This trip came up fast."

At least they were talking about the job now. "I thought it had been planned for a while."

"They talked about it for a while, and Eddie always came up with excuses. Then all of a sudden it was the perfect time," Kyle explained. "Right as David's spring break was coming up. Keep your eyes open."

"Okay. I'm going to try to send you some pictures I've taken around the estate of some of the staff. It's probably nothing, but put them through our facial recognition," she said. She was running out of time, and she'd finally gotten an excellent signal. "I'm texting them to MaeBe's phone as soon as we hang up, and I'll try to get back here tomorrow to pull down the files she's sending me."

She wasn't sure she had enough time to do both. She wanted to make sure the names on Hutch's list were the correct people working in the house now. It seemed like there had been some recent changes.

"Hey, Tessa," Kyle said, his tone softening. "He's a good man."

Yep, they were back to being uncomfortable. And yet she couldn't hang up on him. Something had changed between her and David the night before, and even if she still walked away, there would always be something intimate between them. If…she was starting to use the word if. "I know that."

"Look, I've known something was going on in his head for weeks, but he didn't talk to me about you until the day you two left. He's crazy about you. He might not seem like it, but he is."

She couldn't do this. "I've got to hurry."

"Did you ever think that the reason that voice inside told you to break things off with Michael was because you were waiting for David?"

What the fuck had happened to Kyle? "Did you hit your head?"

"It's the meds," Kyle replied. "They fuck with a guy's brain, which is why I'm not taking any more, and no, you're not going to shove them up my ass. Language, woman. MaeBe's feisty. All I'm saying is I know you're all wounded and shit, but my brother's worth the risk, and he needs someone like you."

"Like me?"

"When you try, Tessa, you give it your all," Kyle said. "I'd be happy to have you watch my back. You'll let him be who he is because you're comfortable with who you are. You think people talk about how you fucked up your engagement, but what they really say is they admire you for knowing it wasn't going to work and ending it with kindness."

That made her stop because he was right about what she'd thought people said behind her back. "They do?"

"Yeah. So stop moping and keep doing my brother. He'll be in a way better mood when he comes back. The last two weeks have been awful, and now I blame you," Kyle began. "You have no idea how broody a professor can get, and when he gets broody he lectures. I swear I caught him lecturing the cat and then we were both trying to claw our way out of the place."

"Ooops, I'm losing you." She hung up because the last thing she needed was Kyle Hawthorne telling her all the things she'd done wrong when she'd walked away from David the first time.

And one thing she'd gotten right. She took a long breath and steadied herself because hearing that no one blamed her, no one thought she'd made a huge mistake was surprisingly emotional.

Or maybe she was in an emotional mood because being around David gave her all kinds of feelings.

He was still giving her feels because she was standing here not sending the stuff she needed to, and she had to leave soon or they would miss her and start asking questions.

She moved the photos she'd surreptitiously taken into a text she sent to Kyle and MaeBe. The files started to send even as she lost a bar.

Damn it. She moved closer to the edge. There wasn't a railing around it but there was a short wall that hit her mid-thigh. She leaned over slightly and managed three bars. The message started to send. Just a bit more.

She leaned again, trying to find the best angle.

That was when she started to lose her balance and tip forward.

An arm went around her waist, and she was pulled back against a hard chest.

"Hey, baby, how about we not find out what kind of medical care is available here?" David asked, his arms tightening as though he was afraid of losing her.

"You find her?" a deep voice asked.

David let her go and turned. Mateo stood there, a frown on his face. "Yes. She's right where I thought she would be." He turned back to her. "I'm so sorry I forgot about our plans to check out the town. When Mateo announced you were gone I realized I'd done it again. I got distracted and lost track of time. I tried to explain you needed a few things."

"We could have sent out for whatever the lady needs. There was no need to walk into town," Mateo replied. "Come and I will take you back."

So David had covered for her. He was fast on his feet, but she felt bad she'd interrupted his day. And worse that Mateo seemed so upset she'd left. She wasn't a prisoner there. "I was about to pick it up when I found this place. I was checking out the view, taking some selfies. We can go."

"Or we can stay." He reached for her hand and pulled her close. "I like this song. '*Zona de Promesas*.' Come here and dance with me."

"What should I tell the boss?" Mateo asked. "He thinks you are coming back."

"Tell him I'm taking the afternoon off to be with my girl," David said, not bothering to look his way. "We'll be back well before dinner. I think we can find our way. Thanks for bringing me out."

"David, you came here…" she began.

He sighed and hauled her closer. "I came here to study. I simply switched subjects. Now hush and dance with me. We're on a romantic island off the coast of Argentina in a bar almost no one in the whole world will ever visit. So be here with me."

She pocketed her phone and rested her head against his shoulder. He'd saved her. She could give him a couple of minutes.

Who the hell was she kidding? She wrapped her arms around him. He was big and strong, and she fit against him perfectly. There wasn't any place else she'd rather be. Certainly not back home where she might have been given the job of forcing Kyle to take his meds. At least he would get the photos since his phone was apparently right on the table next to…

She realized what had bothered her about the picture of Eddie as a baby. There had been a cell phone beside the flowers. A very modern cell. She wasn't absolutely sure, but she would swear it was a model that had come out in the last few years.

It hadn't existed when Eddie was born.

Why would he have lied?

She followed David's lead and let the question go for now. For now she was David Hawthorne's lady, and that seemed like such a nice thing to be. She would worry about the job later.

Chapter Eight

David studied the poem he knew so well. It was the one that all the treasure hunters claimed Montez had written as a siren call to them.

Life begins in the forest where water rushes toward the sea
The green ceiling gives us cover and it was here I buried our treasure
Our greatest gift to the world
But my life began where music plays, where I met with the lamb and the people spoke clearly
Four by four by two

He went back to his notes. The poem was several pages long, but most of it didn't matter. The key was in the first stanza and the last. Montez liked to play around, to bury the important clues inside the noise.

Not noise, exactly, but most of the poem was a restating of his life principles.

The numbers were interesting, though. What he'd discovered in the notebooks was lots of playing around with numbers.

Playing. He glanced at the clock. The sun had gone down a while ago. Could he get them out of dinner and back into their bedroom, where he intended to play with her for the rest of the night?

He needed to focus. This was supposed to be the easy part—the studying.

"Can you grab the blue one?" David asked. Luis was sitting closer to the big stack of notebooks Eddie had discovered.

"Sure." Luis hopped up and had the correct book in his hand. "You got something?"

"I don't know." He took the notebook and flipped through it. "How much do you know about the treasure hunters who come here?"

He forced himself to not look back to where Tessa was sitting, reading a murder mystery and probably thinking about how she would take down the killer.

"A little. I've been following a couple of blogs. Most of them think the actual hunt begins in Buenos Aires, since that's where Montez was born." Luis took the seat in front of him. "They make some pretty farfetched connections. The hospital he was born in is a couple of blocks over from a bar where many of Argentina's great singers played. He lived for the first several years of his life close to it, and his mother worked there as a server for a few years. There's a classic juke box in the club, and if you play the song numbered thirty-two, it's an old Madonna song. 'La Isla Bonita.'"

He rolled his eyes. "I suppose that's what sends them to the island. That's bullshit. First, Montez hated all pop music, especially American pop, and second, it wouldn't be so easy. Four by four by two might equal thirty-two, but it's not a math problem. At least not that easy of one."

Great treasure waits for the one who sees the possibilities, who finds the door and opens it
The truth of my life revealed to the one who searches for it

It wasn't great poetry, but then Montez hadn't been known for creative writing. His political discourse had changed the landscape in some places.

The truth of my life…

The truth of his life hadn't been back in Buenos Aires. He hadn't truly become the man he'd wanted to be until he'd come to this island. This was where he'd lived.

"So you don't think this thing starts on the mainland," Luis prompted.

The annoyance in his assistant's tone made him wonder how long he'd been silent. He'd probably been pretty quiet since he'd gotten back from town. He'd danced with Tessa and then they'd sat on the roof and talked a while. He'd told her it was about giving her some cover for walking away without a word, but he'd wanted that time with her. He'd wanted to pretend they were just another couple enjoying a vacation together.

He glanced over to the window seat where Tessa sat, her e-reader in her hands. She hadn't wanted to go back to their room. She'd walked right in here with him as though she wasn't going to let him out of her sight.

The light from the lamp made her skin a tawny gold, her ebony hair caressing her shoulders. She was the real treasure.

He had so little time with her, and she'd proven that she could walk away.

Something was playing around in her head, but she wasn't ready to talk to him about it yet.

"I think this island was everything to Ricardo Montez," he mused, forcing himself back to the problem at hand. "He had a home in Buenos Aires, but not once did he set up a hunt for Eddie there. It was only here. This was where he lived, where he was happiest."

"What kind of treasure are we talking about?" Tessa had put her tablet down and swung her legs over so she was facing him. "You've mentioned it a couple of times, but I still don't completely understand it. Is there an X marks the spot? Are you looking for a map?"

"The poem is the map. It's not exactly literal the way a pirate map would be. There's definitely no X marks the spot. I don't think a lot of people understand it." The treasure urban legend was the least interesting thing about Montez and the only thing most people had heard of. If they'd heard of him at all.

"Oh, I think they understand that an eccentric genius left a bunch of treasure somewhere on this island," Luis added.

"What kind of treasure are they looking for?" Tessa moved to the table, sinking down on the seat beside his. "Cash could possibly decay or be destroyed if it wasn't properly protected. It rains a lot here. Did he bury it?"

He'd thought a bit about this. There was tons of speculation. "Montez liked to collect lots of things. Art, items of historical relevance. We know he bought items from a shipwreck off the coast of this island. Gold, silver."

"Doesn't he talk about gold in the poem?" Luis asked.

"Yes." He looked down and found the line. "But not in the way one would think. He talks about gold flowing. *Gold flows from the sun and stars but also from my heart.*"

"He seems pretty sentimental." Tessa glanced down at the poem.

"He could be." From what he could tell Montez had gotten more sentimental in his later years. He'd certainly wanted to spend more time with his son at the very moment when Eddie had been pulling away.

"How did the whole thing start? The legend of the treasure, that is?" Tessa asked. "Did Montez release the poem to the press?"

"Absolutely not. Montez didn't have a great relationship with the press. He thought they focused too much on selling papers and not enough on truth. The poem was found with the rest of his papers after his death. It was on his desk, so some people believe it was the last thing he worked on," David explained.

"You're back. I thought you were taking the rest of the day off." Eddie walked into the room. He'd changed, and it looked like he'd had some kind of accident. There was a cut on his face, a butterfly bandage on his left cheek.

"Tess and I wanted to see the village." He wasn't letting go of that excuse. He'd damn near panicked when Mateo had walked in and announced that Tessa was missing. Then the groundskeeper had told them he'd seen her walking down the road to town with one of the maids. He'd had to think fast on his feet.

"And I needed tampons," Tessa said with a shrug. "You know Aunt Flo can strike at any time."

She knew what she was doing since Eddie's eyes widened, and he obviously decided to avoid that subject. "Well, I hope you had a good time."

"What happened?" David gestured to Eddie's cheek. "You have an accident?"

Eddie brushed his fingers over the spot as though remembering it was there. "Oh, this? I was walking in the garden and got too close to some thorns. It's one of the dangers of having a slightly wild garden. The jungle is always encroaching. Have you been in them?"

"We'll have to take a walk through there," Tessa murmured. "David was just telling me about this treasure of your father's. Do you believe it's real?"

"I do," Eddie said, taking a seat at the table. "He told me he was hiding something big. In his last days he told me he wanted to leave something behind, a truth. He was always talking like that though. He was big on truth. He talked about it to more than me. He talked to his doctors and nurses, and I'm fairly certain that one of them is the one who leaked the story to the press. In the last year of his life, we had doctors and nurses here all the time. There were two nurses on rotating shifts and a slew of doctors in and out. I was only here on the weekends, so it would have been easy to get into his office. The poem showed up on the Internet shortly after he died, and that was how the legend began."

"So there might not be anything at all," Tessa offered. "It could all be a crazy misunderstanding."

"I don't think so." Eddie glanced down at the notebooks. "My father wouldn't have told me he'd done it unless he actually followed through. I believe he started the project when he got his first diagnosis. He'd waited a long time to get screened. I think because he knew it was coming. He smoked two packs a day for decades. It wasn't a surprise, though finding out he only had a few months left… Well, that's always a surprise. I know it was for me."

It was never not a surprise, he supposed. Even when one was prepared. "So you don't think he was planning something like this before he found out about the cancer?"

Eddie shrugged. "He might have been thinking about it. Why else would he have done all those treasure hunts with me? It was his final mystery. A way to keep his island relevant."

"I don't think he cared about this island being relevant." He wasn't sure what Eddie was thinking. "I think he wanted to leave something for you."

"Then he could have left me cash." There was a bitterness that dripped from Eddie's lips. He seemed to shake it off. "That would be so much easier than a treasure hunt, but then my father was a complex man."

"You can't sell the island?" Tessa asked. "I mean, I assume if you needed cash, the island would bring some in."

"No. It's in a trust and the board members wouldn't dream of selling it," Eddie said. "My father made sure the trust is full of conservationists and scientists."

"You want to sell the island?" David had wondered, but they hadn't talked about it before beyond the legalities.

"I don't know. I didn't in the beginning. You know I spent time out here when I was growing up. I became a part of this community, but circumstances have changed," Eddie said with a long sigh. "My business keeps me in the city most of the time, and then there are the treasure hunters."

"I thought you controlled a lot of that." Because the island was private, he controlled who could and couldn't come out. It was one of the reasons the tourist situation could be so lucrative. They could charge to even get on the island and provide private experiences.

"There's a management group based here on the island that controls tourism," Luis explained. "I interviewed the head of the board as background for the book. They control the flow of tourism to ensure it doesn't harm the ecosystem, but I think they had a couple of instances of treasure hunters sneaking onto the island or coming in to stay at the beach and then sneaking into the interior without permission."

"Maybe what you need are some park rangers." Tessa sat back, studying Eddie with that look in her eyes that let him know she was thinking. Probably about something he wouldn't like. His lady was on the paranoid side, and she wasn't the glass-is-half-full type. She seemed to believe the glass was actually a bomb and it would kill them all.

"I'll have to consider that, but you can see there are unique problems that come with the island," Eddie replied. "Problems I don't need. Life seems far more complex now."

Because they were adults. It would get even more complex as they found partners and started families. It had been easy when they were kids at university, studying and partying and debating the world's problems without having to solve them.

He could see himself starting a family with Tessa. It was way too early, and she wasn't even ready for a date with him much less letting him put a ring on her finger.

But it had felt so right to dance with her. He didn't dance. He was awkward and weird, and it had been okay to dance with her. No one in the world could pull him out of his work like she could. He'd dreamed of this trip, thought he would do nothing but sit in the library and then go tour the places where the "treasure" was rumored to be found.

He'd hauled ass out of here the minute he'd realized she might be in trouble, and when he'd decided she wasn't, he'd convinced her to spend the afternoon with him. They'd sat on that rooftop bar and had a couple of glasses of Malbec and some empanadas, and they'd talked. She'd talked about her years in the military while he'd given her stories about trying to teach undergrads history.

"Well, a lot of your problems could go away if the professor here can solve the mystery." Luis gestured David's way. "He's got some theories I think are interesting. He definitely thinks it's on the island. If he can find the treasure, everyone wins."

"And if there is no real treasure?" He hadn't thought the treasure would be his primary focus this week. He viewed it as an amusing diversion. "The question is what Ricardo was able to do before he died. From what I've been able to discern, he wasn't capable of hauling some box of treasure into the jungle in the last year of his life."

"He could have done it sooner," Luis said with a nod. "He was a complicated man, and sometimes he could be paranoid. Perhaps he thought his treasure could be stolen."

"That would be exactly like my father," Eddie agreed. "I never saw the gold he bought from the shipwreck. I know he purchased the items. There's a log of what was brought here, but I can't find the actual items in the house, and I've certainly looked. Everything from that shipwreck is somewhere on this island."

The question was where. He'd mapped out the possibilities based on the poem, what he knew about Montez, and what he'd read about the treasure-hunting theories out there. Luis also had a whole list of possibilities. "I only have a couple more days here. I've been thinking we should probably skip the camping so I can spend more time here in the library. It's a small island, but there is still a lot of ground to cover, and the probability of me finding it is pretty low."

"But that's why you came here." Eddie leaned forward. "You came here to find the treasure."

"I came here to research a book." He wasn't sure why this was going sideways. "To honor your father and his life."

Eddie pushed back from the table and stood up. "It would be nice if you honored our friendship and did what I asked you to do. I can't have these bloody idiots sneaking onto the island and getting hurt. They disrupt everything. I thought you would help."

He turned and walked out.

Shit. What had that been about? Eddie had never exploded on him like that before. He didn't have a big temper. Eddie was a laid-back guy. He looked to Luis. "What's wrong with him? What do I not know?"

"He's been stressed about something," Luis replied. "I don't know. He doesn't talk to me. I'm nothing more than your assistant to him. He orders me around like the rest of his staff. But I do know he's been having trouble with people sneaking onto the island. He believes you're the one who can crack the code. He's certain there's some kind of code because no one's found it yet. He doesn't think taking the poem literally works, and no one has decoded the metaphors."

"That's because I think they're not understanding that the metaphors have to do with Montez's private life. I'm not entirely certain this wasn't meant as one last great quest for his son. I think the poem is full of references to their life together as well as Montez's own. I certainly don't think that poem was meant for public consumption, and that means neither was the treasure." He'd been over that poem a couple thousand times, but it was only through being here that he'd started to make the connections.

"Then why wouldn't the poem say 'This is for you, son'?" Luis challenged. "He says the treasure is for the one who finds it."

"Have you looked at how he wrote the clues for the hunts he gave Eddie as a kid? They were written the same way, but there's no question those were only meant for Eddie, and therefore their personal history has to be taken into account," David countered. He sat back with a sigh. This was something between father and son, and while he could help Eddie, he rather thought Eddie should be the one to find it. "It's a four-page document. It could take me weeks to decipher it. I would rather spend the time I have on the background. Looking through those notebooks has been a revelation. I think they really give me insight into what Montez was thinking. This is exactly what I need to get started on the book."

Luis's brows rose. "But the hook for the book is finding the treasure."

"What makes you think that?" Tessa asked. "He's not writing some thriller. He doesn't need a hook. This is a scholarly work, not pop culture."

He loved that part of her that tried to protect him, that was comfortable defending him. "She's right. I'm not trying to make millions. I want to write a good biography. I want to write about the man I admire. The treasure is a minor blip in his personal history. This was a man who brought the Dalai Lama and the leader of the communist party together for a secret meeting. It didn't fix anything, but they had a conversation. You know almost no one knows that happened right here on this island. I only know about it because Eddie was there. Montez never spoke about it publicly. That is a little gem of history. I have the notes Montez took from the meeting. I wish there were photographs, but I've got plenty of eyewitnesses. I was thinking of that meeting as the centerpiece of the biography. I frame everything around that small miracle."

"I think that sounds interesting." Tessa gave him an encouraging smile.

Mostly he wanted to take Tessa to the beach. He could get copies of those notebooks and go over them later when he wasn't so distracted. She was a distraction in the best meaning of the word. She'd made him realize he needed to relax, to focus on something that wasn't work or helping the kids in his family get through Spanish. Tessa was just for him, and she was young and healthy. She was careful. Tessa was starting to show him that everything he'd been worried about before didn't matter.

He sat back, the truth hitting him squarely in the chest. His father's death had haunted him his whole adult life, and he hadn't truly understood the cost.

Oh, shit. Had he honestly held back in other relationships because he'd watched his mother mourn? Because his father had died and his family had felt incomplete? Because he'd been a boy who didn't want to feel that pain again?

It was a revelation that was so simple it made him feel dumb. He'd held back from this new family of his because there was still a kid inside him who lost his dad and was afraid he wouldn't fit in with his mom's new family.

But they'd welcomed him. Not a one of them cared that he hadn't gone into the military the way most Taggarts did. They accepted his talents.

And used them heinously. Why the hell shouldn't he ask Sean to teach him some cooking skills? Or to help him move out of that rattrap he was in and into a better neighborhood? Why didn't he tell Uncle Ian if he wanted him to spend so much time helping his kids, he could have his company install a security system at a reduced rate...or for free.

They were his family, after all.

"But he could make so much more money if he played up the popular angle," Luis argued. "I know the real history is in the leaders and artists who came to this island and Montez's political theories, but no one is making a documentary about political theories."

He'd thought Luis was a practical scholar. He hoped the kid wasn't getting stars in his eyes. Or dollar signs. Since documentaries had become big business through streaming services, some historians had started playing up the more salacious parts of their work in order to garner looks from Hollywood. But he'd seen more than one of those meetings go bad. "You know most of the time they don't actually option the book. They simply read it and count it as research and do their own thing. The author doesn't even get paid."

"Only if you don't have a good agent, which you do," Luis pointed out. "Your family has connections. You can get something out of this, too." He pushed back from the table. "Just think about it. You always think too small. It's a big world and…I'm sorry. I'm overstepping and disappointed in how this trip turned out. I guess I expected more work since we've only got a week here. Are we still going into the jungle to look for the treasure?"

Tessa had sat back, watching Luis. She was perfectly still, reminding him of how a predator watched prey right before she pounced. She didn't like the way Luis was talking to him, and she might have something to say about it.

It was perverted that he was getting aroused at the thought of his pretty predator attacking. He didn't mind at all that some people would consider her the stronger of them, that she could take a man down without breaking a sweat. He was cool with that as long as he got to take her down in a much sweeter way.

She was the beauty and the brawn, and he was the professor who got to study her.

He was perfectly comfortable with his masculinity, and more than comfortable with her femininity. She was his gorgeous, dangerous woman, and she was perfect for him.

It was good that she would defend him physically, but Luis wasn't a threat. He had stars in his eyes and unrealistic expectations. If he gave Luis partial credit in a book that became a huge hit documentary series, Luis's career in academia would be made. Unfortunately, very few people had it that easy. "I think I'm going to spend the rest of my time here in the library. And I'm going to cut the research short. It's been forever since I've had a real vacation, and the bartender in the village was telling us about a beach house we can rent for a few days."

"Are you serious, Hawthorne?" Her lips had curled up like the cat who'd gotten a particularly sweet cup of cream. "You want to sit on a beach with me?"

He wanted to do way more than sit on a beach with her. He wanted to spend every moment convincing her that this was real, that what they had between them was worth fighting for. He reached over and covered her hand with his. "I can't think of anything I'd rather do. I've got some notes to take and copies to make where I can. Luis, you should feel free to do the tour of the possible treasure sites. I've already paid for the gear. You can write it up, and we'll see if it works in the book or if we can get it published for you somewhere else."

Getting work published as a grad student would help him enormously.

"It's not the same and you know it." Luis's head shook and his hands were fists at his sides. "I thought you were different. I thought you were real."

He strode out, slamming the door behind him.

"How am I not real?" He was surprised at his assistant's outburst. The world seemed to have turned upside down today, and he wondered if he was missing some social cues. He could do that.

She stared at the door as though she was worried Luis might come back. "I think he viewed you as some sort of professor god. You know, the kind who would never let a woman fuck up his focus."

"Those guys are sad, and they usually are like that because they're dicks who can't get a woman." He had known the type. They weren't pleasant to be around. He tended to avoid them at faculty mixers.

How would Tessa handle a faculty party? She would likely grab a beer and be herself and tell anyone who didn't like it to fuck off.

He was okay with that, too. Some professors played the game, picked a spouse who fit into the academic world, but he was picking one he loved.

Because he was rapidly falling in love with this woman, and he didn't even want to try to stop.

She stared down at where their hands met. "You aren't any of those things, but apparently you haven't had a girlfriend in a long time."

He'd just realized why. "I've been thinking about that a lot lately, and I've come to the conclusion that I've been a coward. I watched my mom lose my dad. I lost him, too, and it felt like such a fragile thing."

"But your mom found love again. She's happy. At least she seems to be."

"Yes, she is." His mom had found a great life, and she'd tried to make him a part of it. It was his fault he'd been distant. "She's happy, and part of me decided she's happier with Sean than she ever would have been with my dad. And then I wondered if I wasn't the guy a woman had to get through to find a man like Sean. A starter guy."

She gasped, and suddenly she was up and setting herself on his lap. She put her hands on either side of his cheeks, a fierce look on her face. "You are not a starter guy. You are amazing and surprising, and you're kind. Any woman would be lucky to end up with you."

Any woman but you... He didn't say the words, but they sat there between them because she hadn't made that statement personal.

The moment held, and for the briefest time he thought she would admit what she felt because it was all there in her eyes. But then she seemed to make a decision, and she sighed, her hands coming down.

"I need to go upstairs and take a shower. I'm going to think about some things," she said, sliding off his lap. "I don't like how they talked to you."

"They're angry I'm not doing what they thought I would." He wasn't actually sure why Eddie was so upset. His friend had seemed more on edge than he normally was. "To them, I probably look like I'm slacking off or something, though Eddie's always told me I should chill."

"I don't know. I think there's something else."

"Like what?"

"Like I think he lied to me about a picture I saw earlier today," she admitted quietly. "I was looking at a picture of a woman holding a baby and I thought it was probably him with his mother, and he said it was. But there was a cell phone on the table that only recently came out. I know that model. It's maybe three years old if that. There's no way it was around thirty plus years ago."

"This is about a picture of a baby?"

"It's about a lie." She stopped. "Though maybe it is, because why would he lie about a baby picture? I don't know. I need to think about it. Or maybe I don't. Maybe this is the part where I follow my instincts and get you out of here."

"You want to go to the beach tomorrow?" It was late, and he wasn't sure how he would get hold of the property manager after business hours. And without a phone. He'd been planning on going back to the village tomorrow to talk to the bartender who could hook them up with the beach house.

Her jaw tightened, chin tilting up. "No. I think we should leave for home. Tonight."

"What?" It was his day to have things turn around on him. He stood. "Why would we go home?"

"Because I don't like this whole situation."

Because she didn't like how he made her feel? Because she didn't like how close they were becoming? They'd had a blissful afternoon, and now she was upending everything over a single photo she couldn't have seen for more than a few minutes. "What do you think is going to happen?"

"Something bad. I can feel it, and you promised you would leave this part up to me."

He had. He'd told her flat out that he would do what she wanted when it came to his physical protection. He'd promised her. He didn't want to go home because he knew exactly what that meant. It meant no more time with her. No more time to convince her. No more time to woo her.

She stared at him as though waiting for the inevitable argument. He could see it stamped on her face. She was waiting for him to deny her.

"All right." His heart felt heavy in his chest. It was an actual ache. "Can I have a few minutes to make a couple of notes?"

She'd gone still again, but there was nothing predatory about her expression. "You're coming with me?"

He stood up but didn't close the space between them. "You think it's dangerous, then I believe you. I don't feel it, baby, but I don't have the training you have. I agree something's going on, but I don't know what it is. If it were up to me, I would stay."

"David," she began.

He stopped her because there was no argument here. "It's not up to me. We made a deal."

"And you're going to honor it."

"It's more than that. I trust you, Tessa." He shoved aside his worry that she was protecting herself. He did trust her, and she wouldn't lie to him. She wouldn't force him home if she didn't think it was necessary.

"Why?" She breathed the question like she wasn't sure she wanted the answer.

She didn't, and he wasn't going to push her. "Let's leave it at that. I trust you. So I'll make a couple of notes and ask Eddie if we can get a boat out of here before the one that comes in the morning."

"There's not a boat?"

"The one that goes to the mainland left before dark. It won't be back until noon tomorrow," he explained. "I heard there's a storm coming in. Nothing catastrophic, but the seas can be rough. We need a big boat to handle the waves. I'm sure we can pay someone in Mar del Plata to come get us."

"But then we would have to tip off Eddie that we're leaving," she said. "There's no working landline. They said they have a radio, but I wouldn't know what frequency to use without asking. I'm not a comms guy."

"Tip Eddie off?" He had no idea what she thought he would do.

She bit her bottom lip, obviously thinking the problem through. "He's hiding something. Why would Mateo come running after me? Don't tell me it's because the village is dangerous. It's only dangerous if you don't want to learn about sea turtles or hate barbecue. But he came after me the minute he realized I was gone."

"The village isn't dangerous at all. Mateo did seem upset you'd left." David had been upset someone had noticed she'd gone when she'd been trying to keep a low profile, but now that he thought about it, it had been an odd reaction from the butler. She'd tried to get another signal before they'd left the village so she could download some information she'd told him McKay-Taggart was sending. They hadn't been able to get a clear signal. "Does this have something to do with the info you were waiting on?"

"The information I didn't get." She was back to looking at the door and then at him again. "You promise you'll go with me in the morning?"

He sighed. "Tessa, I've done everything you've asked. I'm not going to stop even though it's killing me."

"I know you want to do your research…"

"It's killing me because I want the time with you," he admitted.

She blinked, and he could have sworn he saw a sheen of tears in her eyes. "I can't risk you for some time on the beach. But we can have tonight. It would be dangerous to leave, so we'll stay the night and head out in the morning. But you have to go to dinner and convince them you've changed your mind."

"Changed my mind?"

"About the treasure hunt. They want you working on finding that treasure," she pointed out. "They got upset when you said you wouldn't. So you tell them we talked about it, and I'm enthused at the thought so you'll do it."

Eddie had gotten upset at the thought of him not working on the treasure hunt. Which seemed so odd unless he was missing the obvious. "Do you think he needs the money? He mentioned something about his father should have left him cash."

She nodded. "Something like that. We'll have to figure that out later. The key tonight is to play things cool. Don't even give them a hint that we're leaving tomorrow. I'll talk about the fact that I've never been on a treasure hunt before and I'm excited about it. You say something about how Luis made you think about how it can help you sell the book. Smooth things over. We spend the rest of the night like we'd been planning to before this afternoon. We have dinner and drinks and talk and then we go to bed. We get up tomorrow, have breakfast, and before you settle in for a long day of research, we go for a walk and don't come back."

He wanted to make sure he understood. "We do everything we were planning on doing?"

She looked back to him and seemed to understand what he meant. "Yes, Professor. Everything."

She was giving him one more night, and he intended to make the most of it.

* * * *

Tessa stepped inside their suite, letting the door close behind her and prayed she was doing the right thing. She'd gone over and over this for hours, and he was correct. It would be dangerous to try to make the passage during a storm without the right boat, and she didn't want to make them spend a miserable night in the jungle if they didn't have to.

"Dinner seemed to go well," David said, moving to the desk.

"I think we said all the right things." She took off the shawl she was wearing and settled it over the chair to her left. She couldn't help but notice they'd left the bedroom door open.

How long would it take before she couldn't feel his hands on her? Was she really going to walk away at the end of this?

She shook off the thoughts because she wanted this night with him. One more night with her professor.

Tessa watched him empty his pockets, putting things onto the desk he'd been using when he wasn't in the library. The domesticity of it all was starting to get to her. Earlier they'd gotten ready for dinner together, talking easily and sharing the space. She'd straightened his collar, and he'd zipped her dress up. She could imagine him walking into their little apartment or house and putting his briefcase to the side. He would give her a kiss and they would decide what they wanted for dinner and spend the rest of the night cuddled up together.

"Should I head into the bedroom?" The minute they'd left the dining room, her heart had thudded because she'd known they wouldn't go to sleep. They both knew this might be their last night, and they wouldn't waste it.

"I think the bedroom will do nicely," David said.

She entered the bedroom and put a hand on one of the big four posts, her body already humming because she remembered what it felt like for him to fuck her against it.

He glanced at her over his shoulder, and without looking he reached into his open briefcase on the desk. He pulled out a single sheet of paper. A familiar-looking sheet that was rumpled and creased because they'd landed on it when he had them on the bed after the post fucking.

Post post-fucking.

"You're smiling," David said.

She was sure he expected her to be all nervous and tight because of what had happened earlier in the day. "You're right, I am, Professor. You'll find when I get in this head space I can let go of a lot. We've decided on a course of action. I'm going to stop worrying about it until I have to."

"So we're playing?" He stared at her across the space that separated them. "I want to, but I also need you to know that if you think it's a bad idea, we don't have to. But I can't think of any other way I would want to spend the rest of the evening."

They'd done everything they could to ensure their safety. She would rather be on a plane…

No, she wouldn't. She wanted to be right here with him. "I think I'd like to give up control for a while."

"Are you looking forward to the next part of my study?" His voice had gone deep and deliciously dark.

"Oh yes, Professor." The word felt silky and dangerous, like the tails of a soft flogger. Tessa turned and offered him her back. She wore a dress that skimmed her curves, and she shivered when he eased the zipper down. Her nipples peaked inside the cups of her bra.

He moved back and picked up her dress when she stepped out of it. He set that piece of paper aside and then draped her dress over the vanity chair.

He turned on the nightstand lamp, and soft light illuminated the room as he started to take off the button-down he wore. His hands were slow, methodical.

How was he in such control? Maybe she didn't want to play. Maybe she just wanted him inside her for the rest of the night. She wanted him as hot and needy as she was. She kicked her sandals off and realized she was already slick with arousal. The mere thought of having him got her hot. This man made her feel things she never felt before, and not just sexual things. She wanted intimacy with him, to wind herself around him and not let go.

How the hell was she going to let him go?

"How about I handle those pants for you, Professor?" She took a step toward him, but he retreated, frowning and making her stop.

"I'm disappointed, Tessa." He looked absolutely scrumptious without his shirt on, and she got the feeling he was taking control. If she was sliding into her sub role, he was waking up his inner Dom. He was going to make this hard on her.

"I just wanted to help." She wanted him to want her, and for a moment she wondered if he did.

"Patience is a virtue. And as I informed you, I am in charge of the study. You are the subject of my study." His voice deepened. "And you are also my submissive, aren't you?"

Any embarrassment she felt burned off with a fresh flame of desire. He was setting the ground rules, putting her in her place. It wasn't something she would let any man do in the real world, but this was a space where they made their own rules, followed their desires because it was safe to do so.

She was safe with him.

The fantasy she had earlier about him coming home from work, taking things out of his pockets, setting his briefcase aside, now had a new ending. After he was done shedding the trappings of college professor, he would become her Professor. When he walked into the living room, she'd be waiting. On her knees. Naked. Maybe with a plug in her ass. A plug she'd have to insert herself when he called her from the campus and ordered her to prepare herself for him.

Tessa blinked and shook her head. This was insane. She was a badass security agent.

Who apparently had a previously undiscovered kink, focused around some sort of submissive housewife fetish.

"Tessa."

She jumped, blinking as she looked at him.

David raised a brow. "Did I bore you?"

"No. I was—" She almost confessed what she'd just imagined. She trusted David, enough that she was willing to tell him these things. At least she thought she did. But the words stuck in her throat. She'd never wanted to play at home. She'd always kept it to the club, but she wanted more with him.

"Remove your bra," he ordered.

She did, tossing it aside to land on top of her dress. David nodded in satisfaction.

"It seems that you need help focusing. We're not ready to be in the bedroom yet." David turned to her and pointed at the door that joined the rooms of the suite. "Bend over my desk for your punishment."

Frustration welled inside her. Damn it. She didn't want a spanking. She wanted him to fuck her. The last time she'd wanted a spanking, she'd ended up with the best sex of her life. This time she wanted that sex and was getting a spanking.

"We do not have all day." David sounded disappointed, but his eyes were bright with desire. There was a spark in his eyes she only saw when they were playing. It was for her, for the time they got together.

There was nothing to do but obey because the last thing she was going to do was stop the scene. Every time they were together David surprised her. She'd been shocked to find out the bookish professor was kinky, and even more shocked by the way his touch affected her. She responded to his brand of dominance in a way she never had before. Even after she'd accepted that he played, he'd surprised her. If someone had asked her, she would have said that he probably wasn't much of a sadist. That he wouldn't spank that hard or use heavy impact toys.

But as she walked over to the desk, Tessa had a feeling that her ass was about to hurt.

And she wanted it. Wanted it so bad that when she bent over the desk and her nipples made contact with the bare, slick wood, she couldn't stop the moan of pleasure.

How big was his office back in Dallas? She bet it was small and full of books, and they would have to be creative to make full use of it. It would be worth it. She could visit him for lunch and when she left that little room would smell like sex and for the rest of the day it would remind him that his sub adored him.

"Hold on to the edge," David ordered, one hand on her back, pressing her down firmly.

She grabbed the far edge of the desk, her cheek resting on the cold wood, her breasts compressed. A drugged feeling started to slide over her, the rest of the world slipping away. All that mattered was being here with him.

"Ankles together, please," he said in that stern teacher voice that she shouldn't find hot but absolutely did. "I'm not going to spank your pussy today."

Today.

"Today," which implied that he would spank her other days. That there would be more scenes after this. Maybe that wouldn't be such a terrible thing. He had his club. She could see him there and maybe then it wouldn't affect her work.

Before she could get too lost in finding a way to keep him, he brought her back to the moment by tugging on her simple cotton panties. She hadn't brought any sexy lingerie with her. She wished she at least had a thong. Actually, she wished she had proper fet wear, wished she could kneel at his feet in a corset and tiny skirt. Maybe a tiny little pleated plaid skirt. She would feel sexy and powerful despite the fact that she was on her knees.

David pulled the edges of her panties toward the middle, tucking them between her cheeks so her ass was bare. She felt pressure on her rear entrance and was reminded of his list. She bit her bottom lip to keep from moaning at the thought.

There were a lot of things he wanted to check off that list, and one of the questions he'd written out was about how many fingers she could comfortably take in her ass. His fingers. His callused, talented fingers.

"Comfortable?" he asked.

"Yes, Professor."

"Good." His palm glided from her hip, down her butt cheek and the back of her thigh before jumping to the other leg and repeating the course in reverse.

Everywhere his hand touched her skin felt sensitized.

"I had planned to begin tonight's session with an in-depth study of your breasts." His hand stopped roaming, instead resting on her cheek. "Your nipples in particular."

"That still sounds like a very good idea to me, Professor." The thought of anal play had her on edge. It was so intimate. She'd had anal sex before, but the thought of David touching her there made her breath catch.

"I'm sure it does, and while I value your input, you have no say," he replied simply.

Damn it, that was hot. Tessa arched her back, pushing her ass up into his hand. Why wouldn't he start? Did he know how much this slow study drove her crazy? She needed him to stop talking and spank her. Touch her. Do anything.

She would let this man do anything to her.

"Who is in charge of this study?" David asked.

"You are, Professor." Every word came out breathy and hushed.

"And what does that mean?"

"It means that I do what you say." She licked her dry lips. "I obey you."

It was an easy admission to make since they had a bargain. She was in charge in the field, and he was in charge here. He'd meant it when he'd promised her she was in control of the mission. He hadn't protested or tried to get out of it. When she'd told him they needed to move, he'd given up this precious time he'd longed for.

What he'd been upset about was losing time with her.

He squeezed her ass, hard, an indication her words had affected him the same way they'd affected her.

His hand raised off her butt. "It means that you're mine." *Smack.*

The first spank landed on her right cheek, and it *hurt*. He had a big, heavy hand, and he wasn't fucking around with that smack.

She sucked in air and couldn't stop the groan that came.

The sound was lost in the resounding crack of the second smack, landing on her left cheek. This time she yelped and clenched her backside, an involuntary response.

"Generally when performing a punishment scene, I prefer to spank subs when they have a plug in their ass." He sounded so academic. "Usually with a small amount of ginger oil coating the neck of the plug."

Tessa's eyes went wide, and she lifted her head, neck straining to look back at him. "You know, Prof, you're a dirty pervert."

"Dirty, sadistic pervert, thank you." He spanked her again, just as hard, and then two more swats in quick succession.

"My mentor at The Club was a man named Ben," David explained. "He's a highly intelligent man, a private investigator and former Navy SEAL. He taught me that I should always travel with a full box of condoms, lube, butt plugs, and nylon rope. He thinks they're essentials in everyone's go-bag. I told him that I'm a professor and I don't have a go-bag, but now I think he might have a point."

He stopped talking to spank her some more. Her ass heated, each smack not only stinging the surface of her skin, but making her ache, the heat penetrating deep. This was the kind of spanking that she'd feel tomorrow, the same way she would feel after a heavy squat session at the gym.

The next two swats landed lower, where her butt curved into her thigh.

"Ouch," she hissed.

"Hmm, does that hurt?" He sounded only mildly curious.

"Yes, Professor, the spanking hurts."

He was silent, and she winced. That had sounded more than a little bratty.

She heard the rustle of fabric, and a slick sound, almost like a zipper, but... Wait. She knew that sound. Tessa jerked her head up and looked back over her shoulder.

David had moved to the side so she could see him easier. That sound had been him whipping his belt free of his pant loops. As she watched, he folded it in half, buckle and tip held in one hand.

"Oh, shit," she whispered.

David grinned, hooked a finger in the belt, and snapped it.

Her pussy clenched in reaction to the sound, and she was now so wet that she knew the crotch of her panties was soaked.

"Professor...you know how to use that?" Tessa wasn't used to feeling unsure. That wasn't who she was. She was capable and confident and focused.

His expression softened. "I do, but if you're scared, I won't."

She liked the fact that he could move fluidly between roles, that he didn't get thrown off when she needed to talk. "I'm not scared. I trust you. But you could get this moving."

"I'll move how slow or fast I choose, and you will mind how you speak to me." This mild-mannered stern thing he had going, punctuated by the occasional hard, undeniably Dom-esque commands, were making her crazy. She needed him to rip her panties off and fuck her. She wanted his cock in her, his hips hitting her red, aching ass.

A whole body shiver wracked her, and her nipples, smashed against the desk, tightened painfully. She dropped her head back onto the desk, her breath fanning back against her face.

"Please," she moaned, not even sure if he could hear her.

"Please what?" David's hand smoothed over her ass.

"Please use me. Punish me. Play with me. Study me." The words were raw and way too real. She swallowed, frightened not by him, but by the way he made her feel. Like she was home, like he understood exactly how to handle her.

Kyle's words from earlier crept back into her head. Had she called off her engagement because somewhere deep down she'd prayed this one man existed? Had she longed for him before she'd even known his name?

She'd wanted to say "Stop screwing around and fuck me already." She didn't because she knew better. Knew that submitting to her Dom meant finding a kind of emotional and physical peace that she could never achieve on her own, and she needed it now.

That didn't stop her from being wildly frustrated, and perversely, even more aroused by that frustration. By her lack of control.

"I will, Tessa. I'll do all that and more."

There was a small woosh of air, and then the belt struck her ass. She yelped, head rising, but…it hadn't hurt. It felt like he'd bounced it off her backside rather than actually spanking her with it. He slapped her other cheek, a bit harder, but still not enough to hurt. It was a mind fuck. He knew he'd put her on edge and then proven he could make sure she didn't go over.

Bastard. Sexy bastard.

"The belt is more about the sound than the sensation. I like the way it sounds," he admitted, skimming his fingers down her spine. "I like the way you tense up in anticipation, and then you practically sag because you wanted it harder."

"Damn it, I do." Tessa blew out a frustrated breath.

David stepped up behind her, grinding his pelvis against her backside. She tried to spread her legs so she could feel the hard ridge of his cock against her pussy rather than the seam of her ass. She couldn't because his feet were planted on the outside of her own. It was the first time in her life her legs had been kept closed during a scene rather than her Dom demanding she stay accessible.

He leaned over, his weight grinding his hips into her well-spanked ass. "Not yet. We haven't reached the point in this evening's study where I put my mouth on your sweet pussy. Where I use my tongue to figure out exactly how you like your clit played with."

"Professor..." Her pussy actually ached.

"Yes?"

"Exactly what point *are* we at in your study?"

"We're at the point where I play with your pretty ass." His weight vanished from her back, leaving her feeling cold. She wanted him close again.

His hands rubbed her ass, which had that good post-spank ache. When he squeezed, it caused just enough pain to have her sucking in air. His hands slid up to the waistband of her underwear. He grabbed hold of the gathered fabric which was tucked between her cheeks and lifted.

Tessa yelped as the silky cotton fabric of her panties stroked against her pussy and rubbed the rim of her ass. She danced up on her toes, but that only made him pull harder. It was like the mother of all wedgies, except it hurt in all the right ways.

He released her, and before she had dropped her heels to the ground, he was stripping her panties off her. She lifted her feet when he tapped each ankle in turn. She saw the underwear sail through the air out of the corner of her eye.

"Now I want your legs spread." He was still kneeling behind her.

The urge to grind her pussy against his face was nearly overpowering. She tightened her fingers around the edge of the desk and locked her arms as she stepped wide, spreading her legs. Actual relief flooded her. She wanted to be open to him, needed him to have access to her secret parts.

"You have a lovely pussy," he murmured. "And you're very wet.

You enjoyed your spanking. Enjoyed being bent over my desk, didn't you?"

"Yes, Professor." She liked him bending her over any surface he wanted.

She felt him lean in, and then he blew on her wet pussy. His hot breath felt cool against her flesh, and she didn't bother to stifle her moan. The sound echoed against the wood under her cheek, maybe loudly enough that someone walking by would hear, but she didn't give a damn. She didn't care if Eddie had set the whole group right outside their door to make sure they didn't leave. In that moment all that mattered was David. Her professor. Her lover. Her Dom.

Hers.

David rose to his feet, squeezing her hips. His breathing was labored, and she had a feeling he was nearing the end of his control.

She heard fabric rustle, and a moment later there was a rubbery snap. She looked back to see that he'd put on a pair of latex gloves. "What are you doing, Professor?"

He grinned, a look that made her sigh. "Got these from the kitchen. See, I didn't do what my mentor told me to, but I'm going to prove that I can find the things I need in the field."

He'd done what? She'd thought he'd spent all his time studying, but apparently he'd gone on a kink scavenger hunt. "You prepared?"

The grin became a sexy smirk. "Of course I did. The foundation of academia is prep work. Prepping lectures, writing proposals, finding supplies to use on your sub's ass…"

"Oh, I can feel the students lining up for that class," she snarked.

"You would be surprised. They didn't have lube in the kitchen, but I got this." He held up a small jar of a white substance. "Coconut oil. If you can eat it, it can be used as lube. I will fight anyone who says otherwise."

And she would come out with a supple anus. "David…"

He took off the top then dipped one finger in, thrusting it in and out of the thick, gel-like substance, which she knew would turn slick and liquid with the heat of her body. Watching him finger-fuck the coconut oil was making her jealous…of a jar.

Tessa dropped her head back onto the desk before she completely lost her mind. She gave over to the experience because there was nothing else to do. This man could take her anywhere.

This was what life would be like with him. He would always be thinking of her, always considering how to be her man in the best, kinkiest way possible, and as much thought as he put into sex, he would put into their relationship.

A second later he was spreading her cheeks apart, his touch firm and sure, and she tried to concentrate on that sensation, not the emotion she felt welling inside her. Embarrassment bit at her. No matter how many times she had her ass played with she always felt a little embarrassed. It was ridiculous, and she knew there was no reason for it, but it was there all the same.

David must have sensed her change in mood because he leaned over and kissed her waist. "I want you to relax your ass for me. You know how to take something here, don't you?"

His oil-coated finger swiped over her sensitive flesh, sending a gasp through her.

"Yes, Professor." She held her breath because he was right there, pressing against her with the most delicious pressure.

"And when was the last time you had something up your ass?"

Naturally the bastard wanted to talk at the exact moment she was ready to go.

"It's been a year, maybe a little longer," she admitted.

"And what, specifically, did you have in here?" His finger swirled around her tight ring.

"A plug." She would keep her answers simple and honest and maybe he would move on because she had the feeling this was going to be unlike anything she'd had before.

"Now you're going to take my fingers in your ass, aren't you?" The words were practically a growl.

She arched, lifting her ass, inviting him to use her, fuck her. She didn't want a plug from him. She wanted him. "Yes, please. I want your fingers, your cock, in my ass."

His finger zeroed in on her entrance, and he pressed in with a little shove. Her body gave, and despite knowing she shouldn't, she clenched down around him. He pushed his finger in deeper, past the second ring of muscle, forcing her to open to him.

She cried out when he didn't stop. She went up on her toes, and he kept going, commanding and merciless. His knuckle entered her, opening her more.

"My finger is almost all the way in. How do you feel?"

"Full," she whimpered. "And…"

"And?" he prompted as though he already knew the answer.

Smug bastard. "And it's not enough."

David shoved his finger in, burying the last inch. She felt the knuckles of his other fingers against her pussy.

"Beautiful," he murmured, twisting his finger inside. "Your ass is nice and tight."

"Will you...will you fuck me in the ass?" Tessa loosened her fingers, which ached because she was gripping the desk so tight. She wanted this man every way she could have him.

"Is that a request or a question?"

"I...don't know." And she didn't. She couldn't think past the arousal that was nearly all-consuming.

"I will fuck your ass but not tonight. Tonight you're going to take another finger. Maybe even three," he promised.

His finger withdrew, and her body clenched closed.

Fabric rustled, and when she looked back, David was one-handed stripping out of his clothes.

"I want to feel your skin against mine," he murmured, the words soft and romantic. "But don't think I won't protect you. I'm excellent at putting on a condom one-handed. It was a class at The Club. I passed with flying colors."

Of course he had. Romance was wiped away by kink, when, a moment later, David was back, spreading her ass. The head of his cock rubbed against her thigh. The tip was wet, leaving a damp trail on her skin.

He worked one finger back into her ass, thrusting it in and out a few times before adding more oil and working that around. He withdrew his finger all the way. She felt the broad, blunt force of two fingertips against her. She took a steadying breath and forced herself to relax. David had big hands. She was going to feel this, and she didn't want to miss a moment of the sensation.

The tip of one finger poked in, and a second later the other, shorter finger nudged her. He wiggled and pressed until the tip of the second finger was in. She breathed through it, then whimpered when he pressed them deeper.

"Relax so you can take my fingers in your ass."

"Yes, Professor," she whimpered. His cock jerked against her thigh in reaction, though whether it was to her words, her submission, or the sight of his fingers disappearing into her ass she didn't know.

"I looked for things I could use," he rumbled.

It was hard to concentrate. "Use?"

"In your ass. When I was in the kitchen, I very seriously considered grabbing a banana or a cucumber."

"You were going to fuck me with a cucumber?" Damn that was kinky and weird and hot. And probably not happening.

"They were little cucumbers, so it was more about the banana." He massaged her ass, and she was starting to feel the sweet, hot burn of being stretched.

How could he make her laugh in the middle of something so perverse and hot and intimate? "No bananas. Hard limit, David."

He chuckled. "I decided it would be more fun to use my fingers. I wanted to feel you clench when I did this." His other hand reached between them, and then his thumb brushed her clit. "Just you and me."

Tessa shrieked as the touch sent a sudden bolt of pleasure through her. She'd had full orgasms that hadn't felt as good or had the impact of that one small touch. She was so sensitive.

"I'm close," she gasped. "Professor…David…"

"So am I."

He pulled his fingers from her ass, leaving her aching and empty. She heard the foil of a condom wrapper, and then he was back. The pad of his thumb worked her asshole, which yielded easily to his touch. He pressed the tip in at the same time his other hand, now free of the glove, stroked her pussy, from clit to entrance and back. "I need to feel you around my cock."

Relief flooded her. "Yes, please…I need you."

His thumb sank deeper into her ass, and she rose up on her toes.

"Stay like that," he commanded. "I want your ass up, your pussy right there, ready for my cock."

"Please, please," she gasped.

The head of his cock rubbed her clit, and then he was sliding between her labia to her entrance. She braced herself, ready, so ready to be full, to have him inside her, connected to her. This was what she'd wanted all along. Him. Everywhere.

David shoved his thumb deep at the same time his cock drove into her pussy. She screamed in pleasure, the filling of her sex a sensation so exquisite that it was practically an orgasm. She was still humming with pleasure when he withdrew, only to slam into her again.

And again.

"Mine," he murmured. "You're mine."

His other hand reached between them as he withdrew his cock, his thumb still buried in her ass. He pinched her clit, and the coiled tension, the tight desire, released. Pleasure exploded within her, so hot and intense that she couldn't just lie there. She arched, her head rising, elbows planted on the desk.

David grabbed her by the hair as his cock surged in once more.

The orgasm stretched out, prolonged by his dominance, by the way he possessed her. Her scalp prickled with sweet pain, as did her ass, both from the spanking and his thumb buried in her.

When his thrusts became quick and hard, his breathing labored, she braced herself, welcomed the full power of his need as he slammed into her.

David roared in pleasure, releasing her hair to grab her shoulder, fingers digging in so hard she'd probably have bruises.

Small bruises that would mark her as his.

When David collapsed on top of her, Tessa slid her elbows to the side so she was once more lying on the desk. His breath was labored, his head sweaty where it lay on her shoulder.

"Holy shit." Tessa tried to wiggle out from under him, but his cock and thumb were still inside her.

"No," he said, the word distinct. "You stay here. I'll get up when I'm ready."

Tessa stilled.

"We're…not done with the scene." He sounded out of breath but like he knew what he wanted. "How many fingers you could take up your ass, as well as how you handled a spanking, were only two of my many questions."

Her whole body hummed with pleasure. "Maybe I better see this list."

"Maybe you better behave," he murmured.

"And if I don't want to?" she asked, but she was smiling. She liked to obey this man. Of course, she also like what happened when she misbehaved.

"Well, then I'll have to spank you again," he whispered. "But maybe next time it will be your pussy I spank."

"Oh, god, no more dirty talk. I can't take it."

David finally lifted off of her. She groaned as he took his thumb from her ass and his cock slid out of her pussy.

He stripped off the glove then helped her stand, turning her to face him. He cupped her cheeks in his hands.

"Tessa?"

"Yes, Professor?"

"You're going to take everything I give you."

She would. She might take it forever.

Chapter Nine

"Baby, I need you to wake up now."

Tessa yawned and realized someone had turned on the light. The clock beside her read five in the morning. She'd set a timer on her phone for five thirty. She started to tell him they still had thirty minutes, but then she realized they weren't alone.

"Stay calm, Tessa," David said.

Fuck. She was caught without her pants on. Without anything on.

"Get out of bed, David, and don't move too fast. I don't want to have to shoot the lovely lady," a deep voice said.

Tessa went tense and made a real threat assessment. The question was how many she could take out before one of them got off a lucky shot. Or a professional shot. The trouble was they were in close quarters and she had zero idea who these people really were because she'd come in with no intel.

No real intel because no one thought the danger would be here on the island. All the intel they had had been about a potential kidnapping before they got to the island.

What if the goal of that kidnapping hadn't been ransom? What if it had been to force David to do something? What if this had been the plan all along?

"What the hell is going on?" David had pulled on his pants, and despite the terrible circumstances, she still thought he looked hot. Even as he straightened his glasses, she couldn't help but notice he hadn't put on a shirt yet, and his chest looked good.

And that was why they were here. They were here because she'd lost her head and made the mistake of not leaving when she'd known damn well they should have. They could have taken shelter somewhere else and then gotten off the island in the morning after the storm had passed. But no. She'd wanted one more night with him. She'd wanted to play with him one last time before she gave him up.

If she'd followed her instincts instead of her pussy, they might be on the mainland now. At the very least they would be huddled up somewhere and she wouldn't have a gun to her head and utter impotent rage in her belly.

Mateo held the pistol to her head, and she was aware that she was dressed in nothing but a sheet wrapped around her body. She hadn't had time to grab the semi she'd put in the nightstand drawer.

She should have slept with the sucker in her hand, but then it would have been hard to cuddle with David.

When had she become this girl?

There were five of them in the room, who knew how many outside. She could drop the sheet, kick back and take down Mateo, grab her gun, and kill the guy to her right.

But it left a lot of time for someone to get a shot off David's way. She was hesitating, and she never did that.

"I can explain." Eddie was the only one who didn't have a pistol in his hand. His palms were up as though to show the room he wasn't a threat. He didn't have to be. He had four other threats on his side.

"I'd like to hear it," David said, his voice colder than she'd ever heard.

She had to make sure he survived this. He cared about her. He was the kind of man who would try to sacrifice himself for a woman he cared about. He needed to be reminded that he was the client and she was the one protecting him.

"I need for you to find the treasure." Eddie's hands were shaking, and his eyes went from David back to her and the gun held to her head. And back to David. "You can do it. You found the baseball card. You can find the treasure. You know my father better than anyone. You've read all of his work and know how he thinks. I'll give you anything you need."

David's head shook. "Your men have a gun on my girlfriend. I'm not giving you anything until you let her go."

She had to give it to him. David was steady. He was strong for a guy who'd probably never been in this kind of situation before, but he was reacting exactly like she'd thought he would. "David, I'm not your girlfriend. I'm your bodyguard, and you should fire me after this. I know for damn sure Big Tag will."

David's eyes widened. "I thought we weren't going to mention that part."

Even from here she could feel his hurt at the cold statement she'd made, but she couldn't take it back. They needed to know they couldn't manipulate David this way. They also needed to understand that even if they killed her, someone would come looking for David. "I'm not telling them, David. I suspect they already know I'm not who I said I was. I'm reminding you. I'm not your girlfriend. I had fun with you, but I was already planning on how to avoid you from now on. So you need to make decisions based on what's best for you, not to try to save a woman who was planning on leaving you anyway."

God, it hurt to say the words because now she was pretty sure they weren't true. She was fairly certain that had she played this properly, she would have gotten him off the island and back home, and then the bargaining would have started. She would have told herself that her time with him had been cut short and they should have had at least five more days together, so it was okay to go on a date and spend the night at his place. She would have convinced herself that it was perfectly fine to go to The Club with him because she should have had those nights of play with him. Once those nights were done, she would have given herself one or two more.

And then she simply would have accepted the fact that she was his and he was hers, and it was right this time. She needed David to soften her hard edges, and he needed her to pull him back into the real world from time to time.

If she hadn't screwed everything up and gotten them in this terrible situation.

"Hey, it's okay, baby. You wanted to leave and I convinced you to spend one more night." David completely ignored the men with the guns. His eyes were on her. "I know you're feeling guilty, and you might even be feeling stupid, but you're not. You're the smart one, and you can yell at me when you get us out of this, but don't try to convince me you don't care."

"I don't." He had to be harder than this or he wouldn't survive because she didn't see why they kept her alive.

His face fell, but his eyes stayed on her. "It doesn't matter how you feel about me. What matters is how I feel about you, and they know that. Honestly, it wouldn't matter if I hated you. I would still do what they want. The fact that I'm in love with you only makes it more urgent."

Did he understand nothing? "For a man with as many degrees as you have, you're not very smart."

"She's right." There was obviously a reason Luis didn't have a gun to his head. The "grad student" was watching David with steely eyes. "You're not as impressive as you seem on paper. You spend all your time with a bunch of mewling kids who drag you down."

"Mewling? I assure you Kala Taggart doesn't mewl, though she did threaten to take me down if I didn't stop making her repeat assignments." David's voice was perfectly steady, as though he knew she needed him to be. "She's the one who scares me. I'm fairly certain she's on a path that will lead to a prison or the Agency."

Who the hell was this man? She was the one panicking when she never did. She was cool under pressure. She'd taken plenty of fire and not even had her blood pressure go up. Yet now she could feel her heart in her throat, her eyes starting to water at the idea of losing him.

She needed to be stronger than this.

Or she just needed to not work with her boyfriend. She needed to stop pretending with this man. Stop pretending with herself.

"You could be someone important." Luis paced the room like a caged tiger. "But you spend all your time worried about stupid shit. Your brother is the one dragging you down. I hate listening to you whine about him. You know what I did when my brother got in my way? I took him out because this world isn't about the weak."

"I take it your brother is the real Luis." David shrugged into his shirt. "You probably look a lot like him. He was an academic, but you decided to go a different way?"

"The resemblance is uncanny. When I found out my brother was going to America, I studied up on the university he would be attending. I thought it was useless until I realized the connection between you and Montez's son. You have a picture of you with Montez right there on your faculty page."

"It was the one time I met the man," David explained. "It was a big moment for me. There are also pictures of me with my family and my students."

"Yeah, Montez was the only one I cared about," Luis admitted. "So I studied up on what I would need to, and when it was time, I took my brother's place."

"Did you kill him?" David asked in an academic tone.

"No, I needed him to do the actual work and to coach me on what to say. I broke both his legs, and my friends have kept him and his girlfriend in a safe location," Luis admitted. "As long as he complies, they both live."

"By *friends* he means criminals," she pointed out. "I take it you're part of an established group. I am, too. Do you want to start a war with my group?"

Luis's eyes rolled. "Yeah, I know all about David's stepfamily, and I know he doesn't have much to do with them besides playing tutor. He talks about how he doesn't fit in."

"That won't stop my stepdad, and I assure you it won't stop Ian Taggart," David said flatly. "The minute I don't show up or Tessa doesn't call, he'll move heaven and earth and the CIA to find me. Like I said to Tessa, it won't matter that I'm standoffish. I'm a member of his family, and he will not let me go easily. She's his employee. He won't let her go either. If you want to start a war with a group of ex-Special Forces soldiers and a couple of former CIA operatives, this is the way to do it."

Luis actually seemed to think about that. Had he truly not understood what he was going up against?

She could give him more to think about. "Don't forget the Russians. Charlotte's got ties to the Denisovitch Syndicate. If Dusan can help out his cousin and gain a foothold here in South America, he'll do it."

Mateo's hand shifted slightly. "*No queremos problemas con los rusos.*"

"If you don't want problems with them, then let her go," David commanded.

But they couldn't. This was an act of desperation on all sides.

"Maybe we should think about this," Eddie offered. "You know we could all walk away, and nothing has to happen. I won't go to the cops."

"Why would you go to the cops? You're the reason we're here," David said to the man who'd been his friend.

But he might be wrong about that. A few things slipped into place, and she figured out what was going on. Too late, but at least her powers of reasoning hadn't completely died when her libido took over. "They have your son, right? That picture upstairs. It wasn't you. It's your kid."

Eddie's head fell forward. "I'm not married to his mother. I didn't even know she was pregnant until a few months ago, but he's mine, and I was going to try to work things out with her. He's barely six weeks old and they have him and Camila. We named him after my father."

"Fuck," David said. "They want ransom? Pay it."

Eddie shook his head. "They want the treasure. You think I haven't tried to reason with them? I offered them everything I had."

"You offered two million American dollars," Luis shot back. "The treasure is worth ten times that. Twenty."

"If it even exists," she pointed out.

"It exists," Luis replied. "And we've always known David Hawthorne would be the one to find it. According to my brother, Professor Hawthorne is the expert. No one else has been able to even come close, but he'll find it, and then we won't ever have to worry about money again. We'll crush our enemies and live like kings."

"Or he won't be able to find it and you'll have to kill us all, and you're right back to getting your ass hunted down by my boss." She steadied her breathing. She needed to think about this. They might keep her alive in order to give David a reason to work. They had a couple of days before Big Tag would wonder where they were. He knew about the communications issues here on the island, and that would throw him off. Could David keep them on the hook for a couple of days?

"I have your itinerary," Luis replied. "You're not expected back until late Sunday. That gives us plenty of time to deal with the problem. I also have your phone, and I'll get someone into the village to make sure you send out a message saying you're fine. The question is will the professor do what we need him to do or should I start killing people? I don't really need Eddie or his kid at this point."

David's hands came up. "I'll do it. Don't kill anyone, and that includes Eddie's family. There's no reason to. I'll find it for you and then you can let us all go."

That wasn't the way this would work, but Luis needed to believe that they thought they would survive. This was a standoff of sorts. They needed to buy time. She had to think that most of the staff was in on this. Perhaps not the maids, but the rest of the group would have been brought in or taken care of. She would need to assess her situation and find a way to get David out of here. She didn't care about

Eddie. Oh, he was doing it for his girlfriend and his son, but he could have found a way to let them know. He could have sent a message of some kind and then David would have brought in the troops. If the bastard had shown an ounce of faith in his friend, they wouldn't be in this situation.

David was her only priority.

"I want her with me at all times." David seemed to think that he could negotiate with them. He was naïve. Or maybe a better way to look at it was optimism.

It wouldn't work.

They didn't seem to know about the gun in the nightstand. They'd taken her phone, but they hadn't even looked in the nightstand. At least she knew where one weapon was.

"I don't think so," Luis replied. "I think you'll work faster if we keep you apart. You seem to lose your focus around her, Professor. Mateo, tie the bitch up and then we'll escort Professor Hawthorne to the library. I want him to give me a starting point by this evening."

David shook his head. "That's not enough time."

"It better be or your pretty princess here is going to lose a finger. And she'll lose another one every four hours after that until she runs out and I need to find other body parts you're more fond of. Do I make myself clear?" Luis had a savage expression on his face, and Tessa had no doubt she could lose a couple of digits if this guy had his way.

David's stare had gone stony, all of his emotions shutting down. "I get it. I perform or she gets hurt. We should go to the library, and I'll need Eddie with me. I have questions for him."

Eddie nodded. "Anything you need, man."

David looked her way. "Tessa…"

"I'll be fine." She would be especially fine if they only left Mateo to watch over her. She was almost certain that despite her bodyguard credentials, he would see her as weak.

"I swear to god if anyone hurts her, I'll make sure you never find the treasure," David vowed. "I'll send you on a wild-goose chase that will end in my family as the ones hunting you. Do I make myself clear, whatever the fuck your name is?"

Luis punched him right in the face. "You don't talk to me that way."

It took everything she had not to start fighting.

David merely spat out the blood in his mouth. "I mean it. I find out one of your men laid a hand on her and I'll go down fighting, and you won't see a dime."

How could that man ever doubt that he was the end goal? That he was the man a smart woman would love and never regret giving her heart to?

Stupid tears threatened to fall, and she had to suck it up because he was being her hero.

"Mateo, tie the whore up and make sure she doesn't cause trouble. And don't touch a hair on her pretty head or the professor will get mad," Luis said with a huff. "And be careful in case she really is what she says she is. We know she works for his uncle, but she looks like a secretary to me."

"I think I can handle her," Mateo replied. "She's just a woman."

Ah, misogyny, her old friend.

"Tessa," David began.

"Just do what you need to do, Professor." She used the title she gave him when they were playing. The one she would call him if she was ever brave enough to go to The Club with him. If she was brave enough to let herself love him.

He nodded, and they led him out.

She was left with Mateo and one other bulky man she'd seen walking around the gardens with a shovel he probably used for non-gardening activities. Like burying the bodies of his victims. She should have taken one look at the staff and forced David back on the boat, but no. She hadn't wanted to upset the sexy professor man who she was going to share a bed with.

Big Tag would kill her. She didn't need Mateo to do it. Big Tag would do all kinds of things to her entrails because he liked to talk about them a lot. The only thing he liked to talk about more was not thinking with one's genitals. And he'd said flat out that a pussy could be as dumb as a dick. He was not sexist when it came to doling out lectures on how horniness could get an operative killed.

Mateo didn't move as his friend handed her a robe.

At least they weren't leaving her completely naked. She'd gotten caught without her panties, and she would never, ever hear the end of it.

Of course if she died, her coworkers would likely overlook her mistakes. They would certainly be noted in a file somewhere, and she would become a cautionary tale for newbie recruits, but she wouldn't have to listen to them ragging on her.

She shrugged into the robe and then let the sheet fall to the floor. There were only two of them now, but Mateo had that gun way too close to her head. He would get a shot off, and even if she managed to avoid the bullet, it would alert everyone else, and David would be in the crossfire. She had no idea who was right outside.

"Put your hands together," Mateo ordered as his friend produced a set of zip ties.

Seriously? They were letting her keep her hands in front of her? She loved misogyny so much. Tessa put her wrists together, allowing them to zip-tie her hands. They were tight, but she could work with it.

"Sit down. Stay quiet and let the professor do his work. If you give me trouble I've got something that will make you easy to deal with," Mateo promised.

She could bet what that was, and she didn't want a nice dose of either some kind of sedative or heroin. "Like I said, I'm not his girlfriend. I just want to get out of this alive."

To that end she sat down on the chair they offered and found her ankles tied to the legs. Again, not a problem. The chair wasn't even nailed to the floor, so she could ease those suckers off.

These were not professional kidnappers. She would bet they were used to shoving some screaming victim into a room and not letting them out until they had the cash.

She was going to be a revelation for them because she would also bet that they would get bored real fast, and once their minds started to wander, she could get to the nightstand and get her gun.

"If you want to stay alive, you'll be a good girl," Mateo chided. "I know you think you're some kind of badass, but I don't buy it. Americans hire women to please their media. A woman shouldn't be a bodyguard. You were doing what you did best last night. Stick to fucking from here on out. Maybe get yourself a real man so you don't end up here again."

Oh, she could fuck him up hard, but she knew how to play this game. "I'll be good."

She sat and waited for the right time.

* * * *

David forced himself to walk away from the bedroom he'd shared with Tessa. He couldn't force himself to stop thinking about her.

He'd gotten so close to her. So fucking close, and even if they survived this, he worried she wouldn't forgive herself for not pushing him to leave the night before. She'd known something was wrong. He should have listened to her, but he'd wanted time. Time with her. Time to convince her he was worth taking a chance on.

Now all he wanted was for her to make it out of this alive and whole.

"They won't hurt her." Eddie walked beside him, their captors at their backs.

"Sure they won't." He couldn't believe this was happening. He'd known this man for years, trusted him. Tessa was right. He was naïve, and it might cost him everything he'd ever wanted. He'd thought he wanted tenure and a great career, but now he knew it would all be hollow if he didn't have her to share it with.

"Camila is unharmed, and they've had her for three weeks," Eddie explained.

"So they came to you then? Because Luis has been with me for a semester and a half." They'd been planning this for a long time.

"And they've been infiltrating my house for just as long," Eddie replied, his voice tense.

Well, good he was fucking tense because he was also the reason they were in this situation in the first place. David shoved his way through the library door. "Did it occur to you to maybe shoot me an email. 'Hey, David, got a situation down here and need your help. Why don't you bring the troops in?'"

"Because my son's life is at stake. You can't understand what it means," Eddie shot back.

"I can certainly understand what it means to love someone." He wasn't letting him off easily. Eddie had plenty of time when he could have given David a heads-up. "You didn't even tell me you had a kid."

"I didn't know I wanted one until I met him." Eddie moved into the library.

Luis had two men with him, both with guns, of course. "The lady is a friend of a friend, and that was how I found out about the connection."

"How do you know she's not in on this?" David asked Eddie.

"Does it matter?" Eddie said with a shrug. "He's still my son.

There was a test, and I believe it. Even if she's in on it, he's still my boy, and I want him. She might not kill him, but she could disappear with him. I can't risk it."

But he could risk David's life, and more importantly, Tessa's. "Did they plan to pick me up at the airport?"

"That was a rival group," Luis answered. "Someone in my organization has been talking, but I'll handle it."

"You do understand this is one of the stupidest plans in the history of...do I dare call it organized crime?" He was flabbergasted at the entire idea that they expected him to find a treasure that had eluded everyone else who'd looked for it. And in the matter of a few days. "We don't even know if the treasure exists."

"It better or you're going to be in trouble, Professor." Luis's eyes had narrowed. "I need that money. I owe some people, and the time is coming when I can't make payments anymore. I can give them the treasure or I can give them you. The men I'm dealing with won't treat you with the same respect."

He couldn't tell there was any respect at all. "I meant what I said about Tessa. If she's hurt in any way, I won't do a damn thing for you. It doesn't matter what you do to me. You don't touch her."

"That's a lot to risk for a woman who doesn't care for you," Luis replied.

He didn't think she'd meant all of what she'd said. Oh, he could absolutely see her walking away, but she did care about him. That was precisely why she would walk. If she didn't feel something for him, she would likely offer him a D/s relationship that would be all about sex and kept to their respective clubs. And he would take it on the off chance she might change her mind about him.

Because he was mad crazy in love with her.

"I need a map of the grounds." He wasn't discussing his love life with his kidnapper. And it was also good to know that more than one group wanted to kidnap him. At least it was all for his own skills and not his family connections. That was a plus. Of course his skills would mean nothing if he couldn't translate them into some kind of crazy treasure that probably didn't exist.

"I think we should go into the jungle," Luis insisted.

And waste the time he had? He wasn't about to be farther from Tessa than he already was. There was also the fact that he didn't think the treasure was out in the jungle. "We've gone over this. If there's twenty million dollars out there, it's in a big fucking box, man. Even if it was cash, the container would have to be large and insulated to protect what's inside. The jungle is wet and muddy, and after a couple of years there would be erosion around it. That would make it easier to find. Am I making sense to you?"

"I agree with David." Eddie wouldn't actually look at him. "There's no way my father hauled a large box into the jungle in the last year of his life."

David didn't want to think about it. "Then it's somewhere here on the grounds, and I need a map of them. I would also like any blueprints of planning materials you can find for the house and the grounds. There's a guesthouse as well."

Luis got in his space. "I'm not your errand boy."

"Good, then you'll give me the freedom to go where I need and get the items I need without interference." He wasn't about to back down. All he could think about was Tessa and the fact that she needed him.

He could practically feel Luis's rage, but the man took a step back. "I'll find them for you. But know that you're on thin ice with me. *Vos vigilás.*"

He stalked away, and they were left with the henchmen.

"I don't think those two speak English if you want to talk," Eddie said under his breath. "I'm sorry."

"I know you are, but this isn't some prank that went wrong." Eddie was always sorry about something. "This is our lives and Tessa's, and I'm not even sure there is a treasure to be found."

David walked over to the big table where yesterday he'd made the decision not to pursue some elusive treasure. If he'd listened to Tessa, they wouldn't be in this situation, and she had to be thinking that, too. Could she ever forgive him?

"When he was dying, my dad told me he left something for me." Eddie glanced at their captors. "He said he'd finally figured out what was important, and he hoped I did, too. I thought it was some political ideal. God knows I'd gotten enough of those lectures over the years. I'm worried we're going to find a book or some bullshit."

A new book by Montez would be a true treasure, but only to a historian or political theorist. "How well do you know the grounds?"

Eddie sighed. "You think he hid something here? It's a big place. I know the main house pretty well."

By *pretty well*, David assumed he meant Eddie knew the common areas and likely nothing at all about the parts of the estate the servants spent time in. The truth of the matter was David hadn't spent much time out of the library, dining area, or the bedroom he'd shared with Tessa. He hadn't gotten a real feel for the place because his head had been stuck in a book. "You don't know if there's a safe anywhere?"

"Sure. There's a safe in the master suite, but I've certainly looked through that. There's a gun safe in the garage, but there's only guns and ammo in it, and I scarcely think we'll be able to get to it." Eddie frowned. "I also don't actually know that code since I've never had to fight off a wild animal here."

"You'll know better next time." If they survived. "Have you ever heard anyone talk about hiding places? Were there other kids around when you were younger?"

"I wasn't that friendly unless they were pretty girls," Eddie admitted. "You know I'm an asshole. Trust me. I'm feeling every minute of it. Maybe if I hadn't been such an ass, Camila wouldn't have had to talk to her friends about us. She could have been with me, and I could have taken care of her."

He couldn't think about what Eddie should have done. He had to figure a way out of this.

What was Tessa going through? God, not knowing was an actual ache in his gut.

Was there any way to get a message out to his stepfather? He hoped Eddie was right and their captors wouldn't understand what he was about to ask. He picked up a notebook and opened it, his eyes staring as he lowered his voice. "Are the phone lines really down?"

"They cut them all last week when Luis showed up," Eddie said under his breath. "They blamed a storm, but I know it was them, and they control the radio. They've been slowly getting rid of the important people in the household and replacing them with their own. It's my fault because I left it all up to the manager who hired Mateo, so he's in on it."

Eddie was going to be absolutely no help. David would be surprised if he knew where the radio was much less how to use it. "Is there anyone on the staff that you trust?"

Eddie shrugged. "A couple of the maids. I don't know about Marta. I hired her myself a few months ago. She's worked for me before. I know she's here now. I think Mateo gave the maids the day off, and I'm sure he'll come up with something for tomorrow."

Luis would count on them keeping silent around anyone who came in. After all, they had Tessa and Eddie's kid, so it wasn't like he would go screaming to one of the young women who mopped the floors and changed the bedding.

Though he might be able to slip a note. That could work. He could potentially slip one of the maids a note to let her know to contact his stepdad.

He had no doubt that if he actually found the treasure—if there was one—he would be dead shortly after, and so would Tessa and Eddie. They wouldn't simply let them all go.

There was a knock on the door, and it came open. Marta stepped inside, a big tray in her hand. She glanced over and seemed to take note of the men with guns. If she gave a damn, she didn't show it. The woman who ran the kitchens brought the tray over.

"I was told to bring you coffee and some breakfast, Mr. Montez." Marta's English was good. "You should do what they tell you."

"Of course." David wasn't about to argue with anyone. There was zero point.

"I hired you myself. I'm really shocked that you're with them." Eddie wasn't taking the same view of their situation.

She shrugged. "With them. With you. What is the difference? I don't care as long as I get paid. I don't argue with men who have guns. Do you want the coffee or not? It's not poisoned. They didn't pay me to do that."

The woman was dour but steady. And they wouldn't want to poison him. Not yet. "We'll serve ourselves."

Eddie was shaking his head. "I trusted you."

"You barely talked to me beyond telling me how to cook your steak," she replied in that flat way of hers. "Where is the American girl? Did they kill her?"

"*Vos regresás a la cocina*," one of the men with the guns said.

She didn't flinch at being told to get back to the kitchen, merely sighed as though she was used to the treatment.

"They're keeping her in our bedroom," David said. "Could you make sure she gets some water and something to eat?"

Marta shrugged. "If they tell me to. If not, she can starve for all I care. I'll come back for the tray, but don't expect me to play the maid. Clean up after yourselves since they won't be back until Monday."

She walked away, and David realized there would be no note to sneak. He was well and truly trapped.

"What should we do?" Eddie asked.

David bit back a groan because unfortunately the "we" part was fitting. "We grab a cup of coffee and then I do what I do best."

"And what is that?" Eddie reached for the pot.

"Study."

He had to hope he could study his way out of this.

Chapter Ten

Tessa glanced at the clock. It had been seven hours and the fucker hadn't moved except to allow her to relieve herself, and even then he'd brought in his friend and stood outside the door watching her so she couldn't make a handy weapon out of a lady razor.

She needed to carry more weapons. Why didn't she have a couple of knives in her makeup kit? She'd been forced to allow them to settle her back onto her chair, and then the waiting had begun again.

Mateo sat on the bed, watching the TV he'd turned on shortly after he'd ensured she was tied up and completely helpless. She'd aided in that wrong assumption by crying about how tight the awful zip ties were.

She needed about a minute and a half to get out of them, maybe less if she simply broke the chair to get her legs free. She'd been quiet enough that the word *gag* hadn't been used, and she planned to keep it that way. Not because she had any real issues with gags as a fun way to spend a night, but because she wasn't giving those assholes any other shot at getting near her.

She'd gone over and over this in her head. Patience was the key. She had to shove down all the panic and wait for the best time to move. In her mind she'd gone over everything she knew about the house. Unless they'd brought more people in, she thought she was looking at five to seven possible captors, if the maids were in on it. She kind of thought the cook was. There had been a hard quality to the woman that made Tessa put her on the other side.

Or perhaps she was being paranoid. It didn't matter. The key was to assume everyone was in on it with the exception of David and take them all out as soon as possible.

The waiting was going to kill her, and that was all about him because she was known for her patience. It was her stock in trade.

She wasn't capable of patience when it came to David. He was out there, and she was sure if he stepped out of line they would hurt him. He wasn't a trained operative. He was a college professor. He wasn't supposed to know how to handle physical pain. He was supposed to be dealing with undergrads, not spy shit.

That was her job. She was the one who dealt with security issues, and he would help the kids with homework.

Because as she'd sat here, she'd decided she was a dumbass for even thinking about leaving that man. She was being a coward. What she'd had with Michael had been warm and comfortable and not enough for either of them. What she had with David was a wildfire that they could keep burning for the rest of their lives. It wasn't some ember that one day in the distant future might spark into a fire. It had been a blaze from the second she'd met him. That was what had scared her. Getting burned. But the incendiary nature of their attraction was tempered by the friendship they were growing, by the mutual respect they already shared.

She wasn't willing to let fear of the future cost her what could be the love of her life. He might be upset with her for letting this happen, but she was going to make sure he understood that they were together, and that wasn't going to change.

Kyle was right, and that wasn't something that happened often, so she should honor it. There would always be gossip at work, but she couldn't let that stop her.

She'd made her decision. Now all that was keeping her from the love of her life were five to seven criminals and a big pot of treasure. And a lot of guns. That was all.

A girl did what she had to.

Mateo seemed determined to keep up with the news. He had to go to the bathroom at some point, right? He couldn't simply sit there for the next forty-eight to seventy-two hours. Could he?

There was a knock on the outer door, and she heard someone shuffling around. There was a conversation in Spanish about whether or not she actually needed food. Like she could eat at this point. Marta's voice was gruff as she talked to the guy protecting the door. They agreed he could take a break and she would back up Mateo and feed the sad American who probably couldn't even appreciate her food.

Yep. Definitely in on it, and she was right. She wasn't about to appreciate anything.

Could she refuse? She didn't want to eat or drink anything for fear of it having a sedative in it. It's what she would do. A passed-out captive would be far easier than an awake one.

"After she drinks this juice she won't be much trouble for the next four hours or so," Marta said in Spanish. "We can all take a break. I've got lunch set up in the dining room."

Damn it. She'd known they would try it, but she'd been hoping they would wait until nighttime.

Mateo was suddenly interested in what was happening in the living area. He stood and started to move for the door.

Tessa's heartrate ticked up, and she could feel adrenaline start to pulse. Did she have time? She would bring her hands up over her head and pull them down and apart as hard as she could. Stand up and then slam back and break the chair. Pop up, get her gun in hand, and take them all out.

If Mateo would walk away for a minute and a half it could work. He stopped at the door.

"Let her in." Mateo turned back to Tessa. "Marta is bringing you food. Eat and drink or there will be trouble."

"I'm not hungry." She wasn't going to let herself get sedated. She had to stay in control. If she went under, they could do anything they wanted to her. They could also move her, and she wouldn't have any idea where she was or how far away David was.

Mateo frowned down at her, his big body in tight lines. "You will eat and drink whatever Marta tells you to do. Am I understood?"

She was going to have to risk it, but she needed to wait for the exact right moment. She nodded.

Mateo moved back to the door as Marta walked in with a tray. "*Decís si te da algún problema. Esperaremos hasta que ella haya bebido todo, quiero asegurarme que no esté consciente antes de dejarla en paz.*"

Tessa frowned, hoping she looked like she had no idea what they were saying. Mateo wanted to make sure she drank the whole mug. He wasn't leaving until he knew she was sedated.

"I've been ordered to stay with her even after she's out," Marta replied in Spanish as well. "Luis doesn't want her alone for even a minute, but I think I can handle one drugged girl. Lunch is waiting in the dining room. It might be your only break. Would you rather stay here and I'll bring you a plate?"

Mateo grunted and walked out, his decision obviously made.

Marta walked in and put her tray on the dresser. This might be Tessa's shot. She would have to get to the gun before Mateo got back into the room or it would be over.

Marta turned Tessa's way, the glass of juice in her hand. "You will drink this, girl."

She was ready to head butt Marta then free her hands. She would have to go for the gun with her feet tied to the chair, but she could do it.

Marta stood in front of her. "Yes, that's good."

What?

Marta yawned and then took a drink from the glass herself. "Drink it all up and you can have some food."

Marta swallowed the rest down and sat the empty glass on the tray. She picked up what looked like a bowl of soup as Mateo poked his head back in.

"Do you want to stay and watch me feed her?" Marta asked as though she couldn't care less.

What the hell was going on?

Patience. This was one of those times when she needed to reassess and give this situation a minute to play out because she didn't understand what was going on. She was starting to think what was going on might work in her favor.

Mateo grunted and said something about how Marta better not fuck things up.

She kind of hoped Marta was about to really fuck things up.

Marta simply shrugged again and gave him another yawn.

"What's happening? I feel weird." Tessa slurred her words. Marta had given her a cue and she was going to take it. She yawned. "What was in the juice?"

"Just go to sleep, little girl," Marta said with a long sigh.

Mateo seemed to take that as a good time to get out of there. He told his friend they could grab some lunch. Marta would handle things here.

She heard the door shut and the sound of the men walking down the hall.

"Are you going to do the American operative thing? The one

where you break all the furniture and attack? It's dramatic, but I brought a knife." Marta reached into her pocket and pulled out a small knife. "I can get you out or I can wait for you to look like *Charlie's Angels* or something."

Or Marta could be intelligence. The bitter sarcasm totally gave her away. "Argentinian intelligence?"

She rolled her eyes, and the accent was completely gone when she spoke again. "Agency. You know we're not all twenty-five-year-old models. Eddie Montez has business dealings with some people we're interested in. At least he did until these morons came along. I'd like to keep my cover. I already called in the big guns, but god only knows how long it will take Taggart to get the message."

Hope sprang up inside her. "You called my boss?"

"I had someone call him. I don't know his number. I just thought he would like to know that his brother's stepson was about to be kidnapped. Are you really a bodyguard? You know you shouldn't have told them." Marta...probably not her real name...expertly sliced through the zip ties. "Also, the next time you want to pretend like you don't speak a language you shouldn't smile at jokes you're not supposed to understand."

"I'm a bodyguard, not a damn spy." She didn't want to do undercover. She wanted to stand to the side and jump in front of bullets if she had to. Easy-peasy. Tessa rolled her wrists to get the circulation flowing as Marta worked on her ankles. "When did you send out the message to Ian?"

"Yesterday afternoon, when I realized they were going to make their move. They offered to pay me a lot to help out, and I thought I should take the cash and do what I needed to do," Marta explained.

"Or you could have given us a heads-up so I could have gotten my client out of here."

A brow rose over Marta's eyes. "Seriously?"

"Fine. My boyfriend."

"I had to decide whether or not I wanted to put a year-long op in jeopardy to save your asses," she admitted. "The truth of the matter is it could help me enormously to have something to hold over Eddie's head. It would have given me some real nice leverage to use."

It was good to know her death could have been useful to the Agency. "What changed your mind?"

"I sent your info to my handler and he crapped his pants." Marta straightened up and slid the knife back in her pocket. "I was hoping Taggart would show up and save the day and my op, but we're out of time."

Tessa stood, stretching for the first time in hours. "Why does your op have to be ruined?"

"Well, I don't think you can handle them all on your own. Once Eddie sees me kill a man, he'll wonder where his cook learned to do that."

It was Tessa's turn to roll her eyes. "I might not be a spy, but I can handle these assholes all on my own. You can be the helpful employee who saw something going wrong and waited until you could do something about it. He'll trust you like no one else after this. I won't say a word."

Marta's eyes narrowed. "My handler was clear. He doesn't want Taggart to think we prioritized a mission over his kin."

They wanted Big Tag to owe them a favor. Good luck cashing that one in because Big Tag tended to do what he wanted. "He won't. I'll fill him in on everything you've done, but it's up to you. You want to keep your cover, then tell me what I need to know and let me do my job."

Tessa retrieved her gun and breathed her first deep breath in hours. She could do this. Everything was going to be all right because this was her stage now, and she knew exactly how to perform.

"Don't fuck this up. And use mine. It's got a suppressor." Marta reached behind her and came up with a shiny semi complete with a lovely suppressor that would keep her kills quiet, thereby not alerting anyone that she was on the move. "But get dressed first. I know your boobs might distract those assholes, but it's not seemly. Cover them."

Tessa put hers on the bed and Marta's joined it. She was right. It wasn't seemly to go kill a bunch of dudes in a too-short robe with her ass hanging out. She was a girlfriend, and she had to think about David. She wouldn't want him teaching a class on the rise of democratic socialism in Eastern Chile while showing off his abs. He liked her ass and her boobs and all her other parts, so she would keep the nudity where it belonged. Between the two of them and anyone who happened to belong to one of their clubs.

She reached for some undies. "Tell me what I need to know."

Marta sat back. "I've got most of them in the dining room. Go up the back way and you can pick them off easily from the second floor landing. I'll take out the asshole watching the back door. If anyone asks, you got him first. I want to fuck him up a little because he's been harassing the maids, and those babies are scared of him. I want to make him scared of me before he dies."

"Cool." She had no problem with that. She hooked her bra. "I took out the back guard and then moved to the dining room. Where's Luis?"

"In the library with your boy and Eddie. Don't kill Eddie. I need him. If I do this well, I might be able to shift to a cushy position back home. I miss Mexican food. You know, American Mexican food. My mother would spin in her grave at how my tastes have changed," Marta admitted.

"If you're ever in Dallas, I'll treat you to some Tex-Mex." She put on shorts and a T-shirt.

It was time to save her guy.

* * * *

David glanced up and realized hours had gone by. He'd had his head wrapped around the problem and hadn't felt the passage of time.

Luis was sitting in the window seat where Tessa had been yesterday. He had a walkie-talkie in his hand and had been coordinating movements with his men. So far David had figured out that there were seven of them and they were scattered around the grounds, though he didn't know exactly where they were.

There was another guard on the door that led from the library to the hallway. He wasn't sure if there was another guard outside. Mateo hadn't shown his face for hours. He was probably watching Tessa, and that made David's stomach turn. He'd left her vulnerable. He should have fought, should have done whatever it took to get her out of there.

Or he needed to realize that this was panic and Tessa was a pro who'd wanted him out of that room. She would wait for her best opportunity, and she would come for him.

All he had to do was buy her time. She was smart and brave and deadly. His pretty predator.

What was Tessa going through? It didn't matter how good she was at her job. He would still worry about her, and once they got out of this, he would pamper her and love her and never ask about the more dangerous parts of her job. Unless she wanted to talk about them.

"She's all right," Eddie whispered. "They won't hurt her."

Was Eddie naïve or was he simply trying to make David as comfortable as possible so he got what he wanted? David looked back down at the notes he'd been making. "Of course."

Eddie groaned. "I'm being a fool, aren't I?"

"It doesn't matter." David kept his voice low and didn't look up.

"I'm sorry. I thought you would get here and figure out the puzzle, and you wouldn't even have to know what was going on," Eddie whispered.

He seriously doubted things would have gone that way. "They've been planning this for a long time. They obviously know something we don't. They have to have a reason to believe the treasure exists."

"They told me the old butler knew something. According to Luis, he helped my dad bury the treasure, but before he could tell them anything, he died. That was why they put this plan in motion."

That was interesting. "He used the word bury?"

"I don't know. I wasn't there," Eddie admitted.

Luis's radio crackled, and someone came over the line announcing that there was lunch in the dining room. It was good to know they were keeping a schedule and the cook was still hard at work. He wondered how much they were paying her. Eddie had been surrounded by wolves.

"Because there's nothing in this poem that tells me the treasure was buried." He'd read the thing a thousand times now. "He talks about it being hidden."

There was a knock on the door, and it opened. A man walked in, a stack of files in his hands. He walked up to Luis and handed them off.

"Hidden where? I would think the jungle would be the best place to hide it. He spent a lot of time out there. He called it meditative time," Eddie replied. "Do you think he put it in one of the villages?"

Given some of the rumors he'd heard, David didn't think so. "What do you know about the hidden passageways in this house?"

"I know that I've shown these fuckers all of them. It was the first thing they asked about. The butler knew where the passages are." Eddie glanced back.

Did he? There was a line in the poem that made him think not.

A stream that flows for only one

My secret kept until you are clever enough to find it

He thought he was right about his first impression. The treasure was meant for Eddie and it was personal, and it was here in this house or on the grounds.

Luis had hopped off his seat and moved toward them, the files in his hands. "Here's everything we could find about the house. Montez kept a copy of the blueprints in his office. These are the originals. They don't include the third floor. Hope it helps because you're running out of time."

"I thought you were giving us through the weekend." How hard was Luis going to push because David knew he needed to give Tessa as much time as he could. The last thing he wanted was to actually find this sucker because he was fairly certain a bullet to the back of the head would follow.

Luis frowned. "Someone rented a chopper to take them from the mainland to here. I don't like it."

"It's probably another treasure hunter." Eddie looked up at their captor. "You know this is the tactic they've started to take. We had one of those guys…what do you call it when they have their own channel on social media?"

"I think you're thinking of vloggers." He was right. There were several so-called historians who had their own web pages where they did videos specifically about their adventures trying to locate some of history's mysteries. They usually stuck to the big ones. Atlantis. The Lost City of Z. But there were a few who specialized in recent history's mysteries. It wouldn't surprise him to see someone do a spot on the lost Montez treasure.

Eddie nodded. "Vloggers. We had one two months ago. When they couldn't get permission to come in the proper way, they chartered a small plane and parachuted into the jungle. Naturally one of them broke an ankle, and we had to send a rescue party in. But it won't stop others. Did you get a name?"

Luis shook his head. "A. Rose. That's all we have. I don't know if that stands for Andrew or Albert or what. Three white guys with backpacks. One of them has a limp, and they argued a lot."

David didn't know anyone with the last name of Rose, so Eddie was likely right. "They're vloggers. They won't stop here. They'll go for the jungle where everyone thinks the hunt begins."

"But you don't, do you, Professor?" Luis pocketed the walkie, but the pistol was still in his hand.

"I've explained my thoughts on why I believe the treasure is closer than we think," he murmured. He opened the folder. Despite the panic that was simmering in his gut, there was also a spark of excitement because he knew he was on the right path. He could figure this out.

He spread out the blueprints.

Luis's radio crackled again, and he pulled it back out, walking to the other side of the room before responding.

"Maybe you should slow down," Eddie whispered. "Surely someone will realize there's a problem here at the estate. The maids will be back to work in a few days."

David brought his gaze up to stare at Eddie. "I thought you wanted this over as quickly as possible."

"I'm starting to think that's a bad idea." Eddie leaned in. "I'm sorry I got you into this. I didn't think they would hurt anyone. I thought they wanted to keep everything as quiet as possible. They told me if you found the treasure they would let you go and then they would take what they wanted and I would get my son back. I just want him to be okay. I know this sounds stupid, and I wouldn't have believed it could be true, but I saw that baby and I saw my father's eyes staring back at me. Like I have a second chance."

"I'm glad. I'm happy for you." It was good Eddie seemed to be taking fatherhood seriously, but it didn't change the situation. "I hope this works out and you get what you want."

"What I want is for Camila to not be a part of this." Eddie sat back. "And yet I do because if she is then they're not in danger, you know?"

If she was in on it, Camila would be safe. Unlike Tessa.

He stared down at the blueprints, smoothing them out. He wasn't sure what he was looking for. The dining room had a high ceiling, all the way up to the third floor where a skylight illuminated the room. Anyone walking overhead could look down and see the magnificent space where Montez used to hold court with some of the most fascinating people in the world.

That space was all accounted for. He was looking for missing space, something that wasn't in the plans. Something hidden.

"That boy is my heart, and I think I was my father's," Eddie said with a sigh. "I wish I'd told him I loved him more."

His heart. Montez referenced *heart* and *river* several times.

"I think you're right." Luis walked back up to the table. "My guy on the ground confirms the pilot was told they wanted to fly over the jungle and come back to the mainland. They're not even getting off the chopper, so we're fine. My men are taking a lunch break. When they're done you'll be brought food."

"What about Tessa?" David asked.

Luis shrugged. "Your girlfriend is taking a nap."

Tessa wouldn't sleep. David found himself on his feet. "What the hell did you do to her?"

Luis rolled his eyes, but the gun was up at his side. "Calm down. Marta gave her a sedative so we could all take a break. She's watching over her so no one touches your precious girl. I'm not a monster. I'm a man who owes other people money."

"She's helpless," David heard himself growl. She wouldn't be able to defend herself in any way.

"Hey, sit back down. She's fine. Like I said, Marta is watching her while the others eat. We had to put her down because Marta's an old lady, and I don't trust that your girl couldn't hurt her and get away. We can't have that." Luis pointed the weapon his way. "Now sit back down and get to work. Maybe if you get a good enough lead, I'll let you see her."

The radio crackled and then David would have sworn he heard someone scream in the distance.

Eddie stood up beside him. "What was that?"

"Sit back down." Luis nodded to the man at the door. "*Andá y mirás a los demás.*"

The man rushed out with a nod.

Luis got on his radio, asking for his henchmen to check in.

Nothing but static.

"What's going on?" Eddie asked, his eyes on the door.

Luis started toward it.

"Should we tackle him?" Eddie whispered.

David sighed because he was pretty sure what was coming. "Nah, I want her to have a clear line of sight. Us rushing him would create chaos, and if he got his hands on me that would throw her off her game. Best to let her do her job."

He wasn't sure how he knew, but he did. Tessa was coming for him, and he would make it easy on her. It was obvious that they had their roles in this relationship, and he wasn't going to fight it.

But he was going to fight for her. He would show up at the McKay-Taggart building every day until she couldn't stand it anymore and gave in to fate. He would show that woman that he was the man for her, and it started by trusting her.

"You should take cover now," David said, moving to the side of the room so she didn't have to worry about hitting him when she took Luis out.

The door flew open, and Luis's arm came up, taking his shot right before his body flew back and hit the ground.

"I told you not on the carpets," a disgruntled voice said.

"And I told you to buy a freaking steam cleaner." Tessa came through the door wearing shorts and a T-shirt, all that dark hair piled high on her head. She stalked into the library, her eyes going around the room. "Anyone left in here?"

"No. It was only Luis. You get the one outside?" David stayed where he was, wanting to give her time to come down from what had to be an adrenaline high. His heart had sped up, though, because she was gorgeous.

"She gets them all," a deeply accented voice said. Marta walked in behind her with a frown on her face. She pointed Eddie's way. "I am not cleaning up all this blood, you understand. I am the cook. I do not clean, and especially not after messy Americans."

Tessa picked up the gun Luis had dropped when she'd taken out both his lungs.

Damn. He was going to remember not to piss off his baby.

"I am not messy." Tessa turned on Marta. "You are bossy as hell, and you don't know what you're doing. You're a cook. Leave taking out the trash to the professionals." She turned his way, and a brilliant smile crossed her face. "Hey, Professor. You okay?"

He crossed the space between them, careful to not step in all that blood. Marta was right about the mess, but he wasn't saying a thing. Not about that. He did have a few things to say to Tessa. "I love you."

She went still, and for a moment he thought he was about to get the "it's not you, it's me" speech. He would take it and be patient with her. He wouldn't get angry because she needed some time.

"I love you, too, Hawthorne," she said quietly and took the last step so she was in his arms. She went on her toes and kissed him, and he felt like the whole world was finally right again. Not merely because he was safe from the ones who'd attacked them. Because he'd found the one woman who could make him open up again. Now he could see how much losing his father had made him close off from the world, to try to avoid that pain.

No more. The pain was the cost of the love, and he would accept it.

He kissed her, relief flooding through him because this time was forever.

The *thud thud* of a helicopter forced him to break the kiss.

Tessa's eyes went wide, and she moved in front of him, her whole body on alert. "That's a chopper."

"I thought it was going to go over the jungle." Eddie had gone pale. "Do you think Luis lied?"

"Why would he?" David asked, his mind wrapping around the possibilities. Tessa needed to know everything he did. "Luis told us someone hired a chopper to come out to the island. He told us he'd gotten the information right before you...well..."

"Before I killed his ass and all of his criminal-minded friends?" she asked.

She had a way with words. "Yes, before you killed his ass along with the rest of his body, he was worried about some guy named Rose who hired a chopper to fly over the jungle."

"Rose?" Tessa looked up at him.

"Yeah, some guy named A. Rose chartered a helicopter to tour the island." She needed to know everything he'd learned.

"Axl Rose?"

"I don't think Guns N' Roses is coming to this island. Also, is he still alive?" David asked.

"Your uncle is. You really need to get to know the man." She took off, jogging for the hall. "And he's late."

He followed her.

Eddie was hard on his heels. "What happens to my son?"

"I already called the police, Mr. Montez." Marta had her hands on her hips, shaking her head at the bodies they passed. "The idiots talk a lot around me. They give away everything because they think they can handle me. I found out where they were keeping the child and your woman. And she is your woman. According to what I heard, she had nothing to do with this plot."

"You get a raise, Marta. You get everything," Eddie said with a huge smile.

"I'll just keep my job, which might I point out doesn't include cleaning up bodies," Marta said as they walked past. "The dining room is terrible. She got blood all over the tablecloth."

David hustled to keep up with Tessa. There was something odd about the cook, but he didn't want to think about it now. All that mattered was Tessa and getting her off this island and back home.

The doors that led out to the courtyard had been thrown open, and he could feel the wind blasting from the chopper as a massive man in all black came down a rope, hit the ground, and immediately went into a defensive stance, a gun in his hand.

Was that Ian?

The big guy moved toward them as another muscular body dropped from the chopper.

Was that his stepdad? Where had they come from?

Ian moved forward, his gun coming down. "Hey, you okay?"

What the hell was Ian doing here?

Sean didn't wait. Sean simply ran up and put his hands on David's shoulders, looking him over like he was checking for injuries. "Are you hurt? Where are the fuckers who kidnapped you?"

"I told you I could land on one foot!" Someone was yelling.

Kyle was standing on the ground as the chopper took off again. His brother was in the yard, a big gun strapped to his chest and a medical boot on his left foot.

"Your brother is an idiot, and I'm thinking of killing him myself. He managed to get on the plane. It was going to take us longer to get him off than to take him along." Sean was dressed for war, and David had to admit it looked good on his stepdad. "We thought you were being held at gunpoint. Was our intel wrong?"

He gave his stepdad a big old bear hug. For a moment Sean stood there as though that was the last thing he'd expected, but then his arms enveloped David, and a shuddering sigh of obvious relief went through his stepdad's body.

"I'm good, thanks to Tessa," David said, taking a step back. "Thank you for coming for us, though."

"We brought a sat phone to contact your mom." Sean patted his backpack. "She's so worried about you, and Carys overheard us talking so she's freaked out, too."

It was good to have a family.

"Your cat scratched me," Kyle groused as he hobbled over. "He's irritated that you're not home."

"Santiago, you leave any of them alive?" Ian was asking.

"Why would I do that?" Tessa replied. "Then we would have paperwork, and you know I hate that."

"Good." Ian looked up at the big house. "This place have some food? All that flying made me hungry."

"There's a nice buffet if you don't mind some dead bodies," Tessa offered. "Axl Rose?"

Big Tag shrugged. "I have a certain style."

Kyle frowned. "Seriously? I came all this way to save you and Santiago already took them out?"

"There were only seven," Tessa said with a huff. "Don't act like it was some big deal." Tessa came around and slid her hand in David's. "I couldn't let those assholes get away with scaring my man."

Everyone was suddenly staring at them, but David didn't care. His fingers twined with hers, and he drew her close. "Thanks for the save, baby. I knew you would do it."

"Well, I didn't," Eddie said with a huff.

Ian settled his pack over his shoulder. "Montez, before we took off I gave my people the go-ahead to extract Camila Lopez and your son. The police already have her kidnappers in custody thanks to your cook. I've arranged for transportation for your people. They should be on their way here by now."

Eddie's head fell forward. "Thank you."

"Thank me when you get my bill, buddy," Ian said, walking up the steps. "It's not going to be cheap. You look familiar."

Ian was standing in front of Marta, who simply raised a brow. "You probably watched my pornographic movies. You look like the type."

She turned and walked away.

Ian shrugged. "Probably did. All right, then, let's get some lunch and debrief. I was serious about the bill."

"I could eat." Kyle started to hop up the stairs.

Sean shook his head and went to lend Kyle some balance. "You're going to kill me, son."

"Apparently Santiago is the only one doing the killing," Kyle announced. He glanced back. "And I called this whole romance thing. You always needed a badass chick to balance you. Hope you like cats,

Tessa."

"I like you." Tessa went on her toes as they found themselves alone again. "But next time I want a beach vacay, we're going to Hawaii."

He grinned at her, his heart filled for the first time in forever. "Promise."

He kissed her. She was his heart.

His heart. The heart of the house.

"Shit. I know where the treasure is." David took her hand, and they ran back in the house.

Chapter Eleven

Tessa stood in front of the big mural and studied it carefully. "You think there's something behind this?"

David was running his hands where the mural met with the wall. "Yes. I looked at the blueprints again. The lounge should be behind this wall, but the square footage doesn't add up."

"There's really treasure?" Ian was standing to the side with a sandwich in his big hand. He hadn't minded all the dead bodies. The man was hungry.

He'd also taken the whole "she was now with his nephew" news with pure Taggart calm. He'd patted her on the back and told her to make sure David wore a condom, and now she was part of the family. The man was seriously into safe sex.

"David thinks so." Eddie stood to the side. He'd used the satellite phone to talk to Camila after Sean had gotten Grace on the phone with David.

Tessa had been the one to tell him his treasure hunt could wait long enough for him to assure his mom he was okay. He could be single-minded when he was working. She would be the one to drag her gorgeous professor back into the real world.

"You think the poem refers to the heart on the mural." Sean stood in front of the mural, considering it. "Where the river flows."

That got David's attention. "You've read it?"

Sean nodded. "Yeah, I looked up Ricardo Montez because you're so fascinated with him. I read up on him, and it led to the legends about the treasure."

"Huh, that's nice," David said with a smile. "It's nice that someone in my family knows about my work."

She got the feeling Sean had done that so he could talk to his stepson.

Kyle was sitting on a chair with his leg up. "It wasn't going to be me. That stuff is boring."

"I've never heard anything about a hidden door here." Eddie had lightened up considerably after talking to Camila and ensuring that his son was all right. They would be here in a couple of hours, and he'd already called in a cleaning team to dispose of her afternoon's work.

All in all, not a bad day, and there still might be some treasure.

"Are we talking cash or like art and stuff?" Big Tag asked.

She'd quietly briefed her boss on what had gone down, and he'd agreed to keep Marta's cover even from the rest of the group. They owed her. She was investigating some of the business leaders Eddie was meeting with. There were rumors the businessmen might be involved in some shady shit the government was interested in.

"I think it's the contents of a ship." David was back to running his fingers along the seam. "A couple of years before he died, Montez covered the costs of the recovery of a ship that sank off the coast of the island in 1763. We know he accepted several items from the ship, but they weren't accounted for when he died and the contents of the place became Eddie's."

"Wasn't there something about numbers?" She hadn't expected to feel so comfortable with his family, but the Taggarts made it easy. Ian was distracted with food and or violence. Sean just wanted his stepson happy, and Kyle was half asleep from the pain meds MaeBe had slipped into his backpack.

"I don't know what it meant," David admitted. "There might be a safe we have to get into."

She didn't think so. The numbers had been at the beginning of the poem, so she thought they likely had something to do with the door and getting it open. The mural was painted on a grid, the lines of the grid still visible. "What if one of these squares is a button?"

David stepped back, looking at the whole of the mural again. "That's an interesting idea."

"So you count the squares?" Sean asked. "How do you know where to start?"

"Where the river begins," Eddie said with a sigh. "That's where my father would have started. He did this for me."

David turned to his friend. "You were his heart. It was always for you. That's what dads do. Sometimes they even do it when they don't share a drop of blood."

"Blood doesn't make a family," Sean said quietly.

"No, but sperm does, and you should remember that," Big Tag snarked. "What? You guys know I can ruin any tender moment."

"But he's right about the sperm," Kyle said with a yawn. "I'm not ready to be an uncle. I'm better at being a bad influence big brother."

David had gone back to ignoring his family. He was intently counting squares from the center of the heart down the river.

"What kind of bad influence?" Sean asked, standing over Kyle. "I mean besides ignoring doctor's orders and generally being a pain in the ass to your girlfriend?"

"MaeBe is not my girlfriend," Kyle corrected. "She's a girl who is a friend."

"Good because Charlie's got this cousin she thinks MaeBe should meet," Ian offered.

Kyle's eyes flared. "Absolutely not. Charlotte's cousins are all Russian mob. What the hell is she thinking? MaeBe's not going out with a gangster. And no IT guys either. She's already too invested in her computer. She needs a guy who'll get her outside and take her hiking. Someone who's different from her but has the same values."

"The kind of dude who duct tapes himself up after getting shot?" Tag polished off his last sandwich. "The kind who stows away on a private plane when he's injured?"

"I just think she needs someone to shake her up a little. Or she's happy on her own. You know she doesn't need a man to make her complete," Kyle snapped back. "She's a fully realized person without some dude hanging around."

Except Kyle was the dude who was always hanging around.

There was a *snick*, and the mural moved slightly.

"You did it." She should have known he would find it. He was good at finding lost things. Like her.

The most beautiful smile came over his face. "I did. But not without your help, baby."

David kissed her, seeming to forget that he'd opened a door that had been closed for years, but then the treasure didn't really matter to her guy. It was the journey he cared about.

But she wanted to see the treasure.

"Are you going to let Eddie go first?" she asked.

David kissed her again and then stepped back, sliding the panel to the side and exposing the stairwell. "This was the treasure your dad wanted you to find. The one you can share with your son one day."

There was a sheen of tears in Eddie's eyes as he put a hand on David's shoulder. "The gift was always the game, wasn't it? Not what I found at the end. It was in the hours he put into making the puzzle, into giving us something we could share. That's what my dad truly left for me."

"But it could be money, too, right?" Ian asked. "I'm serious. It was a big bill."

"Ian," Sean admonished.

Eddie shook his head. "I promise, Mr. Taggart. After what you and David have done for me, I'll pay all your bills."

"Don't offer that. He's got five kids and a wife with a shoe addiction," David pointed out.

"We'll work something out," Eddie promised. "Let's go see what my father left for me."

David offered her his hand, and she let him lead her down the narrow staircase.

Low lights came on, probably on a motion detector, and she found herself in a room that looked more like an art museum than a storage room. There were paintings on the walls and glass cabinets that showed off artifacts and jewelry.

"Nice," Big Tag said as he walked in. He took a deep inhale, and his expression went from curious to predatory in a heartbeat. "Is that what I think it is?"

Sean nodded beside him. "Holy shit. That's a bottle of Macallan Fine. I've never seen one before."

"This is from the shipwreck." David was standing over one of the cabinets. "These are Spanish doubloons. They're worth hundreds of thousands now."

"So it's a bunch of old stuff?" Kyle managed to get down the stairs and looked around.

"It's history," David said with that look of wonder on his face she loved so much. "It's more than just the shipwreck. It's all the stuff he collected. This is amazing."

Big Tag was staring at the bottle with a look of longing on his face she'd never seen before. Maybe when he looked at his wife, but there was real desire in the man's eyes. "This is the greatest Scotch in the world. I will trade you the bill for my services for the bottle."

"That bottle is worth almost two million," Sean pointed out. "Don't fall for his bullshit."

Eddie stood in the middle of the room, looking down at the big book left there for him. "This is our family history. Everything he could find. And his journals. David, come and look at this. He took pictures. No one's ever seen them before, and there are recordings from the meetings he conducted."

"Are you serious?" David gasped as he looked down at the books and tapes on the table. "This is a gold mine."

"But this is liquid gold," Big Tag argued.

David laughed. "Well, he did mention liquid gold." He looked back at her. "Baby, do you mind if I look through…"

She wasn't going to keep him from his treasure. She kissed his cheek. "You have at it. I'm going to take your family upstairs and raid the Scotch that isn't worth two million dollars."

"Just a taste," Ian tried.

She frowned his way. She was going to be surrounded by Taggarts. She would have to be tough. "Up those stairs, mister. We need to greet the cleaners and deal with all the bodies. In my family women do the killing and men bury the bodies."

Sean sighed. "Yeah, that's how it mostly works in ours, too. All right. We'll let the professor have his fun."

David suddenly scooped her up in his arms. "The professor's fun can wait. I think I need to take my lady here and make sure she understands how much I appreciate the save."

"David," she began, "it's okay. I know how much this means to you."

"You mean more." He took them up the stairs. "And I'm not done with my study."

She wrapped her arms around him and knew they would never be done. She could study her professor forever.

* * * *

Also from 1001 Dark Nights and Lexi Blake, discover Charmed, Enchanted, Protected, Close Cover, Arranged, Devoted, Adored, and Dungeon Games.

Sign up for the 1001 Dark Nights Newsletter
and be entered to win a Tiffany Key necklace.

There's a contest every month!

Go to www.1001DarkNights.com to subscribe.

**As a bonus, all subscribers can download
FIVE FREE exclusive books!**

Discover 1001 Dark Nights Collection Eight

DRAGON REVEALED by Donna Grant
A Dragon Kings Novella

CAPTURED IN INK by Carrie Ann Ryan
A Montgomery Ink: Boulder Novella

SECURING JANE by Susan Stoker
A SEAL of Protection: Legacy Series Novella

WILD WIND by Kristen Ashley
A Chaos Novella

DARE TO TEASE by Carly Phillips
A Dare Nation Novella

VAMPIRE by Rebecca Zanetti
A Dark Protectors/Rebels Novella

MAFIA KING by Rachel Van Dyken
A Mafia Royals Novella

THE GRAVEDIGGER'S SON by Darynda Jones
A Charley Davidson Novella

FINALE by Skye Warren
A North Security Novella

MEMORIES OF YOU by J. Kenner
A Stark Securities Novella

SLAYED BY DARKNESS by Alexandra Ivy
A Guardians of Eternity Novella

TREASURED by Lexi Blake
A Masters and Mercenaries Novella

THE DAREDEVIL by Dylan Allen
A Rivers Wilde Novella

BOND OF DESTINY by Larissa Ione
A Demonica Novella

THE CLOSE-UP by Kennedy Ryan
A Hollywood Renaissance Novella

MORE THAN POSSESS YOU by Shayla Black
A More Than Words Novella

HAUNTED HOUSE by Heather Graham
A Krewe of Hunters Novella

MAN FOR ME by Laurelin Paige
A Man In Charge Novella

THE RHYTHM METHOD by Kylie Scott
A Stage Dive Novella

JONAH BENNETT by Tijan
A Bennett Mafia Novella

CHANGE WITH ME by Kristen Proby
A With Me In Seattle Novella

THE DARKEST DESTINY by Gena Showalter
A Lords of the Underworld Novella

Also from Blue Box Press

THE LAST TIARA by M.J. Rose

THE CROWN OF GILDED BONES by Jennifer L. Armentrout
A Blood and Ash Novel

THE MISSING SISTER by Lucinda Riley

Discover More Lexi Blake

Charmed: A Masters and Mercenaries Novella

JT Malone is lucky, and he knows it. He is the heir to a billion-dollar petroleum empire, and he has a loving family. Between his good looks and his charm, he can have almost any woman he wants. The world is his oyster, and he really likes oysters. So why does it all feel so empty?

Nina Blunt is pretty sure she's cursed. She worked her way up through the ranks at Interpol, fighting for every step with hard work and discipline. Then she lost it all because she loved the wrong person. Rebuilding her career with McKay-Taggart, she can't help but feel lonely. It seems everyone around her is finding love and starting families. But she knows that isn't for her. She has vowed never to make the mistake of falling in love again.

JT comes to McKay-Taggart for assistance rooting out a corporate spy, and Nina signs on to the job. Their working relationship becomes tricky, however, as their personal chemistry flares like a wildfire. Completing the assignment without giving in to the attraction that threatens to overwhelm them seems like it might be the most difficult part of the job. When danger strikes, will they be able to count on each other when the bullets are flying? If not, JT's charmed life might just come to an end.

* * * *

Enchanted: A Masters and Mercenaries Novella

A snarky submissive princess
Sarah Steven's life is pretty sweet. By day, she's a dedicated trauma nurse and by night, a fun-loving club sub. She adores her job, has a group of friends who have her back, and is a member of the hottest club in Dallas. So why does it all feel hollow? Could it be because she fell for her dream man and can't forgive him for walking away from her? Nope. She's not going there again. No matter how much she wants to.

A prince of the silver screen

Jared Johns might be one of the most popular actors in Hollywood, but he lost more than a fan when he walked away from Sarah. He lost the only woman he's ever loved. He's been trying to get her back, but she won't return his calls. A trip to Dallas to visit his brother might be exactly what he needs to jump-start his quest to claim the woman who holds his heart.

A masquerade to remember

For Charlotte Taggart's birthday, Sanctum becomes a fantasyland of kinky fun and games. Every unattached sub gets a new Dom for the festivities. The twist? The Doms must conceal their identities until the stroke of midnight at the end of the party. It's exactly what Sarah needs to forget the fact that Jared is pursuing her. She can't give in to him, and the mysterious Master D is making her rethink her position when it comes to signing a contract. Jared knows he was born to play this role, dashing suitor by day and dirty Dom at night.

When the masks come off, will she be able to forgive the man who loves her, or will she leave him forever?

* * * *

Protected: A Masters and Mercenaries Novella

A second chance at first love

Years before, Wade Rycroft fell in love with Geneva Harris, the smartest girl in his class. The rodeo star and the shy academic made for an odd pair but their chemistry was undeniable. They made plans to get married after high school but when Genny left him standing in the rain, he joined the Army and vowed to leave that life behind. Genny married the town's golden boy, and Wade knew that he couldn't go home again.

Could become the promise of a lifetime

Fifteen years later, Wade returns to his Texas hometown for his brother's wedding and walks into a storm of scandal. Genny's marriage has dissolved and the town has turned against her. But when someone tries to kill his old love, Wade can't refuse to help her. In his years after the Army, he's found his place in the world. His job at McKay-Taggart keeps him happy and busy but something is missing. When he takes the job watching over Genny, he realizes what it is.

As danger presses in, Wade must decide if he can forgive past sins or let the woman of his dreams walk into a nightmare...

* * * *

Close Cover: A Masters and Mercenaries Novel

Remy Guidry doesn't do relationships. He tried the marriage thing once, back in Louisiana, and learned the hard way that all he really needs in life is a cold beer, some good friends, and the occasional hookup. His job as a bodyguard with McKay-Taggart gives him purpose and lovely perks, like access to Sanctum. The last thing he needs in his life is a woman with stars in her eyes and babies in her future.

Lisa Daley's life is going in the right direction. She has graduated from college after years of putting herself through school. She's got a new job at an accounting firm and she's finished her Sanctum training. Finally on her own and having fun, her life seems pretty perfect. Except she's lonely and the one man she wants won't give her a second look.

There is one other little glitch. Apparently, her new firm is really a front for the mob and now they want her dead. Assassins can really ruin a fun girls' night out. Suddenly strapped to the very same six-foot-five-inch hunk of a bodyguard who makes her heart pound, Lisa can't decide if this situation is a blessing or a curse.

As the mob closes in, Remy takes his tempting new charge back to the safest place he knows—his home in the bayou. Surrounded by his past, he can't help wondering if Lisa is his future. To answer that question, he just has to keep her alive.

* * * *

Arranged: A Masters and Mercenaries Novella

Kash Kamdar is the king of a peaceful but powerful island nation. As Loa Mali's sovereign, he is always in control, the final authority. Until his mother uses an ancient law to force her son into marriage. His prospective queen is a buttoned-up intellectual, nothing like Kash's usual party girl. Still, from the moment of their forced engagement, he can't stop thinking about her.

Dayita Samar comes from one of Loa Mali's most respected families. The Oxford-educated scientist has dedicated her life to her country's future. But under her staid and calm exterior, Day hides a few sexy secrets of her own. She is willing to marry her king, but also agrees that they can circumvent the law. Just because they're married doesn't mean they have to change their lives. It certainly doesn't mean they have to fall in love.

After one wild weekend in Dallas, Kash discovers his bride-to-be is more than she seems. Engulfed in a changing world, Kash finds exciting new possibilities for himself. Could Day help him find respite from the crushing responsibility he's carried all his life? This fairy tale could have a happy ending, if only they can escape Kash's past…

* * * *

Devoted: A Masters and Mercenaries Novella

A woman's work

Amy Slaten has devoted her life to Slaten Industries. After ousting her corrupt father and taking over the CEO role, she thought she could relax and enjoy taking her company to the next level. But an old business rivalry rears its ugly head. The only thing that can possibly take her mind off business is the training class at Sanctum…and her training partner, the gorgeous and funny Flynn Adler. If she can just manage to best her mysterious business rival, life might be perfect.

A man's commitment

Flynn Adler never thought he would fall for the enemy. Business is war, or so his father always claimed. He was raised to be ruthless when it came to the family company, and now he's raising his brother to one day work with him. The first order of business? The hostile takeover of Slaten Industries. It's a stressful job so when his brother offers him a spot in Sanctum's training program, Flynn jumps at the chance.

A lifetime of devotion….
When Flynn realizes the woman he's falling for is none other than the CEO of the firm he needs to take down, he has to make a choice. Does he take care of the woman he's falling in love with or the business he's worked a lifetime to build? And when Amy finally understands the man she's come to trust is none other than the enemy, will she walk away from him or fight for the love she's come to depend on?

* * * *

Adored: A Masters and Mercenaries Novella

A man who gave up on love

Mitch Bradford is an intimidating man. In his professional life, he has a reputation for demolishing his opponents in the courtroom. At the exclusive BDSM club Sanctum, he prefers disciplining pretty submissives with no strings attached. In his line of work, there's no time for a healthy relationship. After a few failed attempts, he knows he's not good for any woman—especially not his best friend's sister.

A woman who always gets what she wants

Laurel Daley knows what she wants, and her sights are set on Mitch. He's smart and sexy, and it doesn't matter that he's a few years older and has a couple of bitter ex-wives. Watching him in action at work and at play, she knows he just needs a little polish to make some woman the perfect lover. She intends to be that woman, but first she has to show him how good it could be.

A killer lurking in the shadows

When an unexpected turn of events throws the two together, Mitch and Laurel are confronted with the perfect opportunity to explore their mutual desire. Night after night of being close breaks down Mitch's defenses. The more he sees of Laurel, the more he knows he wants her. Unfortunately, someone else has their eyes on Laurel and they have murder in mind.

* * * *

Dungeon Games: A Masters and Mercenaries Novella

Obsessed

Derek Brighton has become one of Dallas's finest detectives through a combination of discipline and obsession. Once he has a target in his sights, nothing can stop him. When he isn't solving homicides, he applies the same intensity to his playtime at Sanctum, a secretive BDSM club. Unfortunately, no amount of beautiful submissives can fill the hole that one woman left in his heart.

Unhinged

Karina Mills has a reputation for being reckless, and her clients appreciate her results. As a private investigator, she pursues her cases with nothing holding her back. In her personal life, Karina yearns for something different. Playing at Sanctum has been a safe way to find peace, but the one Dom who could truly master her heart is out of reach.

Enflamed

On the hunt for a killer, Derek enters a shadowy underworld only to find the woman he aches for is working the same case. Karina is searching for a missing girl and won't stop until she finds her. To get close to their prime suspect, they need to pose as a couple. But as their operation goes under the covers, unlikely partners become passionate lovers while the killer prepares to strike.

The Dom Identity

Masters and Mercenaries: Reloaded, Book 2
By Lexi Blake
Coming September 14, 2021

A man with everything

Michael Malone seems to have it all. A wealthy, loving family. A job that fulfills him. Friends he can count on. But something is missing. He's spent years watching his brother and close friends get married and start families, but it hasn't happened for him. When an assignment comes up to investigate fallen Hollywood star Vanessa Hale, he jumps at the chance. She's gorgeous and potentially deadly. Playing the spy game with her might be just the thing to take his mind off his troubles.

A woman with nothing left to lose

Vanessa Hale had big dreams that ended in scandal. She returned home with nothing but heartache and the desire to find her sister's killer. The trail points to someone at Lodge Corp, so taking a job with Julian Lodge's mysterious company is her best option for finding the truth. While she hunts for a killer during the day, she hopes to find some solace at night in The Club. Meeting the gorgeous, sexy and seemingly kind Michael Malone, their chemistry sparks in a way she's never felt before, and Vanessa thinks maybe her luck has finally changed.

A love that might save them both

When Michael's true motives are revealed, she will have to find a way to forgive his betrayal. The killer has made Vanessa their next target. Working together and stopping this monster is the only chance for them to have the real love they both deserve.

About Lexi Blake

New York Times bestselling author Lexi Blake lives in North Texas with her husband and three kids. Since starting her publishing journey in 2010, she's sold over three million copies of her books. She began writing at a young age, concentrating on plays and journalism. It wasn't until she started writing romance that she found success. She likes to find humor in the strangest places and believes in happy endings.

Connect with Lexi online:

Facebook: Lexi Blake
Twitter: authorlexiblake
Website: www.LexiBlake.net
Instagram: www.instagram.com

Discover 1001 Dark Nights

TRICKED by Rebecca Zanetti ~ DIRTY WICKED by Shayla Black ~ THE ONLY ONE by Lauren Blakely ~ SWEET SURRENDER by Liliana Hart

COLLECTION FOUR
ROCK CHICK REAWAKENING by Kristen Ashley ~ ADORING INK by Carrie Ann Ryan ~ SWEET RIVALRY by K. Bromberg ~ SHADE'S LADY by Joanna Wylde ~ RAZR by Larissa Ione ~ ARRANGED by Lexi Blake ~ TANGLED by Rebecca Zanetti ~ HOLD ME by J. Kenner ~ SOMEHOW, SOME WAY by Jennifer Probst ~ TOO CLOSE TO CALL by Tessa Bailey ~ HUNTED by Elisabeth Naughton ~ EYES ON YOU by Laura Kaye ~ BLADE by Alexandra Ivy/Laura Wright ~ DRAGON BURN by Donna Grant ~ TRIPPED OUT by Lorelei James ~ STUD FINDER by Lauren Blakely ~ MIDNIGHT UNLEASHED by Lara Adrian ~ HALLOW BE THE HAUNT by Heather Graham ~ DIRTY FILTHY FIX by Laurelin Paige ~ THE BED MATE by Kendall Ryan ~ NIGHT GAMES by CD Reiss ~ NO RESERVATIONS by Kristen Proby ~ DAWN OF SURRENDER by Liliana Hart

COLLECTION FIVE
BLAZE ERUPTING by Rebecca Zanetti ~ ROUGH RIDE by Kristen Ashley ~ HAWKYN by Larissa Ione ~ RIDE DIRTY by Laura Kaye ~ ROME'S CHANCE by Joanna Wylde ~ THE MARRIAGE ARRANGEMENT by Jennifer Probst ~ SURRENDER by Elisabeth Naughton ~ INKED NIGHTS by Carrie Ann Ryan ~ ENVY by Rachel Van Dyken ~ PROTECTED by Lexi Blake ~ THE PRINCE by Jennifer L. Armentrout ~ PLEASE ME by J. Kenner ~ WOUND TIGHT by Lorelei James ~ STRONG by Kylie Scott ~ DRAGON NIGHT by Donna Grant ~ TEMPTING BROOKE by Kristen Proby ~ HAUNTED BE THE HOLIDAYS by Heather Graham ~ CONTROL by K. Bromberg ~ HUNKY HEARTBREAKER by Kendall Ryan ~ THE DARKEST CAPTIVE by Gena Showalter

COLLECTION SIX
DRAGON CLAIMED by Donna Grant ~ ASHES TO INK by Carrie Ann Ryan ~ ENSNARED by Elisabeth Naughton ~ EVERMORE by Corinne Michaels ~ VENGEANCE by Rebecca

Zanetti ~ ELI'S TRIUMPH by Joanna Wylde ~ CIPHER by Larissa
Ione ~ RESCUING MACIE by Susan Stoker ~ ENCHANTED by
Lexi Blake ~ TAKE THE BRIDE by Carly Phillips ~ INDULGE ME
by J. Kenner ~ THE KING by Jennifer L. Armentrout ~ QUIET
MAN by Kristen Ashley ~ ABANDON by Rachel Van Dyken ~ THE
OPEN DOOR by Laurelin Paige ~ CLOSER by Kylie Scott ~
SOMETHING JUST LIKE THIS by Jennifer Probst ~ BLOOD
NIGHT by Heather Graham ~ TWIST OF FATE by Jill Shalvis ~
MORE THAN PLEASURE YOU by Shayla Black ~ WONDER
WITH ME by Kristen Proby ~ THE DARKEST ASSASSIN by Gena
Showalter

COLLECTION SEVEN
THE BISHOP by Skye Warren ~ TAKEN WITH YOU by Carrie
Ann Ryan ~ DRAGON LOST by Donna Grant ~ SEXY LOVE by
Carly Phillips ~ PROVOKE by Rachel Van Dyken ~ RAFE by
Sawyer Bennett ~ THE NAUGHTY PRINCESS by Claire Contreras
~ THE GRAVEYARD SHIFT by Darynda Jones ~ CHARMED by
Lexi Blake ~ SACRIFICE OF DARKNESS by Alexandra Ivy ~ THE
QUEEN by Jen Armentrout ~ BEGIN AGAIN by Jennifer Probst ~
VIXEN by Rebecca Zanetti ~ SLASH by Laurelin Paige ~ THE
DEAD HEAT OF SUMMER by Heather Graham ~ WILD FIRE by
Kristen Ashley ~ MORE THAN PROTECT YOU by Shayla Black ~
LOVE SONG by Kylie Scott ~ CHERISH ME by J. Kenner ~
SHINE WITH ME by Kristen Proby

Discover Blue Box Press
TAME ME by J. Kenner ~ TEMPT ME by J. Kenner ~ DAMIEN by
J. Kenner ~ TEASE ME by J. Kenner ~ REAPER by Larissa Ione ~
THE SURRENDER GATE by Christopher Rice ~ SERVICING
THE TARGET by Cherise Sinclair ~ THE LAKE OF LEARNING
by Steve Berry and MJ Rose ~ THE MUSEUM OF MYSTERIES by
Steve Berry and MJ Rose ~ TEASE ME by J. Kenner ~ FROM
BLOOD AND ASH by Jennifer L. Armentrout ~ QUEEN MOVE
by Kennedy Ryan ~ THE HOUSE OF LONG AGO by Steve Berry
and MJ Rose ~ THE BUTTERFLY ROOM by Lucinda Riley ~ A
KINGDOM OF FLESH AND FIRE by Jennifer L. Armentrout

On Behalf of 1001 Dark Nights,

Liz Berry, M.J. Rose, and Jillian Stein would like to thank ~

Steve Berry
Doug Scofield
Benjamin Stein
Kim Guidroz
Social Butterfly PR
Ashley Wells
Asha Hossain
Chris Graham
Chelle Olson
Kasi Alexander
Jessica Johns
Dylan Stockton
Richard Blake
and Simon Lipskar

www.ingramcontent.com/pod-product-compliance
Lightning Source LLC
LaVergne TN
LVHW090210311225
828824LV00027B/236